Praise for *New York Times* bestselling author Cynthia Eden

"Eden expertly twines terror and true love in her second Killer Instinct contemporary romantic thriller.... This winning tale is a tightly plotted, expertly characterized adrenaline rush from start to finish."
—*Publishers Weekly* on *Before the Dawn* (starred review)

"Cynthia Eden writes smart, sexy and gripping suspense. Hang on tight while she takes you on a wild ride."
—*New York Times* bestselling author Cindy Gerard

"Sexy, mysterious, and full of heart-pounding suspense!"
—*New York Times* bestselling author Laura Kaye

"Suspenseful, sexy fare that keeps you turning pages until you reach the story's conclusion."
—*RT Book Reviews* on *After the Dark*

"Eden shines with this taut romantic thriller, which opens her Killer Instinct series."
—*Publishers Weekly* on *After the Dark*

"A dynamic and fully vested cast of secondary characters keeps the suspense and intrigue flowing."
—*Smexy Books* on *After the Dark*

"*After the Dark* is an action-packed thrill-ride of a tale that starts with an exciting scene and keeps the tension going for the entire book."
—*Night Owl Reviews*

**Also available by
Cynthia Eden**

HQN Books

Killer Instinct

The Gathering Dusk (prequel to *Abduction*)
After the Dark
Before the Dawn
Into the Night

Harlequin Intrigue

Killer Instinct

Abduction
Hunted

For a complete list of books by Cynthia Eden,
please visit www.cynthiaeden.com.

CYNTHIA
EDEN

INTO THE
NIGHT

HQN™

HQN™

ISBN-13: 978-1-335-01808-3

Into the Night

Recycling programs
for this product may
not exist in your area.

Printed in U.S.A.

First, I want to thank my readers. My readers thrill me every single day. Thank you for your support and your emails and for all of the encouragement that you give to me. My readers keep me typing at the keyboard because I can't wait to share new stories!

I also wanted to send a special shout to my friends... Skyla—lady, you can always make me smile. And for Amy—woman, if you don't write your own book soon, I'll be angry! You ladies are my favorite witches and hanging with you always inspires me.

INTO THE
NIGHT

PROLOGUE

THE LIGHT WAS in her eyes, blinding her. Macey Night couldn't see past that too bright light. She was strapped onto the operating room table, but it wasn't the straps that held her immobile.

He'd drugged her.

"I could stare into your eyes forever." His rumbling voice came from behind the light. "So unusual, but then, you realize just how special you are, right, *Dr. Night*?"

She couldn't talk. He'd gagged her. They were in the basement of the hospital, in a wing that hadn't been used for years. Or at least, she'd thought it hadn't been used. She'd been wrong. About so many things.

"Red hair is always rare, but to find a redhead with heterochromia…it's like I hit the jackpot."

A tear leaked from her eye.

"Don't worry. I've made sure that you will feel everything that happens to you. I just—well, the drugs were to make sure that you wouldn't fight back. That's all. Not to impair the experience for you. Fighting back just ruins everything. I know what I'm talking about, believe me." He sighed. "I had a few patients early on—they were special like you. Well, not *quite* like you, but I think you get the idea. They fought and things got messy."

A whimper sounded behind her gag because he'd just taken his scalpel and cut her on the left arm, a long, slow slice from her inner wrist all the way up to her elbow.

"How was that?" he asked her. His voice was low, deep.

Nausea rolled in her stomach. Nausea from fear, from the drugs, from the absolute horror of realizing she'd been working with a monster and she hadn't even realized it. Day in and day out, he'd been at her side. She'd even thought about dating him. Thought about having *sex* with him. After all, Daniel Haddox was the most respected doctor at the hospital. At thirty-five, he'd already made a name for himself. He was *the* best surgeon at Hartford General Hospital, everyone said so.

He was also, apparently, a sadistic serial killer.

And she was his current victim.

All because I have two different-colored eyes. Two fucking different colors.

"I'll start slowly, just so you know what's going to happen." He'd moved around the table, going to her right side now. "I keep my slices light at first. I like to see how the patient reacts to the pain stimulus."

I'm not a patient! Nothing is wrong with me! Stop! Stop!

But he'd sliced her again. A mirror image of the wound he'd given her before, a slice on her right arm that began at her inner wrist and slid all the way up to her elbow.

"Later, the slices will get deeper. I have a gift with the scalpel, haven't you heard?" He laughed—it was a laugh that she knew too many women had found arousing. Dr. Haddox was attractive, with black hair and gleaming blue eyes. He had perfect white teeth, and the kind of easy, good-looking features that only aged well.

Doesn't matter what he looks like on the outside. He's a monster.

"Every time I work on a patient, I wonder…what is it like without the anesthesia?"

Sick freak.

"But not just any patient works for me. I need the special ones." He moved toward her face and she knew he was going to slice her again. He lifted the scalpel and pressed it to her cheek.

The fingers on her right hand jerked.

Wait—did I do that? Had her hand jerked just because of some reflex or were the drugs wearing off? He'd drugged her when she'd first walked into the basement with him. Then he'd undressed her, put her on the operating table, and strapped her down. But before he could touch her anymore, he'd been called away. The guy had gotten a text and rushed off—to surgery. To save a patient. She wasn't even sure how long he'd been gone. She'd been trapped on that operating table, staring up at the bright light the whole time he'd been gone. In her mind, she'd been screaming again and again for help that never came.

"You and I are going to have so much fun, and those beautiful eyes of yours will show me everything that you feel." He paused. "I'll be taking those eyes before I'm done."

Her right hand moved again. *She'd* made it move. The drugs he'd given her were wearing off. *His* mistake. She often responded in unusual ways to medicine. Hell, that was one of the reasons she'd gone into medicine in the first place. When she was six, she'd almost died after taking an over-the-counter children's pain medication. Her body processed medicines differently. She'd wanted to know why. Wanted to know how to predict who would have adverse reactions after she'd gone into cardiac arrest from a simple aspirin.

It's not just my eyes that are different. I'm different.

But her mother…her mother had been the main reason for her drive to enter the field of medicine. Macey had been forced to watch—helplessly—as cancer destroyed her beautiful mother. She'd wanted to make a change after her mother's death. She'd wanted to help people.

I never wanted to die like this!

But now she could move her left hand. Daniel wasn't paying any attention to her fingers, though. He was holding that scalpel right beneath her eye and staring down at her. She couldn't see his face. He was just a blur of dots—courtesy of that bright light.

She twisted her right hand and caught the edge of the strap. She began to slide her hand loose.

"The eyes will be last," he told her as if he'd just come to some major decision. "I've got to explore every inch of you to see why you're different. It's for the good of science. It's *always* for the good. For the betterment of mankind, a few have to suffer." He made a faint *hmm* sound. "Though I wonder about you…about us. With your mind…maybe…maybe we could have worked together."

And maybe he was insane. No, there wasn't any *maybe* about that. She'd gotten her right hand free, and her left was working diligently on the strap. Her legs were still secured so she wasn't going to be able to just jump off the table. Macey wasn't even sure if her legs would hold her. The drug was still in her body, but it was fading fast.

"But you aren't like that, are you, Dr. Night?" Now his voice had turned hard. "I watched you. Followed you. Kept my gaze on you when you thought no one was looking."

She'd felt hunted for days, for weeks, but she'd tried to tell herself she was just being silly. She worked a lot, and the stress of the job had been making her imagine things. She was in her final few weeks of residency work, and everyone knew those hours were killer.

Only in her case, they literally were.

"You don't get that we can't always save every patient. Sometimes, the patients die and it is a learning experience for everyone."

Bullshit. He was just trying to justify his insanity.

"You see things in black and white. They're not like that, though. The world is full of gray." He moved the scalpel away from her cheek…only to slice into her shoulder. "And red. Lots and lots of red—"

She grabbed the scalpel from him. Because he wasn't expecting her attack, she ripped it right from his fingers and then she shoved it into his chest as deep and as hard as she could.

Daniel staggered back. Macey shot up, then nearly fell off the table because her legs were still strapped and her body was shaking. She yanked at the straps, jerking frantically against them as she heard him moaning on the floor.

The straps gave way. She sprang off the table and immediately collapsed. She fell onto Daniel—and the weight of her body drove the scalpel even deeper into him.

"You…bitch…"

"You bastard," she whispered right back. Then she was heaving off him. Her blood was dripping from her wounds and she crawled to the door. He grabbed her ankle, but she kicked back, slamming her foot into his face, and Macey heard the satisfying crunch as she broke his nose.

He wasn't so perfect any longer.

"Macey!"

She yanked open the door. Her legs felt stronger.

Or maybe adrenaline was just making her stronger. She ran out of the small room and down the hallway. He was going to come after her. She knew it. She needed help. She needed it *fast*. There were no security monitors on that hallway. No cameras to watch her. No help for her.

Her breath heaved out and her blood splattered onto the floor. She didn't look back, too terrified that she'd see Daniel closing in on her. The elevator was up ahead. She hit the button, smearing it with her blood. She waited and waited and—

Ding. The doors slid open. She fell inside and whipped around.

Daniel was coming after her. He still had the scalpel in his chest. *Because he's a freaking doctor. He knows that if he pulls it out, he's done. He'll have massive blood loss right away. But the longer that scalpel stays in...*

It gave him the chance to come for her.

His lips were twisted in a snarl as he lunged for the doors.

She slapped the button to close the elevator, again and again and again, and the doors *closed.*

Macey was shaking, crying, bleeding. But she'd gotten away. The elevator began to move. Gentle instrumental music filled the air.

The doors opened again, spitting her out on the lobby level. She heard the din of voices, phones ringing and a baby crying somewhere in the distance. She walked out of the elevator, naked and bloody.

Silence. Everything just stopped as she staggered down the corridor.

"H-help me..."

A wide-eyed nurse rose from the check-in desk. "Dr. Night?"

Macey looked down at her bloody body. *"H-help me..."*

CHAPTER ONE

"I'VE FOUND HIM." Macey Night exhaled slowly as she faced her team at the FBI headquarters in Washington, DC. All eyes were on her, and she knew just how important this meeting was. She'd spent five years hunting, searching, never giving up, and now, finally... "I believe that I know the location of Daniel Haddox." She cleared her throat and let her gaze drift around the conference room table. "Daniel... the serial killer otherwise known as 'the Doctor' thanks to the media."

A low whistle came from her right—from FBI special agent Bowen Murphy. "I thought he was dead."

Macey had wanted him to be dead. "I never believed that he died from his injuries. That was just a story that circulated in the news. Daniel was the best surgeon I ever met. He knew how to survive."

"And how to vanish," said Samantha Dark. Samantha Dark was in charge of their team. The group had been her brainchild. Samantha had hand selected every member of their unit. The FBI didn't have official profilers—actually "profiler" wasn't even a title that they used. Instead, Samantha and her team were called "behavioral analysis experts." But the people in that conference room were different from the BAU members who worked typical cases in the violent crimes division.

Each person in that small conference room—each person there—had an intimate connection to a serial killer.

Her gaze slid over her team members.

Samantha Dark…so fragile in appearance with her pale skin, dark hair and delicate build, but so strong inside. Samantha's lover had been a killer, but she had brought him down. She'd been the one to realize that personal connections to serial perpetrators weren't a weakness…they could be a strength.

Tucker Frost. The FBI agent's bright blue stare held Macey's. Tucker's brother had been a serial killer. The infamous Iceman who'd taken too many victims in New Orleans. His exploits were legendary—scary stories that children whispered late at night.

Her hands fisted as her gaze slid to the next member of their team. Bowen Murphy. His blond hair was disheveled, and his dark gaze was intense as it rested upon her. Bowen had hunted down a serial killer, a man who the local authorities had sworn didn't exist. But Bowen had known the perp was out there. A civilian, he'd gone on the hunt and killed the monster in the shadows.

And then…then there was Macey herself. She'd worked side by side with a serial killer. She'd been his victim. She'd been the only "patient" to escape his care alive.

Now she'd found him. After five years of always looking over her shoulder and wondering if he'd come for her again. She'd. Found. Him. "You're right, Samantha," Macey acknowledged with a tilt of her head. "Daniel Haddox *did* know how to vanish." Her voice was quiet. Flat. "But I knew he wouldn't turn away from medicine. I knew he would have to return to his patients. He would *have* to pick up a scalpel again." But there had been so many places he could have gone. He could have easily stayed under the radar, opening up a clinic that only dealt in cash. One that didn't have any government oversight because it wasn't legitimate. One that catered to the poorest of communities.

Where he would have even greater control over his victims.

"I also knew that he wouldn't stop killing," Macey said. Once more, her gaze slid back to Bowen. She often found herself doing that—looking to Bowen. She wasn't even sure why, not really. They'd been partners on a few cases, but…

His gaze held hers. Bowen looked angry. That was odd. Bowen usually controlled his emotions so well. It was often hard to figure out just what the guy was truly thinking. He would present a relaxed, casual front to the world, but beneath the surface, he could be boiling with intensity.

"Why didn't you tell me that you were hunting him?" Bowen's words were rough, rumbling. He had a deep voice, strong, and she sucked in a breath as she realized that his anger was fully directed at *her*.

"The Doctor isn't an active case for our group," Macey said. They had more than enough current crimes to keep them busy. "We have other killers that we have been hunting and I didn't want to distract from—"

"Bullshit." His voice had turned into a rasp. "You forgot you were on a team, Macey. What impacts you impacts us all."

She licked her lips. He was right. Her news *did* impact them all. "That's why I called this meeting. Why I am talking to you all now." Even though her instincts had screamed for her to act. For her to race up to the small town of Hiddlewood, North Carolina, and confront the man she believed to be Daniel Haddox. But… "I want backup on this case." Because the dark truth was that Macey didn't trust herself to face Daniel alone.

Samantha's fingers tapped on the table. "How can you be so sure you've found him?"

Macey fumbled a bit and hit her laptop. Immediately, her files projected onto the screen to the right. "This victim was discovered twenty-four hours ago." Her words came a little too fast, so she sucked in another breath, trying to slow herself down. "A victim who is currently in the Hiddlewood ME's office. The autopsy hasn't even begun, but the medical examiner was struck by what she felt was a ritualistic pattern on the victim." She licked her lips. "Look at the victim's arms. The slices, from wrist to elbow. The Doctor always made those marks first on his victims. Those are his test wounds. He makes them to be sure his victims can feel the pain of their injuries, but still not fight him."

Silence. Macey clasped her hands together. "We got lucky on this one because we have a medical examiner who pays close attention to detail—and who seems very familiar with the work of Daniel Haddox. Dr. Sofia Lopez sent those files to the FBI, and I've got...I've got a friend here who knew what I've been looking for in terms of victim pathology." When she'd seen those wounds, Macey had known she'd found the bastard who'd tormented her. "I think the man who killed this victim is Daniel Haddox, and I think we need to get a team up to Hiddlewood right away."

Tucker leaned forward, narrowing his eyes as he stared at the screen. "You think this perp will kill again? You're so sure we're not dealing with some copycat who just heard about Daniel Haddox's crimes and thought he could imitate the murders?" Tucker pressed.

No, she wasn't sure. How could she be? "I think we need to get up there." Her hands twisted in front of her. She wasn't supposed to let cases get personal, Macey knew that, but...how could this case *not* be personal? Haddox had marked her, literally. He'd changed her whole life. She'd left medicine. She'd joined the FBI. She'd hunted killers because...

Because deep down, I'm always hunting him. The one who got away. The one I have to stop.

Samantha stared at her in silence for a moment. A

far-too-long moment. Macey realized she was holding her breath. And then—

"Get on a plane and get up there," Samantha directed curtly. Then she pointed to Bowen. "You, too, Bowen. I want you and Macey working together on this one. Get up there, take a look at the crime scene, and…" Her gaze cut back to Macey. "You work with the ME. If Daniel Haddox really committed this homicide, then you'll know. You know his work better than anyone."

Because she still carried his "work" on her body. And in her mind. In the dark chambers that she fought so hard to keep closed.

But now I've found you, Daniel. You won't get away again.

Tucker rose and came around the table toward her as she fumbled with her laptop. "Macey…" His voice was pitched low so that only she could hear him. "Are you sure you want to be the one going after him? Believe me on this…sometimes confronting the demons from your past doesn't free you. It just pulls you deeper into the darkness."

Her hands stilled on her laptop. She looked into Tucker's eyes and saw the sympathy that filled his stare. If anyone would know about darkness, it would be Tucker. She lifted her chin, hoping she looked confident. "I want to put this particular darkness in a cell and make sure he *never* gets out."

He nodded, but the heaviness never left his expression. "If you and Bowen hit trouble, call in the rest of the team, got it? We always watch out for each other."

Yes, they did.

She put her laptop into her bag. Tucker filed out of the room, but Samantha lingered near the doorway. Bowen wasn't anywhere to be seen. Macey figured that he must have slipped away while she was talking to Tucker. Clutching her bag, she headed toward Samantha.

"How many victims do you think he's claimed?" Samantha's voice was quiet as she asked the question that haunted Macey.

Every single night…when she wondered where Daniel was…when she wondered if he had another patient trapped on his table. *How many?* "We know he killed five patients before he took me." They'd found their remains in that hospital, hidden behind a makeshift wall in the basement. Daniel had made his own crypt for those poor people. He'd killed them, and then he'd sealed them away.

"He's been missing for several years," Macey continued. Her heart drummed too fast in her chest.

"And serial killers don't just stop, not cold turkey." Samantha tilted her head as she studied Macey. "He might have experienced a cooling-off period, but he wouldn't have been able to give up committing the murders. He would have needed the rush that he got when he took a life."

How many victims? "I don't know how many," Macey whispered. And, because she trusted Samantha, because Samantha was more than just her boss—

she was her friend—Macey said, "I'm afraid to find out."

Because every one of those victims would be on *her.* After all, Macey was the one who hadn't stopped him. She'd run away from him, so terrified, and when she'd fled, he'd escaped.

And lived to kill another day.

Samantha's hand rose and she squeezed Macey's shoulder. "You didn't hurt those people—*none* of those people."

"I ran away." She licked her lips.

"You survived. You were a victim then. That's what you were supposed to do—*survive.*"

She wasn't a victim any longer. "I'm an FBI agent now."

"Yes." Samantha held her gaze. "And he won't get away again."

No, he damn well wouldn't.

After a quick planning talk with Samantha, Macey slipped into the hallway and hurried toward her small office. As always, their floor was busy, a hum of activity, and she could hear the rise and fall of voices in the background. She kept her head down and soon she was in her office, shutting the door behind her—

"I would have helped you."

Macey sucked in a sharp breath. Bowen stood next to the sole window in the small room, his gaze on the city below. His hands were clasped behind his back, and she could see the bulk of his weapon and holster beneath the suit jacket he wore.

She put her laptop down on the desk. "Samantha

said we should be ready to fly in an hour. She's giving us the FBI's jet to use—"

He turned toward her. "Do you trust me, Mace?"

Mace. That was the nickname he'd adopted for
her, and half the time, she wasn't even sure that he
realized he was changing her name. But…it was
softer when he said "Mace" and not "Macey." For
some reason, she usually felt good when he used
that nickname.

She didn't feel good right then. *Do you trust
me?* Was that a trick question? She frowned at him.
"You're my partner. I have to trust you." Or else
they'd both be screwed. She was supposed to watch
his back, and he was supposed to watch hers. It was
pretty much the only way the FBI worked.

He crossed his arms over his chest as he considered her. "I have to ask… What will happen if you
come face-to-face with Daniel Haddox?"

She stared up at him, but for a moment, she didn't
see Bowen. She saw Daniel. Smiling. His eyes gleaming. And a scalpel in his hand. The scalpel was covered in her blood.

Bowen's square jaw hardened. "We're on this
team because Samantha thinks our connections
to killers give us special insight into serial crimes.
We're not here because we're trying to follow our
own personal agendas."

Hurt, she took a step back. "My agenda?" Anger
hummed in her blood and, just that fast, she didn't
see Daniel any longer. She just saw Bowen. Bowen
with his handsome face, his dark eyes, his strong

jaw—a jaw that was currently clenched. Bowen with his broad shoulders and his athletic build. Bowen... the guy she'd thought would understand, more than anyone else, exactly why she had to do this. "You're the man who hunted a serial and *killed* him. You're the one who went out for your own justice, not me."

He looked away from her. "There are things you don't know..."

Because Bowen wasn't exactly the sharing sort. That was fine, neither was she. "I'm not going up there to kill him."

Now he turned his stare back on her.

"Isn't that what this whole trust talk is about?" She tugged on her right sleeve, making sure it was perfectly in place, as always. She didn't like for anyone to see her scars. When people saw them, they tended to just—stare. And stare. And then to look at her with sympathy or horror. "You want to know what my plans are? Do you want to know if I'm going up there so that I can exact some vengeance on the man who tried to *kill* me?" Her words hung in the air between them.

He was supposed to say something.

He didn't.

Damn it. He *did* want to know all that.

"Samantha trusts me." So maybe she emphasized *trust* a bit too much there. "You should, too. I'm going up there to stop a killer. I'm not going to Hiddlewood so that I can become one."

He took a step closer to her. "Is that what you think *I* am? Do you look at me and see a killer?"

She thought she'd lost control of the conversation. Total control. She smoothed a hand over her hair. "No, look…we need to get packed, okay? There's a lot of work to do and not a lot of time. I'll just—I'll see you on the jet." Macey backed away from him.

She started checking her desk, grabbing any notes she needed and trying to look anywhere but at Bowen as she heard him pace toward the door.

But he didn't leave her office. At her door, he stilled. She knew because she'd snuck a quick glance at him. He filled her doorway, his broad back tense, and his hands on the door frame. He didn't look back at her as he said, "I hate that he hurt you."

Join the club. I hate that he got away. I hate that he's killed someone else. Maybe a whole lot of people. I hate it so much that it makes me sick.

"You aren't the only one who has been looking for him," Bowen rasped. "You think I haven't been searching for the bastard, too?"

Surprise rocked through her. "Samantha assigned you to his case?" Sometimes they did look into the colder cases but—

"No." He'd finally glanced over his shoulder. "This has nothing to do with Samantha or the rest of the team. It's about you. He hurt *you*. And I want him to pay. So I've been looking for the bastard. I've been hunting him." His lips curved in a humorless smile. "You just found him first."

Unease slithered through her. Macey stopped searching through her desk. "Bowen?"

"He won't hurt you again. I'll make sure of that.

Like I was trying to tell you before, you should trust me. I'll always watch your back."

Then he was gone. And she was left staring at the door.

BOWEN MURPHY HAD one weakness in this world, and that weakness was named Macey Night. The beautiful, brilliant and very, very untouchable Macey Night.

He watched her now as she headed down the flight of stairs that led to the medical examiner's office in Hiddlewood. Their flight to North Carolina had been brief—and quiet. Macey wasn't the kind of person who filled the air with idle chitchat. Macey was intense, Macey was focused…and Macey had been driving him insane for years.

Ever since he'd first walked into the FBI's DC office and seen her.

He'd heard her story before he met her. The woman who'd escaped from the infamous Doctor, the MD who'd walked away from her medical career so that she could catch violent criminals. Macey came in a small package, she barely skimmed over five feet three inches, but the woman was pure power. She was dead-on with her gun, and when it came to crime scenes, she always seemed to find details that others overlooked.

And as for the bodies…

No one gets the dead like she does.

They'd reached the end of the stairs. Macey looked back up at him, brushing her hair over her shoulders. Her red hair was straight and fell in a blunt cut that framed her delicate face perfectly. Her gaze drifted to him, and that gaze was as unnerving as always. And not because she had two different-colored eyes—something he found oddly sexy—because it was her. Because he often felt as if Macey could see straight into him.

A bad thing. Because inside? He was dark and twisted.

"Dr. Lopez is supposed to have the victim ready for us. I just need to get a look at the vic's wounds, and then we can go forward from there."

By going forward, he hoped that meant a fast trip to the crime scene. He wanted to get hunting. Because even if the perp wasn't Daniel Haddox, that meant they still had a killer out there. One that needed to be stopped before anyone else was hurt.

Macey adjusted her sleeves, a move he'd seen her do dozens of times, and Bowen's hand flew out, wrapping around her wrist. "You don't need to hide."

He felt her pulse jump beneath his fingers.

"Your scars don't matter, Mace," he continued, staring into her eyes. "Forget about them."

"I can't." He saw a crack in her mask. A glimpse at the pain she always carried on her own. "They remind me that I let him get away. That I didn't stop him."

Fuck that. "You were a victim who escaped a sadistic bastard." And his fingers slid under her right sleeve. He felt the faint line of raised skin there.

"The only thing these scars should do is tell you how strong you are."

Her lips parted. She stared up at him and he was leaning in toward her. *Too close.* He should back away. He should let her go. But her sweet scent—Macey always smelled like lavender—had wrapped around him. He didn't want to back away. He wanted to get closer.

The door opened down the hallway. "Dr. Night?" a feminine voice called.

Macey pulled her wrist from his grip. "Yes, I'm Special Agent Night." She nodded toward Bowen. "And this is my partner, Special Agent Bowen Murphy."

The woman hurried forward as she offered her hand first to Macey, then to Bowen. "Sofia Lopez." She wore a white lab coat and her dark hair was pulled into a bun at the base of her neck. Dr. Lopez was young, probably close to thirty, and her dark gaze was steady. "I'm so glad that you both came down here. As soon as I saw the body…those marks on the arms—" her gaze slid right back to Macey "—I immediately thought of you."

Bowen tensed.

But Dr. Lopez shook her head. "That sounded wrong. Let me try again." She offered Macey a weak smile of apology. "I remembered your story. A few years ago, it was splashed all over the news. I always follow the big crime stories. I'm something of a crime buff. But with my job, guess that makes sense, huh?"

Very few stories had been as big as Daniel Haddox's gory tale. The public had an unquenchable appetite for darkness. At least, that was how it seemed to Bowen. And the handsome doctor who'd been slicing up his patients? Hell, three movies had been made about him.

Dr. Lopez cleared her throat. "The wounds you received on your arms were very specific, and when it was revealed that Dr. Haddox marked *all* of his victims that way—"

"Why don't you show us *this* victim?" Bowen cut in. Macey looked uncomfortable and she was back to tugging at her sleeve.

"This victim, right!" Dr. Lopez said. She spun on her heel. "I have her waiting on my table."

Bowen followed the ME and Macey into the exam room. As soon as he stepped inside, the smell hit him like a punch. He *hated* the odor that he always found waiting within the labs of coroners or medical examiners. Bleach, bodies, hell.

But he approached the exam area determinedly, his gaze sweeping over the woman on the table. The woman had pale blond hair, delicate features and appeared to be in her early twenties. "Do we have an ID for the vic yet?"

"Yes." The ME pulled up a chart. "The crime team actually recovered her driver's license at the scene. She's Gale Collins, twenty-two, a college student at the University of North Carolina."

"Where was she found?" Bowen asked.

The ME's lips pulled down. "She was…she was

dumped in town. Literally. Her body was just tossed behind one of the motels. She wasn't killed there," Dr. Lopez added quickly. "Not enough blood at the scene. Someone just wanted to get rid of her body."

Macey's brows furrowed. "That wasn't part of Daniel's MO. He didn't give up his prey."

No, the sick prick had sealed them in the walls of his hospital. But since the guy didn't have a hospital any longer, maybe he'd had no choice.

"Based on the body decomp and lividity, I think our vic was killed within the last forty-eight hours." The ME blew out a quick breath. "I'll be able to narrow down that time frame with more testing."

"Were there any signs that she'd recently had surgery?" Macey asked quietly as she pulled on a pair of gloves. Bowen stood back. Macey was the one who worked on the bodies. He had a rule about the dead—he gave them justice, but he didn't examine them. Hell, no, that wasn't his department. So Bowen locked his arms over his chest and watched her work.

"Nothing that I could detect with a preliminary exam," Dr. Lopez replied.

Macey pulled back the sheet and her eyes narrowed.

Bowen blew out a hard breath. *The Doctor made a mess of her.* Anger tightened his body. The son of a bitch sure seemed to like hurting women.

Macey's fingers trembled around the sheet. "Well, here, at least, he stuck to his pattern."

A sick, sadistic pattern.

"He hurt her for a very long time," Macey added

softly. She cleared her throat. "I'm assuming you've already started the blood work to find out what mix of drugs he gave to the victim?" Her fingers slid toward the victim's wrist. "The bruising here is consistent with straps being used to secure the patient. He locked the straps very tightly." She swallowed. "Probably because he wanted to be sure that he never made the same mistake again with a victim."

Her gaze slid to Bowen. He knew exactly what she meant. *The mistake he made with you, Macey? When you were able to slip away from the bastard?*

Macey moved around the table and lifted the sheet so that she could study the victim's ankles. "More bruising," she murmured. "The Doctor secured his victims both by their wrists and their ankles so that they could not escape his procedures."

"His procedures?" The words burst from Bowen. "You mean his tortures."

The ME's eyes widened as she stared at him, but Macey's expression never altered.

Shit. Get the control back. He knew how to handle a scene like this. *By the fucking book.* The problem was that when he looked at the victim on that exam table, he kept seeing Macey. Kept seeing what could have happened to Macey five years ago if she hadn't managed to get away.

And he saw what *had* happened to her. And if that perp was up there, if he was still in the small mountain town…

I'm going to find you. I'm going to stop you. You will not hurt another victim.

"So…it's his work, right?" Dr. Lopez's voice sharpened a bit as she came closer to the exam table. She had on gloves, too, and she lifted the victim's right wrist. "I knew it as soon as I saw these slashes. From the inner wrist all the way to the elbow, exactly like yours and—"

He'd growled. The sound had just slipped out but both women glanced at him. Macey's face showed no expression, but she was good at keeping her emotions in check. Far better than he was. Mild alarm had flared in the ME's eyes. "Is there a problem?" Dr. Lopez asked.

Don't talk about her scars.

But Macey had caught the ME's attention once more. "The Doctor liked victims who had unique characteristics," Macey said quietly. "He wanted victims—"

"Like you," Dr. Lopez cut in again, nodding briskly. "With heterochromia. And that threw me about this victim. Because I thought both of her eyes were blue at first glance. I mean, when I called the FBI, I'd just seen the wounds on her body. I hadn't examined her thoroughly at that point. But take a look." Now her hand moved toward the victim's face. She opened the victim's right eye. "Blue. And then…" She opened the left eye.

"Blue." Macey was frowning.

"That's what it looks like." The ME smiled. "But right before you arrived, I realized that our vic was wearing contacts. Or, rather, she is wearing one contact." Very carefully, she removed the contact from the victim's left eye and placed it in an evidence bag. "And now you have brown." Again, her voice held a thread of excitement. "She's just like you, Agent Night! I mean, that must have been what set him off, right? To find another victim with eyes just like yours. That's probably why he started killing again after all this time. The Doctor found a victim he couldn't resist. He found—"

The door to the exam room flew open. Immediately, Bowen tensed and his hand flew toward his holster. But the man standing there, breath heaving, wore a brown deputy's uniform. A star gleamed on his chest. Bowen recognized the guy immediately. Deputy Coleman Quick. Quick had been sent to meet them at the airport. The deputy had been their escort in Hiddlewood, the small town that bordered North Carolina and Tennessee.

"We've got another one," Coleman said, the words tumbling out of his mouth. "The sheriff wanted me to take you two out to the scene right away. Said you *had* to see it."

Another one? Already? Shit, that wasn't good. Two kills so close together showed definite escalation on the part of the perpetrator.

But...

It also means our killer is still here. We can get the bastard because he hasn't fled the area yet.

Without a word, Bowen lunged toward the deputy and he knew Macey was right on his heels.

A SWIRL OF blue lights illuminated the scene as the deputy braked his vehicle. Macey and Bowen were right behind Deputy Quick in their rented SUV and, when their vehicle stopped, Bowen quickly killed his engine. Macey reached for the door handle.

But Bowen grabbed her wrist, holding tight. "You don't have to go in."

What? Her head whipped back toward him. He couldn't be serious. She'd come to finally stop this particular nightmare from playing out again and again.

"It's going to be..." Bowen huffed out a breath. "You know it's going to be bad inside. After the last vic, I just... It may be too personal for you."

Because that victim had been so similar to Macey. *The eyes. God, her eyes are just like mine.*

"I can handle this," Bowen continued, his voice grim. "I can check the scene and report back to you."

"*I* can handle it," she told him flatly. She wasn't about to be cut out of this investigation. Yes, it had hurt to see Gale Collins and the wounds on her body—too familiar wounds. But the pain that woman had endured—it had just made Macey all the more determined to stop Daniel. *As I wish I'd stopped him years ago.* She swallowed. "We have work to do. Let's get moving." She pulled her wrist free of his hold and jumped from the vehicle. Voices were rising all around her. Other deputies were already at the scene, and she was sure the sheriff was inside that little cabin. Such a nondescript place. Not high on a mountain, but nestled down low, in the middle of the woods. In the middle of *nowhere.*

They'd traveled down an old, winding graveled drive to get to the place. And now...

The sheriff appeared in the doorway. His grizzled face was grim and the star on his chest gleamed dully in the light. When he saw her, he tensed a bit, and then his gaze slid behind her to Bowen.

"FBI Special Agents...Night and Murphy, right?" he said. He offered his hand to them. "I'm Sheriff Burt Morris."

Macey shook his hand. She could feel his calluses beneath her touch. His shake was strong, but not too hard.

He briskly shook hands with Bowen, then said, "I never seen anything like this in all my whole life." A Southern twang slipped in and out of his words. "And before I retired up here, I worked homicide in Atlanta. But this... Jesus H. Christ. How does someone decide to do *this* to another human being?"

Daniel's motivations were still shrouded in mystery. Macey still didn't know exactly why he'd one day switched from saving victims to killing them.

Morris ran a hand over his face. "You two are the ones who study these guys, right? Take a look and tell me *how* a person could do that shit. Tell me how. Tell me *why.*"

Macey squared her shoulders and hurried inside. Her gaze swept over the small living room, and she saw what looked like some kind of makeshift medical office. There were rows and rows of medicine bottles, some medical instruments, even an exam chair.

Was he practicing off the grid? Setting up a practice out here, out of his damn home? A practice and a torture parlor—all in the same place.

"Bedroom," Morris said from behind her, his voice cracking a bit. "Go in there, but don't say I didn't warn you."

She could smell the odor coming from that room. The distinct scents of blood and death weren't easy to miss.

The wooden floor creaked beneath her feet. She lifted her chin as she entered the room, squared her shoulders and prepared to find another woman, cut, tortured but—

The Doctor.

Macey took two steps inside the bedroom before she froze.

There was blood. There was so much blood. It was on the ceiling. On the walls. The victim had been restrained, but not on top of an operating room table, as was Haddox's MO. Instead, the victim in that back bedroom had been tied to the four-poster bed. Thick ropes were around the victim's wrists and ankles.

There were wounds on the victim's arms. Long slashes from wrists to elbows. There were deep cuts on the victim's face. On the torso. Horrible, deep abrasions. But...

"That's fucking him, isn't it?" Bowen's whisper. His breath blew lightly against her ear and she could only nod.

They weren't looking at a female victim. They were staring at a male who'd been horrifically tortured before death.

And Macey knew the victim in that bed. The man who'd been murdered…the man who had been a helpless victim, who'd known pain and anguish in his last moments.

That man *was* the notorious Doctor.

She was staring at Daniel Haddox. The killer she'd been so desperate to find was right in front of her. Only…

Someone else found him first. And that someone had made absolutely certain that Daniel would never kill again.

Goose bumps rose to cover Macey's skin, and she couldn't look away from the dead man on the bed.

CHAPTER TWO

SHE STOOD IN front of the motel room door. Door number seven at a small, no-tell-motel-type place. The paint on the door was chipped. The light to her right kept flickering, and Macey knew she should turn around and walk away. Her room was right next door. She was in room number eight. She should go back inside number eight, shut her door and stay in for the night. That was what she *should* do.

But Macey knew that she wasn't going to leave. She couldn't. So she lifted her hand and she banged against that door. *Lucky seven.* As if anything had been lucky. The night air was brisk, sending a chill over her skin as she waited, and a moment later—

The door opened. Bowen stood there, his hair slightly mussed and a five o'clock shadow on his jaw. "Macey? Has something happened?" His dark gaze darted over her shoulder. "Did the sheriff learn anything new?"

"Not yet." She'd been at the crime scene for hours, unable to tear herself away, and Bowen had been right with her. They'd made sure there were no slip-ups at the scene. The Doctor was dead, apparently killed within the past twelve hours judging by the body's lividity. His victims finally had justice.

So why doesn't it feel that way?

"May I come in?" she asked when Bowen continued to stand in the doorway.

He blinked and stepped back. "Right, yes, of course." He motioned for her to come into his room. Like the room next door, her room, the place was small but clean. Clean enough, anyway. Two double beds were in the motel room, and a nightstand was situated between them.

She stared at the nearest bed for a moment.

"Uh, Macey? You all right?"

No, I am far from all right. "I thought we'd put him in jail. I thought we'd catch him and we'd lock him up. He'd go to court, the judge would find him guilty and Daniel would *never* hurt anyone again." Because he'd be locked away for the rest of his life. Caged.

Silence. The kind that stretched too long.

She looked back over her shoulder and found Bowen's dark gaze on her. His blond hair was tousled, as if he'd been running his fingers through it and faint stubble covered his hard jaw.

"He *will* never hurt anyone again," Bowen said.

Because the dead couldn't hurt anyone. Because someone had killed the killer. Her lips wanted to tremble, so she pressed them together. Her stomach was in knots. It had been that way ever since she walked into that bloodstained back room of the cabin. "This isn't the way I wanted it to end."

He just stared at her. No judgment on his face.

"It *isn't.*"

Bowen took a step toward her. "You don't have to explain or justify to anyone." He gave a bitter laugh. "Sure as hell not to me."

Because Bowen was the man who *had* killed a serial murderer…long before Bowen had joined the FBI. He'd hunted down the killer himself when local law enforcement wouldn't help him. When they wouldn't believe him. He'd found the evidence. He'd found the killer.

And in the end, he'd had to kill that man in order to survive.

Her hands clenched into fists at her sides. "Am I supposed to be glad that he's dead?" It wasn't the FBI agent talking. That wasn't who she was right then.

I don't know who I am.

"Am I supposed to be happy that someone found Daniel Haddox and gave him the same pain that Haddox gave to his victims? Is that supposed to make me feel good?"

Bowen was leaning against the wooden motel room door. "I don't think you're *supposed* to feel any way. You just feel—Mace, you *feel* any way you want. You're entitled. You were the guy's victim."

Her shoulders stiffened at that one word. *Victim.* She'd fought hard to stop being a victim. She'd joined the FBI so she would never be a victim. She'd be the one who hunted the killers. The one who brought justice. Not a victim. Never that again.

"He hurt you. He nearly killed you. If you want to be glad, then, damn it, be glad. Be—"

She found herself stumbling toward him. The control she prided herself on was in tatters. No, it had been sliced apart.

Only, not with his scalpel this time.

"Macey?"

She put her hands on his chest. "I need it to stop."

A faint furrow appeared between his brows. "What? What do you want to stop? Tell me, and I'll fix it."

She licked her lips. "I need the pain to stop."

His eyes widened. "Mace…"

"Because it's been eating at me ever since I was on his table." A truth she hadn't shared with anyone else, not even the FBI shrink that her team had to see every now and then to make sure they stayed psychologically healthy while they tackled their cases. When you worked day in and day out with serials, the pressure could get to you. Everyone had to go in for psych evaluations. Only, maybe she didn't share how she really felt during those visits.

I feel more than pressure. I feel pain. It's what I always feel. And I need it to stop. "I thought it would end when we caught him. Closure, right? Isn't that how it works? I catch the man who hurt me, who killed so many others, and then the pain goes away because *he* is locked away." No longer hunting in the dark.

Bowen's hands rose and curled around her shoulders. She liked his touch. It was warm and she felt so cold. But then, she always felt warmer when she was around Bowen. Warmer, safer.

"He's dead," she whispered. "But the pain isn't going away." And Macey felt a tear slide down her cheek. "Why won't it go away?"

His face hardened. "Macey…"

"Make it go away." She shouldn't be saying these things to him. She shouldn't be in his room. She shouldn't be near him, but…

Bowen wants me. I've seen it before. In his eyes. In the way he looks at me when he thinks I'm not watching him. When he thinks no one is watching. He'd never said anything wrong to her. Not a misplaced word. Never done anything wrong. But… she'd sensed the awareness between them. The attraction.

She'd ignored it. Or tried to. Maybe he'd slipped into her dreams some nights. His dark eyes and his strong hands. His sexy mouth. But those had just been dreams. Dreams that worked their way past the nightmares she had so often.

I thought the nightmares would stop when we finally caught Daniel. The nightmares and pain. But the pain Macey felt was still just as strong as ever.

Will the nightmares be just as strong, too? Because maybe she wasn't going to ever get over the attack. She'd wanted to be strong, but she just felt so twisted on the inside.

He's dead. He's dead. And when I first saw the body…the first thing I thought was…

He'd gotten what he deserved.

Pain twisted within her even more. *What am I becoming?* "Make it go away," Macey said again. She tightened her hold on Bowen's shoulders and pushed onto her tiptoes. "Please."

His lips parted as if he would speak, but she didn't give him the chance. Macey pressed her lips to his. Her kiss wasn't seductive or teasing. It was desperate. She was desperate. And he—

His hands tightened on her shoulders and he slowly pushed her back.

Oh. My. God. The pain in her chest just got worse.

His eyes seemed to have gone even darker as he stared at her. "What are you doing?"

She'd thought she was kissing him. Her cheeks burned.

"Do you have any idea how dangerous this is?" His hold on her shoulders didn't ease. If anything, his grip grew harder as a muscle jerked along his jaw. "You don't want to play with me."

She wasn't playing. And she wasn't going to hold back. She couldn't, not then. Macey was far too raw for any sort of games. "Do you want me?"

He sucked in a sharp breath.

"Because I think you do." She was putting it all out there. Macey couldn't think about consequences in that moment. She didn't *want* to think of them. Pain seemed to be eating her up from the inside out, and she wanted to escape that pain.

Pleasure—pleasure would combat pain. But she wasn't going out and hooking up with some random stranger. She couldn't. Not with her past. She was always too afraid of the secrets others might be keeping. Secrets meant danger.

Bowen wasn't some stranger. *Bowen.* She trusted him. He was her partner. Her friend. And that night, she wanted him to be more.

"Yes." He seemed to hiss the word. "I fucking want you." His voice had never sounded so rough to her before. Her heart thudded in her chest. "But I've been doing a damn fine job of keeping my hands off you."

Yes, he had. Never a wrong touch. Never a wrong word. "They aren't off me now," she whispered.

His eyes narrowed. "Macey, you are playing with fire."

Only because she wanted to get burned. "I don't want your hands off me. I want them all over me. I want *you.*" There. She'd done it. Laid her pride bare to him. He'd pushed her away when she kissed him, so maybe she should have just kept her mouth shut, but Macey wasn't herself that night. She felt as if she'd shattered into a million pieces and then been put together all wrong. Everything was wrong and she just needed the world to stop spinning so wildly, for just a few moments. To just *stop.*

"Be careful what you say."

"I'm always careful. Every moment of every single day." Even before her attack, she'd been so careful. The studious college coed. The diligent MD student. The hardworking resident. She'd been the good girl all her life, and what had it gotten her?

Scars. Pain.

I came back together wrong.

"I don't want to be careful tonight." Maybe that was the problem. Maybe he didn't understand— "Tonight," Macey blurted. "That's all I want." She wasn't looking for some kind of a forever promise. She didn't want one. She needed to feel something other than pain. Needed to see something other than Daniel's dead body.

Right then, she was staring into Bowen's eyes. And she could see, she could see—

He wants me.

"Spell it out for me, Mace," he said. "Tell me exactly what you want tonight."

"I want you." She licked her lips. His gaze immediately dropped to her mouth and she swore the darkness of his stare heated. "I want you to make l— have sex." She stumbled over the words. "With me." They wouldn't be making love. Love didn't enter into the equation.

"We're partners. The FBI won't let us cross that line," Bowen said. "You know—"

"We're not dating, Bowen. And the FBI brass isn't here." Yes, she was breaking rules. *Screw it.* "I want to be with you. But if you want me to go—" *Don't, don't, don't.*

He didn't speak. She *wouldn't* fall apart. Her chin lifted and she pulled away from him, stepping back. "I see." He was blocking the door. Another problem. How could she make her not-so-graceful exit when he was in the way? "Will you please move?"

His face was so tight and hard. Angry. But he stepped to the side. She reached for the door. Opened it—

Only to have Bowen's hand fly up and slam that door shut again. Suddenly, he was right behind her, his body surrounding hers. His hand was pressed to the door just above hers, and his face was bent beside hers. "Remember, when this is over—" his words were a rumble "—you came to me. You asked for me."

Slowly, but with her heart racing so fast and hard she feared he could hear the frantic beat, Macey turned to face Bowen. He'd trapped her between the door and the burning heat of his body. "I know exactly what I'm asking for." If he thought she'd regret this in the morning, he was wrong.

But Bowen shook his head. "Not what, Mace." *Mace.* For some reason, when he said her nickname— the nickname that only he used—her breath stuttered a bit. "*Who.* Remember who you asked for. Who you wanted." His eyes never left hers. "You wanted me. You came to me."

He wasn't going to let her leave. She saw that, felt it with utter certainty. She would have smiled but she was having trouble breathing because, yes, this was going to happen. She'd escape her pain for a bit and then she'd wake up tomorrow and the world would be back to its tainted self.

But that was tomorrow.

For the night...

"If I kiss you again, will you push me away?" Macey asked him.

"I'll never let you get the fuck away."

Maybe his words should have scared her. But they didn't. He didn't mean those words. They were only talking about the night. Nothing more than that. Just hours in the dark.

"Open your mouth for me," he told her. "Let *me* in this time."

Then he was the one to kiss her. And she made sure her lips were parted. His tongue swept inside her mouth and there was nothing hesitant about his kiss. It was hot. It was rough. It was consuming. And it was exactly what she wanted.

She gave herself fully to his kiss, holding nothing back. With her eyes closed, with her body pressed to his and her mouth desperate *on* his, she didn't see her past. She didn't see anything at all. Macey just felt. And she liked how she was feeling.

His hands were sliding down her back. Pressing to the curve of her hips, dragging her even closer to him. His arousal thrust toward her, heavy and thick, and there was no doubt that he wanted her. She hadn't been wrong about him. Her instincts had been dead-on. He'd felt the attraction, just as she had. But he'd been following the rules.

Screw the rules. For that night, anyway. They could go back to playing things safe the next day. Dawn would bring safety. For the darkness, though, in the darkness, safety was the last thing she wanted.

Her clothes were in the way. *His* were in the way. She wanted to be skin to skin with him. Wanted to feel every single inch of his body against hers. But...

Scars. She always worked so hard to cover her arms.

She pulled away from him and her lashes lifted as she stared into Bowen's eyes.

"Changing your mind?" Bowen growled. "Better do it now—"

Macey shook her head. No way was she changing her mind. Then, still staring at him, she began to unbutton her blouse. His gaze fell to her chest and then his eyes narrowed. When the shirt hit the floor, he'd see her scars. But...this was Bowen. She trusted him.

Wasn't that why she was there? Because she knew she could trust this one man?

She let the shirt fall, and, by habit, she started to curl her arms inward, but Bowen had stepped forward. He caught her wrists. Held them ever so carefully in his grip. His thumbs feathered over her pulse points. "You are so fucking beautiful."

"And you have on too many clothes," she whispered back.

He laughed. The sound was deep and rumbling and she realized that she hadn't really heard him laugh much. With their job, there wasn't ever much to laugh about but...he had a nice laugh. It made little butterflies swirl inside of her.

"That's an easy problem to solve." Once more, his thumbs slid along her wrists, but then he freed her, and he went to work on his clothes. As she watched, he tore off his shirt and dropped it to the floor. He kicked off his shoes and ditched his socks, and his pants followed as they slid to the floor. She didn't look away. Didn't pretend not to be avidly curious about his body. And what a body it was. Strong and tan. Sexy-as-hell abs. Powerful thighs and—

He pushed down his boxers.

She released a quick breath. He was *exactly* what she wanted. She reached for his cock, but, once more, his hand curled around her wrist.

"Sweetheart, I've been dreaming about you far too long. You touch me like that, and what control I have will be shot straight to hell."

Macey licked her lips and swore she tasted him. "That's okay. You don't need to maintain control with me."

But he shook his head. "You're the one person I need it with the most."

No, he was—

He used his grip to pull her closer. Right before his lips took hers, he said, "I'm going to put my mouth on every single inch of you."

A shiver slid over her. "Promises, promises…"

"Exactly," he told her, and then he took her mouth once more.

MACEY NIGHT AND Bowen Murphy had arrived too late. As soon as the victim had turned up in the FBI's computer system, he'd known that Macey would make the connection to Daniel Haddox. And, just as he'd anticipated, she'd hauled ass getting up to Hiddlewood, North Carolina.

She just hadn't hauled ass quite fast enough. She hadn't beat him to Daniel's cabin. In this particular race, she'd come in dead last.

No, that was Daniel. He's the dead one.

He stared into the night. Macey and Bowen had gone back to their motel. Was Macey happy, now that Daniel was gone? Did she even realize the gift he'd given to her? Macey hadn't needed to face the darkness in herself. She hadn't needed to finally discover...

Will I kill him when I see him? Or will I be able to take him in like a good FBI agent?

He'd saved her the trouble of finding out just what choice she'd make. Though he knew, deep inside, what she'd wanted.

She wanted him dead. I know it. So...he'd made that happen for her. She didn't have to pretend that she wanted to follow the law. Didn't have to be the good FBI agent. She could enjoy Daniel's death.

I gave him exactly what he deserved, Macey. Exactly.

The Doctor had experienced the same torturous pain that he'd given his patients. The bastard had been screaming his fool head off the entire time. He'd also been fighting...because Haddox *hadn't* been drugged. There hadn't been time for that.

Some criminals weren't meant for a jail cell. Why waste time with a trial? Haddox had been guilty as sin, and he'd been punished for his crimes.

Just as others would soon be punished.

Another race, another kill. Maybe the FBI agents would be better prepared this time, now that the game was truly in play.

He turned away from the mountain and headed

for his car. The night was still young. He could easily get to his next target. After all, he knew exactly where his prey was waiting. He'd worked hard to uncover the monsters in the dark.

Now I know where they are. And I will stop them.

When dawn came, Macey and Bowen would get news of another crime. He'd make sure of it. Another race, another killer. He hoped they'd be ready. After all, he had big plans for them both. Very, very big.

Don't disappoint me, Agents.

CHAPTER THREE

BOWEN'S HANDS SLID over Macey's shoulders, then smoothed down her arms. She shivered lightly at his touch and her lips parted.

He had his hands on *Macey*. This wasn't a damn dream. She was real. And he was having her. When he'd opened the door and seen her standing there, he'd thought something was wrong. It was late, it was dark, and Macey—why would she come to him in the middle of the night unless something had happened with their case?

But this wasn't about the case. This was about them. And he did not want to screw this up.

"You're taking too long," Macey said. Her voice was husky and seemed to stroke right over his skin. Her hands went to her waist and her pants were soon sliding down her gorgeous legs. She'd ditched her shoes—he didn't even know when she'd kicked off her heels but now she stood before him clad just in a black bra and a black pair of panties. Her body was freaking perfection to him. High, full breasts, curving hips and legs that would soon be wrapped around his waist as he drove into her again and again and made her scream with pleasure.

Because he wanted Macey to scream for him. Scream, come, repeat—again and again. He was planning for one hell of a night.

Her hands started to slide down her panties.

But he caught her, pulled her into his arms and carried her toward the bed. She gave a little gasp as he held her, and damn but she felt too light. So delicate. He'd have to remember that about Macey. Sometimes, he just saw her strength. But there was more to her. So much more.

He put her on the bed. She stared up at him, her arms braced behind her. The bra she wore was sexy as sin—pushing up her breasts—and he just had to touch her. He followed her onto the bed, and, as promised, he began to taste Macey. *Every single inch.* Because he'd wanted to have his mouth on her for a very long time.

Bowen knew he was breaking the rules. He just didn't care. For Macey, he'd do just about anything. Pity she didn't realize that.

He slid down the straps of her bra. First one, then the other. He put his hands on her breasts, stroking the nipples, teasing them, and then he took one sweet nipple into his mouth and sucked her. She gasped and her body arched up against him.

He licked her. Sucked harder. Lightly used the edge of his teeth on her.

"Bowen!"

Such a good start. He kissed a path to her other breast. Gave it the same attention. Her legs were spread, so he pushed his lower body between them, and every time that she arched up, his cock pushed against the silken crotch of her panties. She was getting wet for him, he could feel that through the scrap of silk.

Good…but it would be even better when she went wild for him.

Her hands slid over his back and he felt the bite of her nails. He wanted her mark on him, and he damn sure wanted to leave his on her.

Macey. Macey Night.

She had no idea how badly he wanted her. He'd tried to do the right thing. When she'd pressed her lips to his for that very first kiss, Bowen had locked down every muscle in his body. He'd tried hard to fight his ferocious need and tried to send her away.

But…

Macey had wanted him.

And he wanted Macey.

He began to kiss a path down her stomach. Down, down…

"No!" Macey's sharp cry. At once, his head lifted.

"No, Bowen, you don't need to—"

Need to? Was she serious? "Hell, yes, I do. I'm *dying* to taste you." Then he bent his head, slid his body back more…and he kissed her, pressing his mouth right to the silk of her panties. Her whole body stiffened and he kissed her again. "Told you, sweetheart, I'll be putting my mouth on every inch of you." He was a man of his word. Macey should have known that about him.

His fingers slipped under the edge of silk and he

touched her—*even softer than the silk*. He eased back so he could pull those panties down her legs and he looked up at her face. Her eyes were on him. Her breath came in quick pants and light spots of red stained her cheeks.

So gorgeous.

He tossed the panties and his hands curved around her thighs. With his eyes still on hers, he pushed her legs even farther apart. He lowered his head and then he licked her.

Macey nearly came off the bed. She jerked beneath him and gave a moan. He was holding her tightly, so she couldn't back away—and he put his mouth on her again. Kissing. Licking. Tasting.

Every inch of you, sweetheart. Every single inch.

Her moans filled his ears. Her taste made him drunk. He kept taking and taking, totally lost because he wanted every-fucking-thing that she had to give him. His cock was aching, and he wanted to shove deep into her, but he didn't want to stop tasting her. Too good. So good and—

"Bowen!" His name broke from her lips. He looked up and saw her bow off the bed. Her climax ripped through her and she clawed at the sheets.

That's the first one, Mace. The first...

He watched her as the pleasure poured through her body and he knew he wouldn't last much longer. Not with her taste on his lips, not with her body shaking from the release he'd given her.

Fuck, no, I won't last. He shoved from the bed.

Grabbed for the condom he kept in his wallet. Then he went back to her. "I can't be easy."

She reached for him. "Good."

He positioned his body between her legs. His cock pushed at the entrance to her body. Staring into her eyes, he thrust deep, and Bowen was lost. She was so fucking hot and wet and tight, and she drove him out of his mind. He grabbed her hips, his hold too rough and hard, but he couldn't slow down. All he could do was drive into her, again and again, sinking balls deep. Her legs were wrapped around him. She shoved back up against him, meeting him thrust for thrust. Her nipples were tight and pink, her lips were swollen and red from his kiss, and she was so sexy that he wanted to fucking *own* her.

Forever.

"Bowen!" She was coming again. He could feel her release all around the length of his cock, and those silken contractions pushed him straight over the edge. Bowen erupted, sinking deep into her one last time as his own orgasm hit—it slammed into him with the force of a tornado and he knew…there was no going back.

SHE WAS TRYING to slip out of his bed.

Bowen cracked open one eye. Macey was oh, so carefully lifting his right arm, the arm that had been curled around her midsection. The room was cast in darkness, and he knew hours had passed. They'd crashed hard together, falling into an exhausted slumber, but now, apparently, Macey thought it was time to leave.

Wrong.

"Not dawn yet," he muttered.

Macey immediately stilled. "I didn't mean to wake you."

"No, you just meant to slip away in the dark."

She didn't deny his claim.

Guilty, huh, Mace? But I caught you.

Her fingers slid over his forearm. That forearm had moved back against her midsection and was pinning her to the bed.

"I should go," she said.

"You should stay." He turned to fully face her. His eyes had already adjusted to the darkness. "Because we aren't done."

"We...aren't?"

"Dawn isn't here yet." And he wasn't even close to being finished with her.

"No." Her voice was soft. "Not yet."

There was another condom waiting on the nightstand. He'd made sure to get that thing out of his wallet because he had plans for Macey. When a guy was given a perfect fucking gift, he held tight to that gift.

He shifted his position so that he could be even closer to her, and Bowen lifted her hand toward his mouth. He pressed a soft kiss to the scar that began near her right wrist.

He heard her swift inhalation.

"Is it wrong," Macey asked him, "that I'm glad he's dead?"

"No." If she thought that he would judge her, then she didn't know him. With his past, no, there was no way he could ever think anything about her was wrong.

"I thought about killing him. More times than I can count."

He pressed another kiss to her scar and tried not to imagine Macey tied down on the freak's operating room table.

"And I had nightmares about him coming back to kill me."

Another kiss. Softer. "He won't hurt *anyone* again."

"No…"

And I wasn't going to let him get to you. Even if that bastard wasn't dead, I would never let him put his hands on you again, Macey.

"Tomorrow, we forget this," she said.

Not damn likely.

"We go back to the way things were."

Maybe he should be clear on this. "There are some things you can't go back from." Because he would never forget the way Macey looked when she came for him.

Before she could speak, he'd wrapped his hands around her waist and he'd lifted her so that she straddled him. Macey's hands flew down and pressed to his abdomen. Her thighs were so soft and her sweet sex…

He stroked her, sliding one finger, then another, into her.

Perfect. No, I won't forget this. Because I'm not an idiot.

He wouldn't forget, and he'd work like mad to get her this way again.

She began to ride his hand, arching up and then sliding down. She tightened her delicate inner muscles around him.

"Put the condom on me, Mace," he urged her, his voice little more than a growl.

She leaned over the bed and he licked her breast. She gave a little gasp—he loved that sexy sound—and then she was grabbing the condom and slipping back to him. Her fingers closed around his cock.

Sweet torture. His eyes squeezed shut. She wasn't just putting that condom on him—she was stroking him, pumping him in her fist, moving her hand from base to tip again and again.

In other words, Macey was driving him out of his fucking mind.

"Do I get to use my mouth, too?"

Now his eyes flew open. *"Hell, yes."*

She gave a laugh and the sound was the sweetest thing he'd ever heard. Macey was so sensual, so hot…and her mouth…

Her lips closed around the tip of his cock.

Fuck, fuck, fuck! His hands fisted and immediately slammed into the wooden headboard.

Macey stilled. Her mouth left him. "Bowen?"

"Don't stop, Mace." Now his voice was inhuman. Too rough. Too fucking wild. Oh, well…

She didn't stop. She put her mouth back on him.

She started licking him and sucking him and he was sure he'd explode. Right then and there.

Bowen tumbled her back onto the bed. He took the condom from her, put it on and was inside her in the next breath. His hands curled around hers and he pushed her wrists back against the bed. He remained there a moment, balls deep in her, his eyes on her, savoring the feel of Macey.

"Are you trying to drive me crazy?" Macey whispered.

Maybe. She'd driven him to the brink more than a few times.

He withdrew, plunged deep—and they fucking wrecked that bed as control was lost for both of them. Harder, deeper, stronger, he took her.

She arched her back and cried out as she climaxed.

Harder, deeper—

The bed slid across the floor.

He came, surging deep into her and holding her as if…as if he'd never let her go.

WHEN DAWN CAME, she eased from the bed—and out of Bowen's arms. She dressed quickly and then tiptoed to the door. Macey glanced back at him, helpless not to do so. He'd given her just what she'd needed that night.

Pleasure.

Oblivion.

Bowen was still in the bed. He was lying on his stomach, with his hand stretched out across the bed. That hand had been around her.

The covers were near his waist and she could easily see his broad back. And the scars there. Bullet wounds. She recognized them for exactly what they were. Bowen hadn't lived an easy life. He wasn't an easy man.

He'd been exactly the man she wanted.

She opened the door and crept outside. Moments later, she was back in her room. She stopped trying to be quiet as she headed straight for the bathroom. She could feel Bowen on her skin. His touch, his mouth.

He'd kept his word. His mouth had explored her, everywhere.

She wrenched on the shower faucet and the water thundered down. As the steam began to fill the bathroom, Macey turned toward the mirror and looked at herself.

What have I done?

HIS EYES OPENED the minute the door closed.

Dawn had come, and Macey had slipped away. She'd asked him for a night. Nothing more. Just the hours in the dark.

He rolled over. The bed smelled like her. Some sweet lavender scent.

Bowen rose and stalked to the bathroom. Then he paused because he could hear Macey's shower through the paper-thin wall. Macey, in the shower. Wet. Naked.

Just hours in the dark.

His hand lifted and pressed to that wall. Macey

might think they were one and done, but he wasn't so sure. Because...the thing about the dark...

It returned again. Every night.

"I WANT TO see the body." Macey squared her shoulders as she faced Dr. Lopez. "I need to study the marks on Daniel Haddox's body."

Dr. Lopez had her hair pinned at the nape of her neck. She wore her lab coat and she had a big mug of coffee gripped in one hand. "Figured you'd be showing up." She glanced at the clock on the wall. "Though I thought you'd at least wait until eight a.m."

"We've got two dead bodies in this town," Macey said. "There didn't seem to be a point in waiting much longer." She'd barely been able to wait until the ME's lab opened.

She'd taken a taxi over, leaving a note for Bowen. Because yes, she'd been a coward that way. But she knew he wanted to go and see the sheriff again. And she'd wanted—needed—to see Daniel's body.

She'd also wanted to avoid an immediate scene with Bowen. Night-afters weren't really her thing.

"Grab a coat and some gloves and let's get to work," Dr. Lopez said.

Right. Macey grabbed the coat and gloves and then she hurried to the table. The body was already in position. Just waiting—

"Is this weird for you?" Dr. Lopez asked, tilting her head as she studied Macey. "I mean, some of the stories say he was your lover."

"He wasn't." Her voice was clipped. "He was just the man who tried to kill me." Her gaze was on his face. *And now he's the man who is dead.*

But she frowned as she stared at him. "Is that… blood…under his eyes?" His eyes were closed, but she swore she could see a faint line of red beneath his lashes. She leaned in closer to get a better view.

The ME did, too. "Looks like it. Could be spatter from his other wounds."

Because he certainly had plenty of those. Macey's gaze slid down his chest. His arms. She hadn't touched him yet and…she was hesitant to do so.

It still doesn't feel real. I'm standing over his body, and I still feel like this is a dream.

"I'd be glad," Dr. Lopez announced.

Macey's gaze jerked toward the ME.

"If it were me," she added, staring at Macey from under the veil of her lashes. "If some guy had started carving me up like some freaking Thanksgiving turkey, I'd be glad when he died."

"*Not* exactly like a turkey," she replied even as her stomach clenched. Her hand hovered over Daniel's wrist. The bruising there was so dark, a deep mix of blue and black. *He fought against his restraints, tried to get free.*

But there was no escape for him. Not this time.

"Sorry. I, um, sometimes I say things without thinking them all the way through."

Macey glanced back at the ME.

Dr. Lopez gave a little wince. "It's why I work

with the dead. You know…they don't care if I say something stupid. The living—they mind."

Macey wasn't sure what to say.

"Are you glad?" Dr. Lopez blurted.

Macey blinked. That was the only expression change that she allowed herself.

The other woman sighed. "I did it again, didn't I?"

Yes. "We should start the exam."

"Right. Sorry."

Once more, Macey's gaze slid back to Daniel's eyes.

"He was as handsome as they said." Dr. Lopez moved closer to the table. "But he looks different from the pictures I've seen. Bleached his hair blond. Interesting touch. With this hair, he looks a bit like your partner, Agent Murphy—"

"He looks *nothing* like Bowen." Her voice had gone arctic.

"Sorry," Dr. Lopez said. She tilted her head. "Do you think he watched any of those movies about himself?"

She thought he had. She thought he'd probably enjoyed them. Macey had been against those films, but no one had listened to her. One slick prick of a producer had even told her movies like that were called "unauthorized" for a reason. They hadn't wanted her approval. They'd just wanted to share her horror with the world.

"Did *you* see the films?" Dr. Lopez pushed.

"Didn't need to. I saw the actual attack." She hadn't needed some Hollywood remake of the worst night of her life. Macey sucked in a quick breath as she squared her shoulders. "I want to look at his eyes."

Because it was bothering her, that swipe of blood that she could see right under each eye. It almost looked as if someone had tried to wipe away the blood.

"What do you think happened?" Dr. Lopez asked. "You think he killed Gale Collins?" She pointed to the cold storage lockers behind her. "You think he had a partner, someone who helped him kill Gale and then that person turned on the good doctor?"

"There was nothing good about him." She reached for a light, and then, steeling herself, she began to reach for Daniel's right eyelid.

Dear God.

She felt a punch right to her stomach. She shined the light into his eye, making sure she wasn't mistaken. Then…then she lifted his left eyelid. "There's something there." Her voice sounded hoarse to her own ears.

Dr. Lopez crowded in close. She'd gone silent. She took the light from Macey, shone it into Daniel's eyes. The left. The right.

Then she grabbed a pair of tweezers.

"WHAT IS HAPPENING in this town?" Sheriff Burt Morris demanded as he paced the small confines of his office. "First, that poor girl's body turns up and now…now this? I thought you FBI agents were going to swarm in and catch the guy."

"Someone else got to Haddox first." Obviously. "Based on the way he was murdered, it's apparent that the killer knew exactly who Daniel Haddox was…and what he'd done to his victims."

Morris stopped pacing. He swung back toward Bowen. "Like…a partner? The guy had a partner? Is that what you mean?"

Macey had never said anyone helped Daniel Haddox when he attacked her. And no signs had ever pointed to the guy working with someone else. But… Haddox had been in hiding for a long time. Perhaps his MO had changed.

But the crime scene didn't feel like some kind of partner-gone-wrong shit. It felt like a vengeance play. Payback.

"The cabin had been wiped clean," Bowen continued. "Our perp made sure he didn't leave any evidence behind."

The sheriff's shoulders sagged. "Is he going to kill again? That's what I need to know, Agent. Are the people in my town safe—or is the killer going to strike again?"

Before he could answer, Bowen's phone rang. "Excuse me." He pulled out the phone and saw Samantha Dark's name on the screen. "I need to take this call. Give me just a moment." He strode into the hall and put the phone to his ear. "Tell me you've got some news we can use up here." *Because things took a serious right-hand turn straight to hell.*

"I need you and Macey in Gatlinburg, Tennessee." Her voice was brisk. "And I need you there now."

"Uh, Samantha, we've got two bodies here. One of those bodies belongs to Daniel Haddox." He knew she didn't need the reminder. But… "And you just want us to pack up? In the middle of our investigation?" He marched down the hall, not wanting the sheriff to overhear. "The local sheriff is worried about another kill, and I have to agree with him. The Haddox scene was a freaking bloodbath, and things *aren't* looking good—"

"Patrick Remus."

At the name, ice tightened around his heart. "Patrick the Pyro? Shit, don't tell me he's in action again." Because Patrick was a killer the FBI had been hunting for months. The guy was an ex-firefighter who liked the flames too much. He picked victims and trapped them in isolated locations. Then he set those poor souls on fire.

"He may not be in action very much longer." Her voice was quiet. "A video went up on the internet one hour ago. A video that one of our techs picked up. In that video, Patrick Remus is tied to a chair and someone is pouring gasoline on him."

"You're fucking kidding me."

"No, I'm not."

Shit.

"The FBI was able to track down the location of the person who posted that video. We traced the IP address and we know the individual is in Tennessee." Her voice carried easily to him. "Local law enforcement is closing in, but you're less than an hour and a half away from the scene at your current location. I need you to get your ass over there. Get to the scene. I need your eyes. I need you and Macey to see what's happening there." Her rough expulsion of breath crackled over the phone. "Two serial killers. Haddox and Remus. Two of the worst out there... both seemingly targeted. And both within such a close distance of one another? *I do not like this*."

Someone was hunting serials? *We're the ones who hunt the serials.* That was the whole purpose of their group. They were the ones who went in. They were the ones who got the job done.

"Check out the scene in Gatlinburg. Haddox is already dead," Samantha continued grimly. "We don't have to hunt him any longer."

But they did need to hunt the bastard who'd killed him. Was he just supposed to walk away?

"I think the cases are connected," she said. "My gut—every instinct I possess—tells me that two serial killers...both of them in such close proximity... both of them targeted..."

He knew where she was going. "You believe Haddox's killer moved to Gatlinburg."

"He finished his work in North Carolina, and yes, I think he could have moved on."

Shit.

"I'm sending Tucker up to North Carolina so that we can keep a team member with the sheriff and his team there. It will take Tucker a few hours to arrive, but he'll be there by nightfall. In the meantime, I *need* you and Macey in Gatlinburg. Right now, we have to operate under the assumption that Remus is still alive and that he *is* still in Gatlinburg."

He understood. "We'll be there," he told her.

He ended the call and headed back in to see Sheriff Morris. "There's…been a development," he began quietly. "Another case nearby. Agent Night and I need to head out for the day, but the FBI will continue to provide you with backup on this case."

"What?" The sheriff's jaw dropped. "You're leaving? With two bodies here?"

I may have another victim close by. Another killer turned victim. "We're needed in Gatlinburg."

Morris's eyes widened. "Why? Is there another body there?"

A soft knock sounded behind Bowen. He glanced over his shoulder and saw Macey standing there. A Macey who looked too pale and wouldn't quite meet his eyes. Had Samantha already called her? Was that why she'd come to the sheriff's office?

"We found something. Dr. Lopez and I…" Macey cleared her throat. She had a manila file clasped in her hand. "I wanted you both to know about it. It's… very distinct. Could be our killer's signature." She headed toward the sheriff's desk. Her hands trembled a bit as she opened the file. Then she swallowed. "The killer…he put nails into Daniel Haddox's eyes."

What the actual fuck?

"Dr. Lopez made pictures for you." Her fingers pushed the photos across the desk. "This is…this is *not* something that Daniel Haddox ever did to his own victims. And this did not happen with Gale

Collins. Dr. Lopez and I checked. The nails…" She straightened her shoulders. "It's specific to Daniel's killer."

"Why would someone drive nails into the guy's eyes?" the sheriff demanded.

Macey finally turned her stare onto Bowen. One brown eye. One blue. Just like Gale. "He picked me because of my eyes," she said, her voice strained as she glanced back at the sheriff. "And I suspect that is the same reason he picked Gale. The killer knew that. The eyes—I think he made Daniel regret that he'd ever looked into our eyes."

Son of a bitch.

"This is why you can't leave!" the sheriff exploded. "We need you *here*. This case needs you! You understand this sick bastard out there!"

"Leave?" Macey blinked. "But…why would we be leaving?"

Because another serial is out there…and he's about to die. "Samantha needs us in Gatlinburg. She thinks—" he cleared his throat "—there is a possibility that a victim there may be related to these kills."

Her lips parted in surprise. "Another victim? Already?" And he knew by the tone of her voice that she carried the same fears he did.

The killer is accelerating too fast. There is no cooling-down time between his kills. He'd already been working to build a profile on this guy…and it wasn't looking good.

Highly intelligent, extremely organized, with

knowledge of crime scene analysis and police investigations.

In other words, a killer who would be very hard to catch.

And *that* was why Samantha wanted them to get in a chopper and get their asses over to Gatlinburg right then. Because if the guy was still there, they had to take him out.

He nodded toward the sheriff. "Our colleague Tucker Frost will be arriving in town by this evening. He'll make sure to provide you with support until we return." Because they weren't just going to leave and not look back. That wasn't how they worked.

Then he turned and followed Macey out of the sheriff's office. They didn't speak again until they were outside. The sunlight fell down on them as they approached the SUV.

"Who's the victim?" Macey asked him.

"Patrick Remus."

She stopped, then swung toward him. "What? The Pyro?"

He nodded, grimly. "Now you see why Samantha wants us over there? We're looking at two high-profile criminals...two men who appear to have been targeted by the same individual."

"What is the perp doing?" Macey whispered as her brow furrowed. "It's almost like he's..."

"Taking out the predators. Hunting them..."

Her gaze met his.

"Just like we are," Bowen finished.

"YOU'VE…GOT…THE wrong man…" Patrick Remus gritted out. He hurt—he fucking hurt. The bastard holding him had doused his legs with gasoline and then lit them on *fire*. Then the SOB had stood back and just watched while he burned. While the flames ate at Patrick's pants and his legs.

Then, when Patrick had been screaming, the guy had lifted a fire extinguisher and sprayed at the flames.

"You're the right man, Remus. I know. The FBI has been searching for you a very long time."

Patrick's breath heaved out. "No…no… I—I didn't do that shit. None of it. *Wasn't* m-me…"

The wooden floor creaked as his attacker began to stalk around him. The guy had a mask over his face—a black ski mask—so Patrick couldn't tell anything about him.

"Of course, it was you. Your prints were found at two of your arson scenes. In Orlando, Florida, where you killed that father of two. In Atlanta, Georgia, at the home of the elderly grandmother you sent to a fiery grave."

His teeth clenched. "I'm…a different man. I was *sick* back then. I'm better now! I haven't burned… anything…" Like this bastard would know the truth.

The floor creaked again. "You think that stopping absolves you of your crimes?"

His legs *hurt*. "I need a doctor."

His attacker laughed. "Too bad, he's dead. I finished him first."

What?

"I've been watching you... I *do* know that you've still been starting your fires."

Fuck.

"And I don't like it when people try to lie to me."

Patrick yanked at the ropes around his wrists. That jerk had tied his arms behind him, securing him to the wooden chair. This shit couldn't be happening. It *couldn't*. He'd been living a normal life in Alabama, even had a girl he was thinking about marrying. She'd won this fucking trip up to Gatlinburg, and they'd come together— "Lydia," he whispered. "What did you do to Lydia?" Because this bastard before him had taken Patrick right out of his cabin.

The guy laughed. Patrick jerked against the ropes. His legs *burned*.

"She doesn't know about you, does she? Poor Lydia...she thought she'd found her prince charming."

"If you've hurt her..."

More laughter. "What? You'll *burn* me?"

And he heard the slosh of a liquid. He couldn't see the other guy, but he knew the man had picked up the gasoline again. "The only one who will get burned," he told Patrick. "That's you..."

CHAPTER FOUR

"PLEASE, PLEASE, I need help!" The woman with the long black hair was ringing her hands as she stood in front of the check-in desk at the Gatlinburg police station. "My boyfriend is missing!"

Macey slanted a quick glance her way. She and Bowen had arrived at the station moments before—to a scene of pretty much chaos. The police captain had greeted them at the door. Captain Henry Harwell was young, probably in his late twenties, with close-cropped brown hair. He wore a pair of glasses and his gun was holstered at his side.

Right then, he motioned toward another uniformed officer and pointed to the woman. "Help her, now."

The officer bustled to the woman's side.

"We searched the cabin," Captain Harwell said as he began to lead Macey and Bowen back into the station. "Your Special Agent Dark helped coordinate with our team here and we went to the location that the FBI had pinpointed, but no one was there. I don't know if this is just some damn trick or what is happening—"

"No!" It was the woman's voice, rising over the

din in the station. "You're not listening to me! I think someone *took* him! He's not just off drunk somewhere or lost in your damn mountains! He needs *help!*"

Macey paused and glanced back at her.

"The cabin had been swept clean," Harwell continued. "I had my men check and double-check the place, but there wasn't any sign of anyone. It was a rental, one that had been taken off rotation while some repairs were being made. No one should have been there..." He exhaled. "And sure as shit not some serial arsonist! Damn it, do you know what will happen if word gets out that Patrick Remus is in this town? Do you know how many tourists come here?"

Macey found herself sliding away from the captain and from Bowen. There was something about that woman at the counter. Her certainty that her boyfriend wasn't just lost or drinking it off...that he'd been *taken*.

Macey touched her shoulder. "Miss?"

The woman swung toward her. Mascara smudges darkened her eyes.

"Why do you think your boyfriend was taken?"

"Because Patrick wouldn't just leave me!"

Macey tensed. "Patrick?"

"Patrick Grace." Now the woman turned to grab Macey's shoulder. "He was there last night, I swear, he was asleep in that bed next to me. But...but when I woke up, he was gone. The front door was wide-open. Our car was still there. But he wasn't." A tear slid down her cheek. "He left his phone, his wallet. Everything. I *know* something happened to him."

"Do you happen to have a picture of Patrick?" The name was too much of a coincidence to ignore. When individuals went into the Witness Protection Program, they often tried to keep their new first names as similar as possible to their real ones—it helped them to transition.

And Patrick Remus—the serial arsonist who'd been hiding from the FBI for over two years—must have adopted a new identity while he'd been in hiding. Perhaps that new identity involved a new last name—

"Here he is." The woman pushed her phone toward Macey. "See him? What will you do now? Get an APB out for him? Put his face on all the news channels?"

Macey stared at the photo before her. On the way there, she'd pulled up Patrick's old case file and photos on her tablet. The man she was looking at right then had shaved his head and put on about twenty pounds... but she was staring at a face she knew.

Patrick Remus.

"Macey?" Bowen strode toward her. "We need to go back with the sheriff—"

"No." She took the phone from the woman. "We need to put this man's face on every news outlet in the area."

Patrick's girlfriend gave a quick sob.

"Because he's been taken," Macey continued. "And we need to find him."

Macey turned the phone so that Bowen could see the screen. "Meet Patrick Grace."

Bowen swore.

"He disappeared from his cabin last night."

His gaze met Macey's and Bowen nodded.

"SHE HAS NO clue who her lover really is," Macey said as she stared through the one-way mirror at Lydia Chasing. Lydia was in the interrogation room at the police station, a mug of coffee cradled in her hand. Captain Harwell had just finished interviewing her, and Lydia…she seemed on the verge of collapse.

"The perp we're after…you really think he snuck into her cabin and took Patrick without her knowing?" Bowen's arm brushed against Macey's.

"I think he could have done that." She'd been considering the matter. "He attacked Daniel Haddox first." She turned to stare up at Bowen. "You saw Daniel's place—there were plenty of drugs there." *Syringes, medicines…things Daniel shouldn't have been able to access, but he had. He'd made his own office in the middle of nowhere. He'd probably catered to low-income families, promising them treatment but…had he just taken more victims? Were there more victims out there waiting to be found?* "Maybe our killer helped himself to supplies while he was at Daniel's. Then all he would have needed to do was sneak into Lydia's cabin, inject her while she was asleep, and he would have been sure she didn't wake up and…interrupt his work."

Bowen raked a hand over his face. "And if he

didn't want Patrick fighting back against him, then he probably drugged that guy, too."

"It's always easier to transport prey that doesn't fight back."

His gaze jerked up to hers.

"We should get blood work done on Lydia. See if anything turns up."

"Macey…"

"It's good that he didn't hurt her," she continued quickly. "I mean, it's showing us that he's focused on specific victims. If he'd wanted Lydia dead, she never would have woken up." She drew in a deep breath. "This goes along with him being so organized. He knew exactly who he wanted, and he took that prey."

"What are the fucking odds?" Bowen muttered. "The Doctor. The Pyro. Both so close together…"

"The odds are against that." She wet her lips. "So I think we have to assume that our perp set this up."

Now Bowen's eyes narrowed. "When the captain was interviewing Lydia, she said she'd won this cabin vacation."

"And that's something else we need to investigate because my money—" Macey gave a sad shake of her head "—is on the fact that the killer brought Patrick up here. He lured him here because he wanted to kill him. He wanted him close enough that he could bring him into the plan, the trap that was waiting."

"First Daniel Haddox, then Patrick Remus." Bowen blew out a slow breath. "Who is going to be next? And how is this guy finding these serials?"

He's a step ahead of us. More than a step. "He won't move onto the *next* one, not until he's finished with Patrick."

A knock sounded at the door. It opened a moment later to reveal Captain Harwell. "Local news is here. They're going to be running the pics of Patrick." His jaw hardened. "You two going to tell that woman in there the truth about her boyfriend before the press conference?"

Yes, they were. Because Macey didn't want Lydia finding out when she turned on a TV. Macey nodded, once, and relief flashed across the captain's face. She knew he was relieved he wasn't going to be the one who had to shatter that woman's world.

The FBI has a lead because of Patrick's real identity. The serials go to us... And they were going to be the ones to reveal the truth to Lydia. The captain exited and Macey squared her shoulders. She took a step toward the door—

Bowen moved into her path and she couldn't help but tense.

But he didn't say anything personal, didn't bring up the night before, and she tried to act as if she couldn't still feel him on her skin.

"She's not going to believe you, not at first." His voice was quiet. "People never want to believe that they've chosen the wrong lover."

She eased out a slow breath and forced herself to hold his stare. *I knew exactly who I was choosing when I went to you last night.* "I have pictures. We'll make her believe us."

His jaw hardened. "Lydia told the captain she'd been living with Patrick for over a year. A *year*, spent with a cold-blooded killer. And she never had a clue."

"I think some people are very, very good at hiding their true selves."

His lashes lowered over his eyes. "Yes." That was all, just that one word. Something about his tone nagged at her, but Bowen had already turned away and exited the room. She followed him out, hurrying her steps, and soon they were walking into the interrogation room. As soon as they entered, Lydia looked up, hope on her face.

That hope is about to turn to horror.

"Lydia," Macey began, trying to keep her tone kind. "I didn't get to properly introduce myself earlier. My name is FBI Special Agent Macey Night." She pointed to Bowen. "And this is my partner, Bowen Murphy."

Lydia frowned at them.

"We were brought to Gatlinburg because we were actually looking for a man named Patrick Remus." Macey set her manila file on the table and pulled out the first photo to show Lydia. "This man."

Lydia stared at the picture and a furrow appeared between her brows. "That's my Pat. Patrick Grace." She pushed the photo back toward Macey as she gave a nervous laugh. "Him with a whole lot more hair." She shook her head. "But you've got his last name wrong. Get that right before the reporters go live—"

Macey pushed the photo back toward her. And this time, she pulled out another photo, a crime scene photograph that showed the remains of Patrick's first victim.

"What in the hell?" Lydia shot to her feet. The chair slammed to the floor behind her. "Why are you showing me that? Are you crazy?"

"That is a photo of Patrick Remus's first victim, a thirty-nine-year-old father of two named Kent Powell." She tapped the photo of Patrick once more. "And this man…this man *is* Patrick Remus."

Lydia shook her head, frantically. "No, no, you're wrong. You have the wrong man—"

"Patrick Remus is a serial arsonist," Bowen said, his voice quiet and calm. Unrelenting. "He's wanted in connection with the murders of five people."

All of the color bled from Lydia's face. "That's… that's Patrick *Remus*. Not my Pat. Not my—"

"They're the same man," Macey interrupted. "And we have reason to believe…" She swallowed. "We believe someone found out who your Patrick really is…and that individual has taken him."

Lydia scrambled back. "He took the wrong man!"
No, he took the right one.

"You needed to know the truth," Macey continued. "Before the reporters arrived."

A tear leaked down Lydia's cheek. "Not my Pat…"

Macey stared at her and she saw the horror that began to grow in Lydia's gaze.

BOWEN GAZED AT the dark cabin. Sunset had come fast in the Smoky Mountains, and the night had chased its way across the sky. He'd spent the afternoon and evening searching for Patrick Remus—and for the man who'd taken the infamous Pyro.

Lydia had told them her story, again and again. She'd gotten a notice in the mail that she'd won a cabin in Gatlinburg. A three-day getaway. She hadn't remembered entering the contest, but she'd been too excited to question the win.

Bowen had figured that if the killer had lured Patrick and Lydia to the mountains with the cabin that had been taken off rental rotation, then perhaps he'd been using another, similar cabin as base. A cabin that was off the beaten path, a place that would give him privacy... Another cabin that was empty because it was part of the rental program, but perhaps a place that had also been removed from potential listings because repair work needed to be done on it, too.

Using that criteria, Bowen had hoped to compile a small list of possible locations.

But this was Gatlinburg...and there were dozens of rental agencies in the area. The simple search had turned up results that had taken hours to evaluate. He'd divided up the local law enforcement team and sent them out while he and Macey also searched. So far, they'd all turned up nothing.

"It doesn't look as if anyone has been here lately," Macey said, her quiet voice breaking into his thoughts. They were right beside their rented SUV, and she'd already pulled out her weapon as she stared at the little cabin. Nestled at the very top of a mountain, they'd spent twenty minutes going up the twisting, winding roads that led to this place.

No other vehicle was parked near the cabin. All of the lights were out. Macey was right, the place did look empty.

Just as the others had.

But they were still going to search it. He took a few steps toward the cabin, and the wind seemed to shift as he felt the breeze stir against his cheek and then—

"Gasoline," Bowen rasped. He could smell it. His eyes strained to see in the darkness. The cabin didn't appear damaged in any way, but he could sure as hell smell that gasoline odor. His nostrils flared as battle-ready tension swept through him.

An empty cabin *shouldn't* smell like gasoline.

He motioned to Macey, indicating that they'd be heading toward the front door. She moved quickly with him, their steps silent as they approached. And when they drew closer, he was able to tell that the front door was ajar, just a bit. Barely an inch.

This is the place. Bowen flashed another quick signal to Macey. He'd go in first, and he knew she'd cover him. Bowen pulled the flashlight from his pocket even as he silently counted down. *Three, two, one...*

He went in fast, crouching low. He kept the flashlight above his gun as he swept the room, sending out the light to check the corners and the darkness, and he heard the faint rustle of Macey's footsteps behind him. The scent of gasoline was even stronger inside the cabin. He glanced down and saw that the floors were...

"Wet," Macey whispered.

Not from water, though, not based on that smell. Someone had soaked the place with gasoline.

Fuck. That was Patrick's MO. He'd always poured gasoline all over the places where he kept his victims. On the floor, on the walls, on the furniture.

"Stay alert, Mace," he rasped. She wouldn't need the warning, of course, but, shit, he had to give it. This scene had *nightmare* written all over it. Bowen followed that trail, snaking down the narrow hallway and then turning right into a room at the back—

His light swept inside and fell on the slouched figure of the man in the chair. The guy's head hung forward and Bowen could easily see the blood that dripped from his wounds. "Patrick," Bowen said even as he rushed forward. His hand immediately went to the man's throat.

Blood. Blood every-freaking-where. They'd arrived too late. Patrick was dead.

A rough exhalation escaped from Bowen as he stared at the man's body. Jesus Christ. Burns covered him. His skin—what remained on his arms—was red and raw with oozing blisters. Blood had spilled down his shirt because the bastard's throat had been cut. And the wounds in his head...

Bowen's light slid over them. Patrick's head was shaved, just like in Lydia's picture, but there were two distinct wounds on his forehead. At first, Bowen thought those might be bullet wounds.

"Nails," Macey said, and there was horror in her voice. "*Just like with Daniel.*"

Damn it. The press didn't know about the nails. Their team had been careful not to leak that information. And for this guy to use them on Patrick Remus...

Same perp. We are absolutely looking at the same man who took out Daniel Haddox.

Shit, shit. It was—

Whoosh. He heard the sound and his blood iced. That whoosh of air was low and long and the very cabin itself seemed to tremble around them. He looked down at that stain of wet gasoline on the floor. It was a trail that led right to the dead man.

Patrick's body was fucking soaked in gasoline. Dripping with it.

So when he heard that whoosh, Bowen didn't stop to think. He just reacted. He grabbed Macey's hand and he yanked her with him as they ran toward the window in the back of the room.

The fire was coming. The perp who'd killed Patrick? He'd set a trap for Bowen and Macey. He was burning the cabin down, sending the flames running through the whole place.

He was going to bury his victims in the flames— just like Patrick had done. *His victims... Patrick. Macey. Me.*

This SOB wants to take out FBI agents.

The window wouldn't open. The damn thing had been nailed shut.

Organized killer. Planning, always two steps ahead...

Since the window wouldn't open, Bowen just broke the glass. It shot outward as he used his gun to knock out more chunks. He could feel the flames heating the air, and Bowen was afraid the whole cabin would go down at any moment. *Get Macey out. Get her to safety. Take care of Macey first.*

He pushed her toward the window. "Go!" Smoke was already thick in the room. The flames— *Shit, they are everywhere!*

She coughed as she jumped through the window. He started to follow her, but Bowen glanced back.

The flames were destroying Patrick Remus.

"Bowen!" Macey shouted.

And those flames were coming for him.

He followed Macey through the broken window. There had been too much gasoline in that cabin. *Too much.* They ran together, rushing toward their vehicle, racing away from the scene—

The explosion seemed to rock the whole mountain. The blast's impact came flying at Bowen. The force of it sent him surging into the air. He grabbed for Macey, trying to hold her tight and shield her. They hadn't moved fast enough. They hadn't gotten away in time.

I'm sorry, Macey.

Then he slammed into the ground.

HE COULD ALMOST understand why Patrick Remus had used fire. The flames were quite beautiful. And very, very powerful.

From the woods, he watched as the cabin exploded. The windows blew out, sending glass shards everywhere. Chunks of the roof flew into the sky.

Burning wood littered the ground. And those flames just kept raging, destroying everything in sight.

The FBI agents had arrived and they'd done exactly what he wanted. They'd gone into the cabin. They'd stepped right into his trap.

And he'd sent the fire after them. Fire to consume Patrick. Fire to teach the agents a lesson.

No one is above my justice. The agents thought they were so good at hunting killers. *Knowing them,* from the inside out.

They knew nothing. He was the one with the answers. He was the one who could see the killers. And now, thanks to the work he'd done, everyone would be seeing *him.*

He backed away, knowing that he couldn't linger. The agents had gotten out. He'd watched their frantic race to safety. Their escape hadn't upset him. After all, it was what he'd wanted. He hadn't intended for them to die in that cabin, but he had wanted to teach them a lesson. Maybe they'd have a few scars to help them remember this night.

The night I proved I was better than you.

If he'd wanted them to die, he would have boarded up that back window. Covered all the glass. Covered the windows for every room in that cabin. Instead, he'd just nailed them shut. He'd given them a challenge. Not death.

He was smiling as he backed away.

The flames kept shooting into the sky. He knew those flames would attract attention, and it was the attention he deserved. His time to shine. *His.*

He'd taken out two of the FBI's most wanted. The world owed him a debt of thanks. He'd collect on it. On that, and *everything* else that he was owed.

It was finally his time to shine.

CHAPTER FIVE

"MACEY!" BOWEN SHOOK her once, fear twisting in his gut because she was so still. Flames raged behind him but he couldn't take his gaze off her. He'd tried to shield her as best he could when the blast launched them into the air, but they'd hit the ground hard. Had she hit her head? His fingers slid into the silk of her hair, searching for a wound.

"I'm okay," she whispered. "Breath was just knocked out of me." Then she was pushing at him. *"I'm okay."*

But the fear in his gut wasn't lessening.

They both grabbed their guns and their flashlights. They'd dropped both in the chaos of the explosion.

The fire was crackling as orange and red flames shot into the air. "He's here." Bowen kept his voice as low as hers had been. "The bastard waited for us to go inside and then he set the place on fire." He'd nearly killed two FBI agents.

He nearly killed Macey.

"We have to search," she said, her voice a husky breath in the dark. "Each minute that passes is a chance for him to escape."

If the guy wasn't already long gone.

There hadn't been any sign of another vehicle when they arrived, so their perp was either on foot or he'd hidden an off-road vehicle in the woods. During the explosion, he could easily have slipped away on an ATV without Bowen hearing him.

He was watching the place. He waited for us to go in.

The whole scene had been one big trap.

"We need to search," Macey said again.

He looked back into the darkness. They couldn't just run into the woods, no plan in place.

They couldn't—

Then he heard it. The growl of an engine. The bastard *was* still there. He'd been waiting and watching all along. *Did you want to see if we survived?* Bowen made sure he had his flashlight and gun at the ready as he lunged toward the woods—and toward that growling engine. Macey's footsteps pounded behind.

"FBI!" Bowen bellowed. *"Stop!"*

His flashlight hit on the back of an ATV. He had a quick impression of a man's broad shoulders, of a black ski mask covering the guy's head, and then that ATV zipped forward.

"Freeze!" Bowen shouted, but the guy wasn't stopping. He was rushing right through the woods, twisting and snaking down the mountain. Bowen took aim, firing, and the bullet slammed into the back of the all-terrain vehicle. He heard the clink as the bullet hit metal, and for an instant, the driver swerved.

But the ski mask–covered asshole didn't stop.

Bowen raced after him, shoving branches and bushes out of his way. Macey was with him, giving chase at full speed. He lifted his hand, firing again at the fleeing man.

The ATV vanished.

What? He rushed forward, running as fast as he could and he saw that the woods seemed to just damn well drop. He threw out his arm, but Macey had already staggered to a stop next to him. From that vantage point, Bowen could see the ATV hurtling right down that slope as the driver moved like a fucking madman. He was zigging and zagging so that they didn't have a shot. Bowen pulled out his phone and dialed the captain. As soon as Harwell answered, Bowen filled him in on what had just happened, demanding backup so they could try to intercept the fleeing perpetrator.

"Maybe we can catch him at the base of the mountain," Macey said as soon as Bowen finished the call. "Come on!" She whirled and they raced back for their SUV.

And that was when they realized that the perp had slashed their tires. All fucking four of them.

THE KILLER HAD gotten away.

Macey stood near the remains of the cabin, watching the firefighters do their best to contain the blaze. She knew that the last thing they wanted was for that fire to get out of control and reach the woods. The firefighters had set up a strong perimeter to contain the flames, and the men and women in uniform were working like mad to douse the cabin.

Smoke drifted into the air, mingling with the darkness of the night. Cold air had settled around them, heavy and thick.

The local authorities hadn't been able to intercept the perp on the ATV, and the guy had made sure that Macey and Bowen couldn't follow him. *He's as organized as we suspected. Planning every move in advance.*

"Can't believe he tried to kill you two." Captain Harwell strode toward her, giving a rough shake of his head. "*Federal* agents, I mean…the guy doesn't fear anything or anyone, does he? Talk about a piece of work."

Her gaze slid to the thickness of the woods. "I'm not so sure he was trying to kill us."

"Uh, got to disagree there. He set the cabin on fire *around* you. To me, that seems like a pretty straightforward murder attempt."

She swallowed. "If he'd wanted us dead, there were easier methods. He could have shot us while we were going into the cabin or waited until we came out and then fired."

The captain put his hands on his hips. "So then what the hell was he doing?"

"He wanted us to see his work." She'd been thinking about this as she watched the firefighters battle the flames. "He didn't destroy the cabin until we got inside. He wanted us to find Patrick Remus. Wanted us to see his body and what he'd done to it." *The nails. Again.* The nails had significance. Terrible, horrible significance. "And he could have killed us with the fire, yes, but I think he knew we'd get out. *That's* why he went ahead and disabled our vehicle. He was… I think he was almost testing us."

Harwell gave a low whistle. "Did you pass his test?"

Once more, her attention slid back to the cabin. The flames. The smoke. Macey bit her lip for a moment and then replied, "I'm not so sure that we did."

THE FBI HAD booked Macey and Bowen a cabin just outside Gatlinburg, an A-frame perched high atop a mountain. It was too late to see the view beyond her balcony, too late to see anything but darkness. Macey knew she should crash into the bed, but when she closed her eyes, she just kept seeing Patrick's dead body. Daniel's body.

The fire.

The nails.

So she wasn't closing her eyes.

She was upstairs, in the loft bedroom. The loft bedroom consisted of a four-poster wooden bed, a chest of drawers that appeared to be hand-carved, an overstuffed chair and a pool table. Pool tables seemed to be standard fare in the local cabins, an extra activity for families on vacation. The pool table was situated about five feet from the bottom of the bed. She could look past that pool table and see the floor-to-ceiling windows that separated the interior of the cabin from the sweeping balcony. She could see the darkness.

The darkness was better than seeing the dead.

Her steps were slow as she headed toward the windows and the French doors that led outside. The wood creaked beneath her feet, and Macey froze.

Was Bowen awake downstairs? He'd taken the downstairs bedroom. He'd looked as tired as she had when they arrived. Tired, but furious. She'd seen the rage glittering in his gaze. He was pissed that their perp had gotten away.

So was she.

She didn't hear a sound from downstairs, so Macey slowly opened one of the French doors. The cool air slipped inside, swirling over her legs. She wore an old FBI T-shirt and a pair of jogging shorts. When she stepped onto the balcony, her bare toes curled against the wood. There were stars out there, so many, glittering in the sky. She moved to the edge of the balcony and her hands pressed to the wooden railing. A hot tub was to her left, another staple of cabins in the area. Local cabins seemed to come equipped with all the bells and whistles. The cover was on the hot tub, but she could hear the low hum coming from beneath it—a sure sign that the tub was working. Two rocking chairs were to her right, but Macey didn't go toward them. She stood exactly where she was and stared into the night.

And she thought about killers.

About the killers who hid in plain sight.

About the killers she'd known. The monsters who'd come into her path while she was at the FBI.

The monster who'd found her long before her Bureau days.

She thought about the man they were hunting now—the perp who'd beaten them to the two most wanted killers.

And Macey thought about Lydia... Poor Lydia Chasing, who'd been in love with a killer and she hadn't even known it. Now Lydia would be burying her lover.

A lover who'd had nails embedded into his body. *Nails. Why did he use those nails?*

She heard the creak of the door opening, and Macey spun around, her heart racing. She hadn't turned on any exterior lights, so she just saw a big, dark shadow standing in the doorway. But...

"Didn't mean to scare you," Bowen rasped. "I heard you moving around up here, and I just wanted to check and make sure you were all right."

Because that was Bowen. Taking care of the world. "I'm fine."

At her words, he didn't back away and ease into the cabin. Instead, he came toward her, silently stalking forward. Macey tensed, and her back bumped into the wood of the balcony railing. Instantly, he reached out and his hands curled around her shoulders. "Careful there," he said, and she could feel the warmth of his fingers pressing through her shirt. "You take a tumble and that's one very long way down."

"I'm not going to fall."

He didn't let her go. If anything, his hold tightened on her. "I'll make sure of that."

His words sounded like a dark promise. She tilted back her head as she gazed up at him. So much darkness, but she could see him now—thanks to the stars. Big, strong Bowen. Dangerous Bowen. "You shielded me today."

He didn't speak.

"You don't have to do that," she continued, trying to make her voice brisk. "You don't need to take the fire for me." Because that was exactly what he'd done. He'd put himself between her and the blaze. And when the cabin had exploded, he'd grabbed her and held tight, using his body to block hers so that she wouldn't get burned. She knew he'd gotten some blisters. They'd both gotten bruises. It could have been much worse. *And if it had been, Bowen would have taken those injuries. All because he was trying to protect me.*

"You're my partner. I'm supposed to look out for my partner." He was still holding her, but his hands had moved down to wrap around her wrists now. Macey shivered, and it had nothing to do with the cold.

And everything to do with him.

He'd been the perfect agent all day, not saying a single word about the previous night. As if it had never happened. As if she'd never gone wild in bed with him. His gaze had barely seemed to glance over her. His tone had been almost painfully polite before they'd gotten to that crime scene at the cabin.

When she'd gone to him in North Carolina, Macey had told Bowen it would just be for one night. She'd promised him that nothing would change. It sure looked as if he were following her rules.

So why do I want him to break those rules so badly?

"He's...he's going to attack again." She pulled away from Bowen because she found that she liked his touch too much. Something she hadn't expected at all. Since her attack, she hadn't liked to be touched. But with Bowen, it was different. He touched her, and she ached—she *wanted*. "The perp we're after isn't going to stop. Obviously, he's planned all of this in advance. I mean, getting Lydia and Patrick up here, then killing Patrick right after his attack on Daniel—"

"You think he deliberately scheduled his attacks so that one would follow right after the other."

She'd been considering this, again and again. While the firefighters had battled the blaze, she'd tried to get inside the killer's head. "If he did that—" Macey exhaled on a slow breath "—then he would have needed to plan Daniel's murder in advance, too. He would have needed to know that Daniel was hiding in North Carolina the whole time."

His body tensed before her. "And the bastard was what—waiting for us to find Daniel?" But he didn't give her a chance to answer. Instead, he growled, an angry, rough sound, and said, "That would mean that our perp let Gale Collins die. He knew exactly what Daniel Haddox was. He knew *where* Daniel was, and he didn't tell anyone. He just waited until he'd lined up all his little chess pieces."

"He waited until we entered the game." She licked her lips. "And then he went in for the kill." Macey hesitated a moment, and then she made herself say the suspicion that wouldn't leave her alone. "Our perp could have even used Gale as bait, to lure Daniel into an attack. Her eyes, Bowen. *Her eyes.* When she crossed his path, he would have immediately been drawn to her. Our perp would know that, if he had studied Haddox's work." And she was betting he had.

If Macey was right, then the perp had viewed Gale as disposable. A perfect victim to be used so that he could spring his trap.

He wanted the FBI to know where Daniel was... In order to do that, he needed the perfect victim. A victim that Daniel wouldn't be able to resist.

"The bastard profiled Daniel Haddox," Bowen said.

Yes, she feared that was exactly what he'd done.

"He found the perfect victim for Haddox, and then he waited to see what would happen." He took a step back. "He profiled *you*."

Her heart lurched in her chest. "What?"

"He knew you were looking for Haddox. Knew you were studying victims, always searching for a kill that could be Haddox's. Our perp knew you'd bring Gale's murder to the attention of the team.

He was counting on it." He gave a low whistle. "He wanted us here. He wanted *you* here. Whatever he's doing, I think the bastard is just getting started."

That scared her, and FBI agents weren't supposed to be afraid, were they? They were supposed to be the ones always ready to act. The ones eager to find the danger and stop the monsters.

But the more she learned about the monsters out there, the more she feared them.

The human monsters are far worse than any fairytale nightmare that children fear.

"We should get some sleep, Mace." Bowen's voice had become even rougher. "Something tells me tomorrow is going to be another long day."

Right. Sleep. Too bad that when she closed her eyes, Macey saw all the things she didn't want to face. *The Doctor is finally gone, but nothing is better.* "Good night, Bowen."

He turned away and paced back toward the door, but then he stopped. Tension seemed to fill the air between them. In the next breath, he'd spun back to face her. "We're not going to talk about it at all, huh?"

Her lips parted.

"I'm not supposed to bring it up? Supposed to act like things are normal between us?"

She wasn't sure things had ever been "normal." That was a bit of a stretch. Things had always been a bit strained between them. The awareness—that primitive attraction—had always been there simmering just beneath the surface.

"Nothing to say, Macey? That's not like you."

She swallowed. "I wasn't…myself last night."

"Really? Because I sure thought I was fucking you."

Macey flinched.

He swore. "That's not what I… *Hell.* I don't ever say the right thing with you. Don't ever do the right thing with you."

She thought he'd done things pretty right last night. She wrapped her arms around her stomach and tried to explain things better. Macey figured he deserved an explanation. "Daniel's death…it messed me up."

"Understandable." He stalked toward her.

"I felt like I was being torn apart on the inside." Her voice had dropped to a husky whisper. "I wanted to escape the pain. You were my escape."

A beat of silence. The uncomfortable kind, and then he asked, "Is that all I was?"

Her cheeks burned, and she was glad he wouldn't be able to see her blush in the darkness. "You're my partner. You're my friend." One of the few friends she had because Macey had learned not to let people get too close. If you let the wrong person close…

His hand lifted and his fingers slid over her cheek. "I am your partner. I am your friend." His hand curled under her chin. "And I'm your lover."

One night. Just one.

"Remember that," he said as his head came toward her. She thought he was going to kiss her. Macey tensed but she didn't back away. *I want his kiss. I want his mouth.*

I want him.

"Remember that," he whispered. "When you need someone to take away the pain again."

Then he let her go and he backed away. Bowen walked off the balcony and went back into the cabin. Macey waited a few moments, pulling in deep breaths of that crisp, mountain air before she crept into the room. Her steps were almost sluggish. She turned off the lights. She climbed into the bed.

She closed her eyes—

She saw death.

HE WAS A fucking idiot.

Bowen glared at the darkness above him. He was stretched out in the bed—a king-size four-poster. He'd stripped. He'd crashed. He should be asleep.

Instead, he was wishing he'd put his mouth on Macey.

Fucking. Idiot. Her lips had parted. He'd heard the little catch in her breathing, the slight moan. She'd wanted to be kissed by him.

Why did I walk away?

His hands were fisted beside his body. And he *ached.* His cock was hard and swollen and Macey's sweet scent was in his head. *She* was in his head. The woman was making him crazy.

The floor creaked. The faintest sound near the door. In a flash, he was up, the bedside lamp was on, and he grabbed his weapon from the nightstand.

And he had that weapon aimed—at Macey.

Macey in her sexy T-shirt, the soft cotton clinging so well to her curves. Macey with her shorts skimming the top of her gorgeous legs. Macey with her eyes so wide as she stared at him.

"Sorry," he rasped, aware that his voice was far too rough. That was how he often felt around her—too rough. "Reflex." A by-product of the job. Sometimes he just couldn't turn things off. He lowered the gun and put it back on the nightstand.

Macey took a step closer to him. "I can't sleep."

Because she'd had one hell of a forty-eight hours. Seeing the bastard who'd tortured her again...finding the guy's body. He knew that had taken a toll on her. Then today—shit, the explosion had been far too close for comfort and—

"I keep thinking about you."

Bowen shook his head, sure he hadn't heard her right.

"One night was supposed to be enough."

He'd never thought one night with her would be enough. Not with the voracious hunger he had for her. He wanted his hands on her body. Wanted his mouth on her. Wanted his cock *in* her. But he was trying to play by Macey's rules.

"But I want more." She took another step closer.

His body felt as if it had turned to stone.

He watched her as she closed the distance between them, and then her soft hands were rising to press against his chest. "I know we're crossing lines."

They were destroying lines.

"But it's just you and it's just me here right now." She licked her lower lip. His cock jerked. He wanted to be the one licking. "And I really need you tonight."

She was using him. He got that. Macey wanted the rush she felt in his bed to banish the darkness around her. He might not have as many fancy degrees as Macey or Samantha did, but he understood people. He understood criminals and he understood victims.

Macey rose onto her toes and her lips pressed lightly to his.

His hands clamped down on her hips. "Wait."

A shudder went through her body and he realized just how hard this was for her. Did the woman think he'd actually turn her away? *Her?*

Fuck, no.

"Want to make sure I'm clear on this…" His voice was even deeper. Closer to a growl now. "During the day, it's hands-off."

"If the FBI brass finds out we're together, we won't be partners any longer."

No. They'd be separated.

"So, yes." She swallowed. "Hands-off during the day. But at night…"

Her words had trailed away.

"Anything goes?" His hands tightened around her hips. He knew his hold was probably too hard, but he couldn't help it. When a guy held his wet dream in his hands, he was going to hold on tight. *And never let go.*

"Anything goes," she whispered back, and he was *done*. He took her mouth, his need for her clawing to the surface. The kiss was hard, desperate—because it had truly been one bitch of a day. Adrenaline still rode him hard with the kind of charge that even three showers hadn't been able to cool. In the dark, he'd thought far too much about what *could* have happened in that gasoline-soaked cabin.

He could have lost her.

His tongue thrust into her mouth. He loved her taste. Sweet and wild at the same time. Her little tongue flicked against his, and he lifted her up against him, carrying her to the bed. The first time wasn't going to be soft and gentle, wasn't going to be long.

Something was different that night. *He* was different. His control was barely in check.

She could have died. Fucking died right beside me.

He lowered her onto the bed, and her legs dangled over the side. Bowen grabbed the top of her shorts and he yanked them down.

No underwear.

"You're trying to make me insane."

His hands went to her thighs and he shoved them apart. Then he was touching her, stroking her clit and sliding two fingers into the hot heaven of her sex. Her hips arched against him, and she moaned. He worked her with his fingers, making sure she was ready, needing her to be wet and open for him. His fingers drove in and out, in—

"I want you inside when I come."

He grabbed a condom and rolled it on. She still had her T-shirt on and her long legs still sprawled over the edge of the bed. It was a high bed, putting her at just the perfect location.

He yanked her hips a bit closer to the edge of the

mattress. Her legs wrapped around his hips, and he plunged deep, standing up as he took her that way. His hands slammed down, locked with hers, and he pinned her hands to the mattress. In and out he drove, thrusting deep because he could fill her so completely from that angle. Her moans broke into the air, her hips shoved up against him, and her sex closed greedily around him.

Tight.

Hot.

Fuck.

She came—a fast, hard release that had her nearly screaming his name. He kissed her, taking her mouth even as he took her body. Her climax had her inner muscles contracting around him, and he let go. He drove into her and held nothing back. Wild and deep. Again and again.

His climax ripped through him, a release heavy and hard, and he didn't think it would ever fucking end.

When it did, when the pleasure ebbed and he could suck in a deep breath, Bowen stared down at Macey. He was still holding her hands in his. Still buried balls deep in her.

"Again," she whispered.

Fuck, yes.

SHE SLIPPED FROM his bed before dawn. Bowen let her go, keeping his eyes closed even though he'd woken the instant she'd pulled away from him.

Bowen could hear the softest rustles as she dressed. Then the creak of the stairs as she slipped back to the loft. When he was sure she was gone, his eyes opened.

The day was coming. That meant…

Hands off.

His jaw locked.

For now.

CHAPTER SIX

"I NEED TO see Patrick's remains," Macey said as she stood in front of Henry Harwell's desk the next morning. A line of dark shadow coated the young captain's jaw and the shadows under his eyes testified to the long night he'd had.

"Wish I could help you with that, ma'am," Harwell replied as he rubbed his hand across his jaw, making a faint scraping sound as his fingers hit the stubble. "But the body isn't ready. Hell, *what's left* of the body. The medical examiner just got it about an hour ago. The firefighters and arson investigators wouldn't let anyone close to the scene before that. We just... I'm sorry, but I'll get you access as soon as I can, all right? It's just going to take some time."

Time was something they didn't have, and that issue was why Macey was already at the police station, even though it was barely seven a.m. Time was not a luxury they could afford to waste. Not with this perp. He'd already shown he didn't have any sort of cooling-off period between his crimes, and Macey knew he *would* be taking another victim.

"We'll be creating a task force," Bowen said, his voice smooth and deep. "The FBI will be taking point. Based on the evidence at the scene last night, we strongly believe the death of Patrick Remus is linked to the recent murder of Daniel Haddox."

"Linked…" Harwell squeezed his eyes shut. "I know who you and Macey are, all right? I know what *team* you work for at the Bureau. You're thinking a serial is hunting, aren't you? Here. Shit, *shit*. Here, in my town."

"We have two bodies so far," Macey said. The nails were what linked them. And, after she'd left Bowen, she hadn't been able to sleep. So she'd been doing research online and she'd come up with some chilling possibilities. "We want to make sure there aren't more bodies out there." *Or that there wouldn't be more.*

"We'll be working with your department," Bowen continued as his dark eyes narrowed. "With the fire investigation team, with the ME… We'll need all hands on deck on this one. Cooperation is key." He nodded toward Harwell. "Let me be clear. This isn't a pissing match. We want to work together so that we can find the perp that we are after."

"And who is this guy? I mean, do you have any clue?" Captain Harwell rose and began to pace around his office.

"We're developing the profile." Bowen's reply was measured. "The more we know about the victims, the more we learn about the man committing the crimes."

"And that's why I need access to the body as soon as possible." Access to the body and she'd want to talk with Lydia again, too. Lydia would be key for Macey.

"The victims, huh?" Harwell's lips tightened. "From what you told me, the victims are two killers. Hardly like we're going to have a line of grievers for them." He crossed his arms over his chest. "I don't think you all realize...tourism is a very, very big deal in this city. We were named as the number one family destination in the US by one of the big news shows a few months back. You can't say that a serial is hunting in a place and *keep* it the number one destination. You'll scare people and they don't need to be scared." The faint lines near his mouth tightened. "I mean, hey, he's not even after regular folks, now, is he? Is that what your profile is saying? If he's only hunting killers, then everyone else is safe. We need the people in this area to feel safe." His gaze slid to his desk and the phone there. "The mayor spent an hour on the phone this morning telling me that very thing."

Macey's shoulders had tensed. "We're *not* saying that everyone else is safe. We can't make that sort of leap with the intel we possess."

Harwell's dark brows rose. "Seems like we can make the leap. I mean, the perp took out two sadistic—"

"The fire last night could have killed two federal agents." Bowen's voice was tight, striking like a whip. His face had hardened and his eyes glittered. "That single act tells us that our perpetrator isn't concerned with collateral damage. Innocent targets who get in his way will be taken out."

The captain's Adam's apple bobbed. A trickle of sweat had collected near his temple.

"He's a very dangerous man," Bowen continued darkly. A muscle jerked along his clenched jaw. "And, yes, we believe we are looking for a male." His gaze slid to Macey's and she nodded. They'd worked out this part together before coming to the captain's office. "We're looking for a white male, fit, probably between the ages of twenty-five and thirty-five. It would be someone who knows the area, someone who has a background in criminal investigation. A real crime buff. He would—"

"How do you know this stuff?" Harwell squinted at him. "How can you tell what race the guy is just by the way he killed? I mean, seriously, that's just crazy. That's like voodoo, psychic shit. You *don't* know that."

"Not all serial killers are white," Macey responded, as she walked toward the window and glanced outside. "Serial killers span all ethnicities but…in general— actually, by a very, very large percentage—murder victims are the same race as their killer."

"Ninety percent of the time," Bowen added.

And since all of their victims had been Caucasian, then they had a real high chance of being after a Caucasian killer.

"We're looking for a male," Macey said. "Obviously, we saw a male on the ATV, but we're looking for a male who is fit. One who is physically strong enough to transport Patrick Remus. It is possible that the killer had an accomplice but…"

"Serials don't usually work together," Bowen finished for her. "That's rare."

Right. She exhaled. "That's why we said he was fit—Patrick Remus was a big guy, and moving him wouldn't be an easy task. If the perp wasn't in top shape, it wouldn't be possible."

Harwell nodded, slowly. "And he knows the area because he was able to get away so quickly last night."

"On an ATV." Bowen rolled back his shoulders. "He was comfortable on the ride, indicating that he'd probably gone through the mountains that way before. He knew where the trails were so he knew exactly how to vanish."

"He's smart." Macey had no doubt of that. "He's what we call an organized killer."

A furrow had appeared between Harwell's heavy brows.

"Organized killers have higher IQs, and they tend to plan out their attacks in advance. They have controlled crime scenes." She ticked through the list. "They don't leave a lot of physical evidence behind for the authorities to find. When they aren't murdering, organized killers can blend in pretty well with everyone else. They're the killers you never see coming because they'll have normal jobs, be in relationships and maybe even have a spouse or children."

"In other words," Bowen said, "they look just like everyone else. They don't kill in some furious rage. Instead, they plan out everything. They can stalk their victims. They can hunt for days, weeks or even months." He inclined his head. "Considering the timing of both Daniel Haddox's death *and* Patrick Remus's murder, it's obvious this perp has been planning his attacks for a while. He moved his game pieces into play, and then he sprang his trap."

Harwell was quiet for a moment, and then he muttered, "Guess you two… Guess you know your killers."

Some they knew too well. And it wasn't because of psychic voodoo shit.

"So what's he gonna do next?" Captain Harwell's face had tensed up. "If he's some serial killer—"

"To get the moniker, the perp would need to kill three people," Bowen interjected.

Harwell's frown grew heavier. "What?"

"The term…*serial killer*…usually the perp murders three or more people. And as far as what we think he's going to do next…" Bowen glanced at Macey.

Her stomach twisted. They were in absolute agreement on this point.

"He's going to kill again," Bowen replied. "Our job is to find out *who* he's going after. Like Macey said, the more we learn about the victims, the more we learn about the killer."

THEY'D GONE BACK to the Remus crime scene. Macey slammed the SUV's door behind her and turned to look at the remains of the cabin. The fire had burned hot and hard, and the structure was barely standing. The wood remaining was blackened, and the scent of ash hung heavily in the air.

A line of yellow police tape blocked off the area. There was no sign of a crime scene team or an arson investigator. It was just her and Bowen. Macey had her gun holstered at her side as she approached the cabin.

"I want to look around the perimeter," Bowen announced. "Find out just where the hell our guy was when he watched us go inside."

Macey nodded and she followed him. The ground was covered in tire tracks and footprints. Dozens of law enforcement personnel had combed the area, and as the firefighters battled the blaze, she feared their hoses and powerful bursts of water might have destroyed any evidence that had been left behind.

Bowen paced away from her and began walking through the line of trees that surrounded the little cabin. His gaze was on the ground as he walked. She knew that he was looking for signs that might have been missed during the darkness. When he paused and then crouched low, she hurried to his side.

"Oil," he said.

She could see the faint brown stain on the grass.

"He could have parked his four-wheeler here, it would have been covered by the bushes."

A thick growth surrounded the spot. Perfect for hiding.

Bowen rose. His gaze was on the cabin. "He would have been able to see us perfectly."

She knew that the search team had found gasoline canisters in the woods near the cabin. The perp had watched them go in, and while they'd been searching the cabin and finding the body, he'd sprung his trap. "We need to get the evidence collection team out here again." She'd already spoken with the local FBI bureau, too. She wanted more feet on the ground on this case.

She wanted—

Bowen's phone rang.

The guy had service? Her phone connection had been spotty since they'd made it to Gatlinburg.

He frowned but quickly pulled out his phone. "Murphy," he said as he put the phone to his ear.

But in the next moment, his eyes had turned to slits of fury. He'd lowered the phone and tapped his finger on the screen so that she could hear...

"There's someone else...here for you to find." The voice was low and rasping. Static crackled. "But, really, if you'd done your job right...sooner, you would have found him...by now."

Macey stepped closer to Bowen—and to his phone—even as her gaze swept the area.

"Who is this?" Bowen demanded.

"I'm the man who beat you...to Daniel Haddox." More static. The connection seemed to be weakening. "I'm the man who...beat you to Patrick Remus." A pause. "And if you aren't good enough, I'll beat... you to the next one, too."

"This isn't a fucking race," Bowen growled.

"Isn't it?" His rasping taunt drifted over the crackling line. "I think...it is. And I think you're...losing. The big, bad profilers. Guess you aren't so...special. I do your job better."

"We don't kill," Macey said, driven to speak. "That isn't what the FBI does—"

Mocking laughter broke through her words. "It's what…he does. Bowen kills. That's how he got into…the FBI in the first place."

Her gaze flew back to Bowen's face and she saw that his expression was a mask of hard fury.

"I learned…from watching you, Bowen." That distorted voice continued, "But I'm better than you now. Everyone…will know that."

The line went dead.

"Son of a fucking bitch." Bowen immediately tapped the screen to call the number again and—

"You've reached the Gatlinburg Police Department. If this is an emergency…"

It was an automated voice, one that rattled off instructions for the caller.

Bowen's gaze glinted as he stared at Macey.

And the robotic voice kept speaking. "If you know the extension you wish to reach…"

THEY'D TAKE THE BAIT. He knew it. Bowen wouldn't be able to resist. He'd studied the other man, that part hadn't been a lie. Once upon a time, he'd even admired the guy.

Not anymore.

Bowen would hunt because that was who he was. He'd hunt and he'd lose.

Because that is who I am. I'm the better hunter.

And Macey…Macey always thought she was

doing what was right. Her self-righteous words rang in his ears. *We don't kill. That isn't what the FBI does.*

Before he was done with her, she would kill. And she'd see *exactly* what the FBI did—what she would do.

He whistled as he walked down the busy street. Tourists were fucking everywhere, but that was good. It was always easy to disappear into a crowd.

He knew what move Bowen would make next. Bowen would try to trace the call, but that shit wouldn't happen. He'd planned, oh, he'd planned well. The call would just connect back to the police department. He didn't leave traces behind.

If Bowen wanted him, he'd have to work harder.

Harder and smarter.

MACEY STARED DOWN at the remains. What little was left, anyway.

"Bad, isn't it?" a male voice behind her said, sympathy heavy in his tone. "But not the worst I've seen, unfortunately."

Macey glanced over her shoulder at the ME. Dr. Shamus McKinley's wire-framed glasses were perched on his nose. His skin was a warm brown, his eyes were a deep gold that glinted with intelligence and the silver at his temples was the only hint at his age. He'd struck her as being a no-nonsense ME. Straight to business, but still sympathetic to his victims.

"Not a whole lot to go by," he added as he rounded

the table and pointed to the remains with a gloved finger. "The body was severely burned."

Burned until nearly nothing was left. "Were the nails recovered?"

Shamus looked up at her. "Yes." His jaw locked. "*That* was something new."

"Because of the damage, will you be able to tell if they were delivered postmortem?" She suspected the answer based on her own medical training.

He shook his head.

But I'd hoped to be wrong.

"I will say, the victim's lower extremities were burned far more severely than his torso and his head."

She nodded and forced herself to look away from the remains. *The smell*... Macey swallowed. "When Special Agent Murphy and I arrived on scene, the victim's upper body hadn't been ignited. There were obvious signs that his lower body had been burned, though."

Shamus exhaled. "He was tortured before death."

"Yes. The burns on his upper body... I can confirm those happened postmortem." She turned away from the body and saw the evidence bag with the nails. She picked up the bag, studying them carefully. They looked to be the same size as the nails retrieved from Daniel's body, but she measured them, just in case. Measured the head of the nail. The length...

The same.

"We'll be sending these to the FBI's lab." Not that she meant any disrespect to the local authorities. "Our lab can get a faster turnaround for us, and they've already got the materials from the crime scene in North Carolina."

Behind her, he was silent.

Then he let out a long sigh. "There's this…museum in town…" Shamus's voice was low, hesitant. "You know Gatlinburg, we've got all kinds of things to bring in the tourists. This place—it's full of strange things. Oddities and stuff."

She turned back toward him but found that his gaze was on the remains.

She kept her stare on him.

"I took my grandson there over the summer." For a moment, his lips thinned. "He's a little thing, just turned six, and he got scared by one of the exhibits."

She waited, knowing this story would go somewhere.

His gaze finally lifted to hers. "They had this skull in there, supposedly from some old tribe in Africa that practiced voodoo magic. The skull scared him so much, not because he thought it was real, but because the skull had nails driven into it."

Macey sucked in a quick breath. What he was saying—her own research had uncovered a link between nails in the body and voodoo rituals.

"Not typical voodoo," he continued. "This was to *hurt* someone. According to the chart there, every time you wanted something bad to happen to a person, you drove a nail into the skull." Once more, his gaze slid back to the body. "Guess someone really wanted something bad to happen to that guy."

"I'm going to want the name of that museum."

He nodded. "Thought you might."

"I've been researching cultures that use nails. In the Congo region, there's a tribe that has a religious idol." She licked her lips. "Nkondi. But…what they do to the statues, it's nothing like this." She gestured to the body. "This is personal. This is an attack. This is…*hate*."

Shamus took a step back. "That's what they were called at the museum. Hate nails."

Her phone rang then, vibrating in her pocket. She pulled it out quickly and stared at the text from Bowen.

Need to see you ASAP. Got a hit on NamUS.

NamUS—the National Missing and Unidentified Persons System.

Her phone vibrated again.

Actually got more than one hit…too many.

A shiver slid over her.

BOWEN HAD TAKEN over the conference room in the police station. As soon as Macey entered the room, he dropped his news. "Ten."

She froze, her unusual eyes flaring wide. "Excuse me?"

He rose and stalked toward the map he'd pinned

to the wall—and he pointed to the bright circles he'd made on the map. "I found a pattern."

She shut the door behind her and hurried forward. "What kind of pattern?"

"Over the last two years, there are ten hikers that fit a profile—young males, all in their early twenties. They left hiking alone, and then they vanished. Most of them weren't even reported missing for several weeks because they didn't have close ties to their families."

"You're telling me *ten* people have gone missing here in the last two years?"

His brows climbed. "Actually, almost twenty have gone missing in the area."

Her lips parted.

"But only ten fit my pattern based on age and sex."

She shook her head. "What about the others?"

"Some were older, some were female, some disappeared in a group...and they used different trails."

"Different trails," she repeated. "Okay."

He pointed to the red trail he'd marked. "Eight of our missing ten males departed on *this* trail."

"And the other two?"

"No one knows what trail they were supposed to use, but my money says they took the same one."

She leaned in closer to the map. Her sweet scent teased his nose and her arm brushed against him. "With so many victims, why didn't someone point this out sooner?"

"Their disappearances *were* reported, but they

were just listed as missing persons. Hikers who got lost in the mountains and never returned home. Most of these guys were amateurs, this was their first or second big hike…so it just seemed like a tragic accident when they went missing. They were considered people who got lost in the woods, nothing more." And he wouldn't have even looked at the puzzle pieces if it hadn't been for that damn call. "But the perp…he brought us to Gatlinburg for a reason. He brought Patrick up here for a reason. So I knew that I needed to look closer at this area. And when I went into NamUS, the hits wouldn't stop."

Her head turned and she was staring into his eyes. "You're saying you think a serial has been operating up here—"

"For years." Now he was grim. "Operating right under the nose of the park rangers, of the local cops, of everyone, because the disappearances weren't thought to be linked to foul play. Every single one of them went down as an accident. A lost hiker."

"Were any remains found?"

He shook his head. "But that isn't unexpected. There are so many bears up here, coyotes… They could have destroyed anything they came across."

She pulled her lower lip between her teeth and he could practically see the wheels spinning in her head. "This guy we're after…he found the pattern, that's what you think, right?"

Hell, yes, it was. "He found it. He saw what no one else did."

Now she backed up a step. "Maybe…or maybe

he's responsible for that pattern. That's an option
we can't overlook." She began to pace and her shoes
clicked on the floor. "That could be the very reason
he brought us to this town. He was tired of his work
not being noticed. He wanted attention, so he made
sure he got it."

That was one possibility, yes. "My gut says no.
This guy we're after, I swear, it's like he's profiling,
too. Only he's one step ahead of us."

Once more, her gaze darted to the map. "Have
you told Samantha?"

"Called her right after I texted you. She's sending Tucker Frost over this way. Tucker *and* Jonah
Loxley."

Her gaze shot to him. "She added Jonah to the
team?" Her eyes gleamed. He knew she liked the
other agent.

"Looks that way." And he wasn't sure how he felt
about that addition right now. "She thinks Jonah's
tech knowledge can help us out. Considering the way
the perp had us chasing our asses with that phone
call…" The clever bastard had made it seem as if his
phone call had come from the police department.
"Well, we need someone who comes from a strong
tech background on our side." Jonah had worked in
cyber crimes for years.

But the guy had been a desk jockey that time. He
hadn't seen a lot of field action. This case would be
different for him. And sometimes, when agents got
in the field…

There's no safety net out here.

"I've been trying to convince Samantha that Jonah should be added. We needed someone with his skill set and…he's like us."

Like us. She meant the ties that they all had to killers.

"He has a personal stake in these investigations," Macey added. "And that stake can make all the difference in the world. That's something we've all learned. That's the whole reason Samantha made her team."

He nodded. And Bowen didn't want to admit that maybe—hell—maybe he was jealous of Jonah. He knew that Jonah and Macey were close, and he didn't like that fucking fact. *Suck it up, Murphy. Do the job.*

But if Jonah so much as looked at Macey the wrong way when Bowen was near…

Her shoulders tensed as she turned to look at his tactical board once more. "I think we need to go out on a few stops. We have plenty of daylight left. No sense wasting it." The morning was gone, but they had the afternoon and evening to use.

Bowen cleared his throat and said, "We're going to need some equipment." He tapped the red trail on the map. "Because we're going hiking." The best way to learn from the victims was to try to re-create their steps, at least as much as possible. They could get out into the field and talk to the park rangers. See if anyone remembered *anything* about those disappearances.

"I made a discovery, too. Thanks to the ME."

His head craned toward her.

"The nails struck me as being very important to this killer. Driving them into the victims seemed symbolic. I did research earlier, and I found a link to a group of individuals living in the Congo..." Her words trailed away. "While I was with the ME, he told me about a visit he'd had to one of the 'oddity' museums in the area. Turns out, they have a skull there on display, one that is filled with hate nails."

"Hate nails?" He did a double take and forgot Jonah Loxley for the moment.

"Each nail that you drive into the skull is supposedly a wish for ill luck to befall your enemy. It's... it's like a voodoo doll. Every nail is a bad wish. An ill thought." Her shoulders straightened. "With that skull here in the city, we can't overlook the connection. We need to see it for ourselves. The killer could have been inspired by it, and that could have made him use the nails as his—"

"Signature." Yeah, Bowen got exactly where this was going. "So we had a budding serial on our hands, someone who'd learned to track other killers. He wanted to stand out, he needed a signature, and inspiration struck him."

She nodded. "After our visit into the mountains and our chat with the rangers, I'll arrange for us to get an after-hours view of the museum. And I'll have the local FBI agents check out all the employees there." But she still hesitated and he saw the worry in her eyes.

"What is it?"

Her head cocked to the right as she studied him. "It's you."

Now he was the one to close the distance between them. But he didn't touch her. He wanted his hands on her, but they were working the case. And during the day...*hands off.*

"He called *you*, Bowen. And when he spoke to you, he didn't address you as Agent Murphy. To him, you were Bowen."

He'd noticed the same thing.

"You're personal to him."

"I'm a challenge. The asshole knows about my past." He forced a shrug. "Nothing to worry about."

But she touched him. Macey put her soft hand against his chest. "Liar." She said the word almost as if it were a caress.

He looked down at her hand. He could feel the heat of her touch running straight through him.

"It's personal," she said again. "He called you. He taunted *you.* This guy is pitting himself against you, like a test to see who's better."

But better at what? Profiling? Or killing? As a rule, Bowen didn't talk about his past. It was ugly and twisted because the things he'd done were ugly and twisted. At the time, the media had tried to make it look otherwise, but Bowen knew the truth.

He might lie to other people, but not to himself.

"I don't like his focus on you." Her voice had dropped. "He had your personal line, Bowen. He could have been watching you, for a very long time.

And last night, that fire…maybe he did want to trap you inside. Maybe he wanted to kill you."

"You think I'm one of his targets?"

She didn't answer, but then, with Macey, her silence was an answer. He leaned in close to her. "Don't worry. I know how to take care of myself."

Before she could reply, the door swung open. Her hand was still on his chest, and he was still bent far too close to her. Captain Harwell stood in the doorway and surprise flashed on his face.

But Macey hurriedly stepped away from Bowen. "Captain, there have been some developments you need to hear about."

Hesitant now, Harwell slowly entered the room. "This isn't going to be news I want to hear, is it?"

Grimly, Bowen shook his head. "It looks like a serial may have been operating in your town."

"Right, yeah, we know that. That's the reason you've got a task force happening and my office is being swarmed by FBI agents—"

"No," Bowen cut in, voice flat. "I'm talking about a serial who has been hunting in this area, undetected, for years." Briefly, he went over his theory and the missing men.

But Harwell started shaking his head halfway through Bowen's explanation. "No, they're just lost hikers. It's tragic, but it happens. We get several missing each year."

"And that's why you didn't notice the killer." Bowen was certain on this. "That's why he slipped by undetected for so long. Because hikers do go miss-

ing, it happens, like you said. But these ten men...
they're all similar victim types. They stand out because the perp picked them specifically. They're his
targets."

The captain paled. "You...you're serious?"

"Dead serious."

His eyes squeezed shut. "The mayor will have a
heart attack."

"Then you'd better get him to a fucking doctor...
because we've got victims out in those mountains.
Ten of them, so far."

HE WAS SO THIRSTY.

Curtis Zale licked his dry, busted lips, but the
move did no good. He couldn't remember the last
time he'd had more than a few sips of water to drink.

*Because the bastard is keeping me weak. Giving
me just enough to live, but not enough water or food
to get stronger.*

His hands were tied behind him. His feet were
roped to the legs of the chair. Roped and—*no, don't
think about it. Not now.*

He'd screamed until he was hoarse, but no one
had come for him. No one had come to help him.
His backpack was just a few feet away. Easy enough
to see, but impossible to get. He had a knife in that
pack. A knife, food...water. His whole damn life
was in that pack.

If he could get to it, he could survive.

*The SOB put it just out of my reach. He wanted
to taunt me.*

How long had it been since Curtis had seen the bastard? One day? Two?

More?

So fucking thirsty. If he didn't get a drink soon…

How long could a person go without water?

Maybe the prick wanted him to suffer a slow, torturous death. Maybe the guy got off on that. Curtis had just been walking, hiking, exploring the damn trail when he'd seen the guy. *Just another day.*

But the day hadn't ended like others. He'd been hit, slammed with a freakin' hammer, of all things. Curtis had gone down and when he'd woken up… he'd been in the cabin. He'd been a prisoner.

His body shuddered. For a moment, he wished that he had a family. That his wife would be looking for him. Or that his parents would be sending out a search party.

But there was no family. There was no one to give a shit about him. Never had been.

He'd been in the woods too long, but no one would know where to look for him. As he often did, he'd gone off on his own. Only this time…

I'm going to die alone.

The thought ripped through him and he tried to scream. But no sound emerged.

CHAPTER SEVEN

THERE WAS A "Missing" sign near the ranger station. It had taken longer than she'd wanted to reach that remote station. The mountain road had been treacherous and twisting, and her ears had popped as they'd gone higher and higher up the narrow road. There had been trees all around the road—and a deep plunge to nowhere that waited just past the old guardrails that lined the path.

But now Macey stared at the rough, wooden sign, and her gaze trekked over the photos posted there. Men, women. Even a few teens…barely more than children. Their photos were tacked up along with notes from family members. People begging for information on those who'd vanished.

Seeing those photos made her heart race faster because after reviewing more of the files, she'd become certain Bowen was right. The victims all shared too many similarities. They formed a perfect victim profile. Many serials had a type. Scary, but true.

When dating, certain men preferred brunettes. Or redheads.

Some women always fell for the guy who was tall, dark and handsome.

And some killers...they had a preferred victim.

Her hand rose and pressed to one of the photos. It was of Glen Young, age twenty-one. His mother had left a note.

My Glen has been missing for a year. Please, please if you see him, get him to call his mother. I swear, I'm not mad any longer. I want him to come home.

A number was below the photo.

"Sad, aren't they?"

Macey looked back and saw a park ranger staring at her. His hair was a dark blond, his eyes a pale blue. His hands were on his hips as he studied her. No, not her—the sign. "Had a supervisor once who thought we should remove that but—" he shrugged "—removing the board takes away the family's hope, you know? Their loved ones went missing here, so they pray they can be found here, too."

"You don't sound like you have much faith in that happening."

The ranger shook his head. "Never seen one of the missing walk out of the woods. You go off the trail, you get lost, and it's only a matter of time before you run out of food. Before the cold gets you. Or the animals do." His gaze raked over her. "You're Agent Macey Night, right?"

Bowen approached behind the ranger. They were both of a similar height and build.

The ranger looked back over his shoulder at Bowen.

His head inclined. "Your partner said you two had some questions. Wanted me to come out here so the tourists wouldn't listen in." He put his hands on his hips. "So I *know* that can't be good."

"Good has nothing to do with this," Bowen murmured.

No, it didn't.

"I'm Zack Douglas," the ranger said. He offered Macey his hand.

Her fingers closed around his. "Thanks for taking the time to talk with us today." When he released her hand, Macey pulled a list of the ten profiled missing men—and their photos—from her bag. "We'd like for you to look at these men. Look and see if you recognize any of them."

He started thumbing through the photos. But then he looked back at her. "Course I recognize them… Most of these guys are on my board."

The board behind her.

My board. "Did you talk to any of them? Learn where they were going? Did anything stand out in your mind about these individuals?"

"I think we have most of their permits on file," Zack mused. When he saw her frown, he said, "If you're going backcountry hiking, you have to make a reservation and get a permit. They're required for all overnight stays. Most of the guys—once I found out they were missing—I pulled their permits. A few didn't have them, but, like I said, most did." He glanced back at the photos. "I can give you the permits, but not a lot of information is on them."

Macey and Bowen shared a long look. "Those permits—did they outline where the hikers were going?"

"Yeah…and the shelters or campsites that the hikers were hoping to use."

"That information would be extremely helpful."

"People don't get it." Zack sighed as he put his hands on his hips and looked out at the woods that surrounded the ranger station. "It's beautiful up here, God's country, but it's dangerous. Streams swell, bridges wash out, trees fall down…and the bears, it's their home, you know? You have to respect nature. You have to be prepared for it. We tell hikers that they shouldn't try the longer, more dangerous trails if they don't have experience." A sad smile twisted his lips. "Some people just don't want to listen, you know?"

Her gaze slid back to the photos. "I know."

"Always tell people…make sure you triple-check your route. And *be* at your campsite before dark. Hiking in the dark can be downright deadly."

There were a few other things out there that could be deadly, too.

"Can you take us out on the trail that most of these missing men used?" Bowen asked. "Our research has already shown us that they generally set out on one particular path."

Zack rubbed the back of his neck. "Setting out on the path is one thing…staying on the path is another. A few steps off, and then you're lost. You don't come back."

No, you didn't.

Especially not when you had help.

"Let me make sure my post is covered, and then I'll take you all out." He turned and headed back to the small brown building. "I'll pull up the permits on the computer."

Macey glanced up at the sky. It was just after one p.m. If the hikers had gone out too far, they wouldn't be able to follow their full path. "There's no way a search team can check the entire national park."

"No, but we're not hitting the whole park." Bowen had moved to her side. The ranger was a few feet away. "If these men were all heading for the same campsite—or hell, even if just five or six of them had the same campsite in mind—*that's* where we need to go. I want to check it out. And I want to see if any particular visitor has gone to that site again and again over the years."

A visitor who could just be their killer.

CURTIS TWISTED HIS HANDS. Was he still bleeding? The rope had cut into his wrists, slicing deep into his skin. He didn't think that he could feel his finger-tips any longer.

He rasped out a breath. He was so fucking thirsty. So—

The door opened, a long slow crack of sound. His head lifted up and he blinked against the light that spilled through that doorway. The light fell around the man there—the man who wore the black ski mask.

"Didn't think I'd just leave you, did you?"

Actually, that was exactly what he'd thought. That the bastard had left him to rot.

Laughter rolled as the man stepped into the old cabin. And then he was right in front of Curtis. He lifted a water bottle and held it gripped in his gloved hands. The guy always wore gloves. Always had himself covered.

Maybe...maybe that means he will let me go. Since I haven't seen his face, maybe he's planning to let me go. He knew hope always came to the desperate.

The guy slowly untwisted the bottle cap and then he held that water near Curtis's mouth. Curtis twisted and jerked his head forward, but he couldn't get to the water. The son of a bitch held it just out of his reach.

"You want it badly, don't you? So badly. I bet you'd do just about anything...for a drink."

Wild, frantic, Curtis could only nod.

That taunting laughter came again. "You're not the first, and you won't be the last."

What was that supposed to even mean?

But the water was pouring down, finally hitting his mouth because the guy in the ski mask had brought it closer to Curtis. He opened his mouth wide, greedily gulping the water down his parched throat. Curtis took and he took and the water hit his face and his shirt and he hated the waste. *I want it all.*

"Even brought a special treat for you." The guy tossed aside the now-empty bottle. It bounced on the floor. His captor pulled out a sandwich bag. *A fucking sandwich!* "Have some…"

Curtis tore into the sandwich. His tongue was swollen, though, and his throat was still dry even though he'd had the water, so he almost choked on the bread.

"That's right, eat up. Because I've got big plans for you."

Curtis had big plans, too. He was going to escape. He was going to get to his pack. And he was going to drive his knife right into the bastard's throat.

"THIS ISN'T A COME-ON…"

Bowen glanced up at Zack's words and saw that the ranger was staring at Macey. Staring a bit too hard at her.

"But I swear," Zack continued as he moved around the counter at the ranger station and slid to Macey's side, "I've seen your face before." His head tilted as he studied her. "Those eyes of yours are pretty unforgettable."

Bowen narrowed his own eyes.

"Have we met?" Zack pressed.

Macey's gaze jerked toward Bowen.

He wondered what his expression looked like. *We're on a murder investigation, and that's totally a fucking come-on.* The ranger needed to get his shit in check.

"We haven't met," Macey replied. "Sorry." Her gaze slid back to his computer. "Those files almost ready?"

"Printing now." But Bowen saw that the guy didn't take his stare off Macey. "I know I've seen you before. Those eyes…they are really something." Then he laughed, seeming to catch himself. "Though I'm guessing you get told that all the time."

Once more, her gaze darted to Bowen. This time, Zack followed her stare.

Bowen crossed his arms over his chest. *Move away from her, asshole. Move. Away.*

But the ranger didn't get the hint. He turned back to Macey. "Are you sure—" he began.

"A few years ago, my face was splashed in every paper along the East Coast. I was the only victim to get away from Daniel Haddox. He came after me—" her voice was flat, almost brittle "—because of my 'unforgettable' eyes."

Fury pumped through Bowen's body.

"That's probably where you saw me," she added, voice softer. "Because, no, as I said, I don't think we've met before."

He didn't back away. Didn't apologize. If anything, his stare seemed to warm as he focused on her. Bowen moved closer to them. *Back away, Ranger. Back away.*

"I wish we had met before." Zack's voice was gentle. *Dick.* "And I wish we were meeting under better circumstances now. Because I think you're a very interesting woman, Special Agent Night."

"You like women who escape from killers?" Her words were crisp.

"I like strong women. Smart woman. I think you're both."

The printer beeped. Ranger Jackass finally turned away from her and snagged the papers that had just pushed from the machine. Then the guy was leaning over the counter as he pored over them. Looking for similarities, and Macey crowded in closer.

Bowen didn't like it when Macey got close to the guy.

Shit. It's getting personal. Hands-off. No strings.

She looked back at Bowen.

He wanted his hands on her.

"Five of them were planning a brief stop at Rainbow Falls." Zack glanced up at Bowen. "But you knew that, right?"

Bowen inclined his head.

"After Rainbow Falls, the trail keeps going up to the summit of Mount LeConte. That's where they were supposed to be headed. The end goal." He thumbed through the pages. "Actually, now that I think about it…there was a guy here, maybe three, four days ago? He was going on the same path." Zack moved away and tapped on his computer again. "Right. Curtis Zale. He was heading up there, too."

"We need to get there," Bowen said. He wanted to see that trail.

But Zack glanced toward the windows. "Yeah, I don't think you quite get how things work out here." He rolled one shoulder. "Here's a little rule to help you… In the Smokies, it takes hikers an hour to make it about 1.5 miles. Rainbow Falls? It's 2.7 miles away—that's one way. So say two hours to get there. That's *just* to the falls. If you want to reach the summit, you're looking at nightfall by the time you get to the top of Mount LeConte. And you two—you aren't prepared for that kind of hike. Not today." He drummed his fingers on the countertop. "Why don't you come back tomorrow, at first light? I can take you out then. We'll have enough time to get to the summit."

"We have gear in the truck," Bowen told him. "And no, this isn't my first hike. Macey and I will head up to Rainbow Falls. We need to see that scene today." And they had just enough time to do it before the sun set, barely. They'd go up the full summit tomorrow, with the ranger. "The trailheads are marked, we'll get there."

Because every moment counted. They had a killer out there—two killers, if he wasn't mistaken. The bastard who'd been hunting hikers and the perp who'd made death into a game.

"I'll guide you," Zack said quickly, "just like I promised."

"Then let's get moving." Because he didn't want to waste any more daylight. Time was precious, and he had the sinking feeling that he was already far behind in this deadly race.

THE TRAIL WAS QUIET. Almost too quiet. Or at least, it seemed that way to Macey. Maybe she'd just spent too long in DC—too long surrounded by the sights and the sounds of the city. But the forest put her on edge.

Her steps didn't falter as she hiked. She and Bowen had both changed before heading to the ranger's station. She wore jeans and a loose coat. Hiking boots. And she had her gun.

Never leave home without it. Especially not after last night.

"We're turning up here," Zack called out. "There's a log foot bridge that crosses over the creek. Once we get past that, it won't be much farther until we hit the falls."

He'd kept up a brisk, unrelenting pace, but Macey and Bowen had both followed him easily. She glanced around, trying to peer through the trees. So many trees. So many shadows. It was all too easy to imagine a lone hiker going through those woods, unaware that he was being watched.

Hunted.

Because predators didn't always walk on four legs. The most dangerous predator…he walked on two.

They passed another sign on the trail. "During times of high stream flow, Rainbow Falls Trail is impassable. Use Bullhead Trail."

Macey stilled, her foot near one of the large boulders that often seemed to line the side of the trail. "Is the Bullhead Trail as well traveled?"

"Nah, not at all," Zack told her. "Folks just use it when they have to do it—they're going for the falls, you know? They don't want to miss the view. Plenty more people use the Rainbow Falls Trail."

So if their killer was looking to isolate prey, he

would be less likely to use the Rainbow Falls path…
and more likely to focus on the Bullhead Trail. *Because he has a better chance of not being spotted by anyone else.* "Maybe the missing hikers were diverted." She glanced around, trying to see through the trees. Thin trees, thick trees, twisting trees that seemed to wind into the sky. "Maybe they had to go off their original path because the stream was too high." She could hear the flow of the water.

Maybe it hadn't even been the stream that had caused them to divert, though. *Perhaps they changed routes because they had some help.* The kind of help that had gotten them killed?

Zack glanced back at her. "Even though it's not as well used, the Bullhead Trail is easily marked, too. Even amateur hikers should have known to stick to it."

"But what if it was late…darkness falls fast here. They could have turned toward the Bullhead Trail and gotten lost." Excitement pulsed through her. "Show us the way, okay?" Because every instinct that she had was screaming at her.

Zack cast a quick glance toward Bowen.

"Show us the way," Bowen said.

So they diverted paths. They went deeper into the woods and then…she saw a cabin's roof, barely visible over the trees. If it hadn't been so late into the fall season, she probably wouldn't have seen it. But many of the leaves had fallen off the trees, and in the distance, she could just make out the slanting roof of a cabin. "Bowen!" Her voice sharpened. They were at least a mile from the cabin, maybe two. It was far away, but the thinning trees had enabled her to see it as soon as they shifted to the other trail.

He immediately followed her gaze. "Who owns that cabin?"

"No one," Zack answered slowly. "It's an old abandoned place. No one is in there." He paced closer to Macey and pointed at the area. "Every now and then, hikers will take shelter there for a night or so. It's not an official campground because the place really should be torn down. The wood is rotting and the forest is trying to reclaim the cabin, but…we had cutbacks so we haven't gotten around to demolishing it." He gave a low whistle. "But we should get going. That cabin is—"

"It's in our killer's operation zone." Tension had tightened Macey's body. "It's a prime spot for him to set up his base." She pinned Zack with a hard glance. "Are there any other cabins in a two-mile radius of this location?"

"No, just that one." He rubbed his chin. "But I mean, you can't seriously think—what? That some guy has been killing in that place?" He laughed, but it was a nervous sound.

"I want to see that cabin." She glanced up at the sky. They had time to make it.

"This is what happens." Now Zack sounded sad. "There is no trail that leads to that place, not anymore. People get urges to see things. They go off the trail. They get lost when night sneaks up on them."

She braced her legs. Every instinct she possessed

screamed for her to get to that cabin. *It's in his kill zone. We could have found his safe place.* A place where he might have left evidence behind. "Today we're searching the cabin." Tomorrow, at first light, they could start out and head up to Mount LeConte.

"Have it your way." Zack pulled out his radio and made a quick call in to base. "Let's go."

THE BASTARD IN the ski mask had left him again.

Curtis could feel his stomach cramping. The food was sitting heavy on him… *Food.* The guy had given him food, so that had to mean he wasn't planning on killing Curtis. It *had* to mean that. So he just had to stay alive longer. Just had to escape…

His gaze strayed to his pack. Still fucking out of reach. But…

I feel stronger.

He began to tug on his ropes once more. And maybe it was his imagination, but Curtis could have sworn the ropes were starting to feel…looser.

I'm going to get out of here. Then I'll find you, you fucking bastard. I will hurt you so badly. I will make you pay.

As soon as he was free. That prick in the mask— He'd picked the wrong man to mess with. Curtis Zale wasn't anyone's bitch. He didn't give up easily and he wouldn't die easily.

He had too many plans.

There were too many things that he wanted to do with his life.

And dying isn't one of those things.

"TOLD YOU," ZACK said as they drew to a stop right outside the cabin. They'd hiked for an hour and the sun had slid across the sky. "It's abandoned."

The place sure looked that way. The windows were boarded up, vines snaked up the sides of the cabin and the slanting walls looked as if they might fall in any moment.

"Can't usually even see this place, not in the spring and summer. The trees cover it too completely. Most folks will pass by and never even know it's here." Zack strode toward the door. "Could have been some historic spot, but there isn't any funding to repair it. No funding to repair it, and no funding to destroy it. So the place sits."

Macey cast a quick glance at Bowen. He was near the front door, just steps away from Zack.

"Mind stepping aside, Ranger?" Bowen drawled. He'd dropped his pack. Macey did the same.

Zack blinked, but then he stepped aside.

"Thanks." Bowen reached for the door. There wasn't a handle there, no lock, nothing. He shoved against the door and it opened with a long creak of sound.

"See?" Zack announced. "I told you, the place is completely empty—"

"Help me!" A desperate, choked cry. One that had come from inside the cabin. Instantly, Bowen was springing forward, and Macey was right on his heels. She grabbed her gun from her holster even as she shoved Zack out of her way. She bounded into

the cabin after Bowen, her gaze sweeping the scene for signs of a threat but…

No threat. Just a victim. She saw the man tied to the chair, heaving and struggling desperately. As she watched him, his mouth opened and closed, but only a hoarse whisper escaped when she knew he was trying to scream. A backpack lay on the floor a few feet from him.

"Help…" the bound man managed again. Macey rushed to his side. Bowen was checking the rest of the small cabin, and she knew he was searching for the perp.

"It's okay," Macey told the man tied to the chair. "I'm FBI Agent Macey Night. You're going to be all right."

"Promise?" A desperate rasp.

She grabbed for the ropes around his wrists. The ropes were soaked with blood and she saw the deep cuts on his wrists where the ropes had sliced into him as he struggled to break free.

"Oh, shit!" Zack cried out. He stood just inside the doorway.

"Get back!" Macey yelled. This was a crime scene. They couldn't afford to contaminate any evidence, and for all she knew, the killer could be hiding in that ramshackle cabin.

Or he could be outside, watching. Just like before, at the other cabin.

Zack started to retreat.

"Stay near the door!" Macey shouted. "Get cover, okay?"

"Cover?" Then Zack seemed to understand because he looked over his shoulder and immediately crouched.

She yanked at the ropes. Damn it, they weren't coming loose.

"Clear," Bowen barked as he came back into the narrow room. "No one else is in the cabin." He hurried to her side and he pulled a knife from his boot. He sliced right through the ropes at the guy's wrists, and the man in the chair let out a weak cry.

"Circulation has to come back," Macey said, understanding exactly what he was going through. "It's going to be painful at first, but it won't last."

Bowen slid to the front of the chair. He started to cut through the ropes that bound the man's ankles, then he paused.

"Bowen?" Macey prompted.

He looked up at her. "The chair was nailed to the floor. And there are… Hell, one of the nails…no, two of them—"

"Are in me," the guy rasped. "In…my feet… Help…"

Oh, God. "Get him loose," Macey demanded. Then she was there, helping Bowen, working hard to free the man who'd been bound. And *nailed to the floor.*

"He took me." The man's voice was a broken whisper. "I—I was hiking… He took me. H-hit me… Why did he h-hit me? Wh-why did he hurt me?"

She looked up at him just as Bowen pried the guy loose. The ropes were cut and the nails… *They're still in him, but he can move.* They'd pried the long nails from the wooden floor. "We're going to get you medical attention." She turned her head toward Bowen. She moved closer to him, and her lips feathered over his ear as she warned, "The killer could be watching, just like last time. We need to get backup out here and we need to search the woods."

"You read my fucking mind, Mace." He pulled out his phone, but then swore. "No service."

"Go outside." She nodded toward a watchful— and still crouching—Zack. "Use his radio or see if you can get service. I'll stay with the victim."

Bowen's gaze swung back to the man in the chair. The man who was clutching his stomach and crying. "How long were you here?" Bowen demanded.

The guy shuddered. His lips were raw and blistered. His face too pale. His pupils were pinpricks and sweat covered his body. "Wh-what day is…it?"

"Thursday."

The man's eyes closed. "Left…for my hike…on *Sunday*."

He'd been trapped here for that long? Macey curled her hand around Bowen's. "Get him help. I'll stay with him." She was the doctor. She could check his vitals, make sure he didn't do anything to hurt himself.

"S-starved…me… No f-food… B-barely any… w-water…"

"Go," Macey said to Bowen.

He slipped away. She rose, moving to press her fingers to the man's throat. His pulse was thready. "What's your name?"

"C-Curtis…"

That was the name Zack had given them…the guy who fit their profile. The man who'd gone out on the trail that the killer loved.

She put her gun on the floor, making sure to keep it within easy access, and she knelt in front of him. "Did you see the man who did this to you?"

Curtis shook his head, but then his bloody hand lifted and he pointed to his bag. "F-food…in there. Water…"

When she'd run into the cabin, she'd left her pack outside. She had extra water—water that this man desperately needed.

Before she could speak, Curtis lurched up. He stumbled toward his pack even as she grabbed for him. "Curtis, no, you'll hurt yourself!" The nails were still in his feet, near his ankles, and his blood dripped onto the floor.

"Water…" Such a desperate plea.

She helped him toward the backpack. He fell, sinking to his knees, and then he was reaching his trembling hands inside the bag. She saw the water bottle, several of them, and his shaking fingers hovered over those bottles.

But then his hand shoved deeper into the bag and when his fingers came up, he was clutching a knife. A knife that he drove straight at her.

CHAPTER EIGHT

"BOWEN!" MACEY'S FRANTIC shout reached him just as Bowen and Zack managed to contact the ranger station. There was still no damn cell signal, but Zack's radio had worked to connect.

At her cry, Bowen whirled back toward the cabin. His heart raced in his chest and adrenaline pounded in his blood as he raced for the open door. His gun was gripped tightly in his hand.

He burst into the cabin but then Bowen froze. *Froze.*

The guy who'd been bound—the victim who had been so desperate—stood behind Macey. And the jerk had a knife at her throat. Bowen could see a trickle of blood sliding down her neck.

"Let her go," Bowen snarled. "She's FBI. She's here to *help* you." *You dumb son of a bitch.*

But the man shook his head. "No..." His voice was still that broken whisper, and Bowen had to strain to hear him. "She's gonna...lock me up."

"We're not the bad guys," Bowen said. He didn't let his gaze stray to Macey's face. Not then—he couldn't. He had to focus on the man who held her. A man who'd been pushed too far. A man who—

"I am," the guy rasped.

I am. A cold chill slid over Bowen's skin. He stared into the "victim's" eyes…and he didn't see fear staring back at him. He saw rage. Hate.

And he realized just what had happened.

The bastard on the phone… The perp did beat us. He beat us again. He said there was another serial out here. And I think I'm looking at him.

Bowen and Macey had been told that another killer was hunting in the area, but when they'd gone into the cabin, he'd thought they were looking at a victim. The man had been tied, dehydrated, held captive, tortured…

"He did to you," Bowen said quietly, "what you did to the others."

Curtis flinched. "Fucking SOB. I'm gonna…find him. I'm gonna *kill* him."

Bowen took a step toward him.

"Don't!" And Curtis jerked Macey closer to himself. "I will slit her throat from ear to ear." The threat was low and whispery, but Bowen heard it. His whole focus was on the man who held Macey. "Not my first kill…so don't think I'll…hesitate."

Bowen's weapon was aimed at the bastard's head. Unfortunately, he didn't have a clear shot. Macey was too close. One move of *her* head to the left, and the bullet would hit her. And Curtis kept jerking her, so there was no way Bowen could take that risk.

I also can't let him kill her. "Ten," he said, throwing out the number.

Curtis squinted at him.

"Is that how many people you've killed, Curtis? Ten people? Ten hikers who never made it out of these mountains."

Curtis laughed, a rusty, weak sound. "A few more than that…"

"How?" Bowen asked. He wanted the guy to keep talking. If he kept talking, Curtis would be focusing on Bowen and not Macey. If he kept talking, Curtis's hold on Macey might ease. Bowen knew Macey would be waiting for her chance to escape. As soon as the guy's hold weakened, she'd act. Bowen had to give her that opportunity.

Helplessly, Bowen's gaze jerked to her face. Her eyes were wide, emotionless and locked on him. The blood was still trailing down her neck. His rage boiled inside of him, a white-hot fury that demanded he end the son of a bitch who'd dared to hurt her. Jaw locking, he forced his stare back on the man before him. "How," Bowen snapped. "How did you take them all?"

"Wandered away," Curtis rasped. But as he spoke, his shoulders straightened. His slightly pointed chin lifted. The guy was proud, Bowen realized. Proud and he wanted to brag about what he'd done. "The stream rose too high, and they wanted an…easier path." He licked his busted lips. "I told them one… told them I would help, share supplies."

"And, what, as soon as you were safely away, as soon as you had them where no one else could hear them scream, you attacked?"

"Put something in the coffee…" Curtis's wrecked

lips twisted. His eyes gleamed. "Brought 'em here. Said it was shelter. Gave 'em coffee and when they woke up…" He laughed. "That was when the f-fun began."

Macey's hand rose, and she pulled at his wrist.

"Stop it, bitch," he said, his words croaking out. The knife sliced deeper into her.

"Put the fucking weapon down!" Bowen shouted. "Or I will shoot you right here."

Curtis still wore that sadistic smile on his face. "I know…how you agents work. You can't let…one of your own…get hurt."

Macey was very much *his*. The truth of that settled into Bowen's bones.

"So you drop *your* weapon," Curtis ordered in his weak, broken voice. "And you…tell the ranger outside that I want transportation. I want an ATV. I want *out* of here…or the pretty lady is going to be bleeding a whole lot more."

Bowen opened his mouth to reply.

"That's not happening," Macey said, her voice calm. Quiet. "You're not getting away. Bowen is the best shot at the Bureau. He can shoot you between the eyes right now, and he'd never so much as come close to my skin."

She sounded so very certain. She was also lying. Macey was the best shot, not him.

Curtis's attention flew back to Bowen and his eyes widened in alarm.

"I'm giving you to three," Bowen warned him. "One, two—"

Curtis's hold on Macey eased, just a bit. "No, no, you bast—"

"Three," Macey said. She drove her elbow back into Curtis's midsection. He grunted and the knife sliced at her, but she was whirling and she punched him hard in the face. Then Macey was free. She ran toward Bowen and he grabbed her arm, jerking her close with his left hand even as his right still held the gun.

Curtis let out a weak scream and lunged at them, the knife swiping down.

Three.

Bowen fired. The bullet blasted straight into Curtis's heart. His mouth dropped in surprise, and he looked down at his chest. Curtis even shook his head, as if this *couldn't* be happening.

You were a dead man the minute you put the knife to her throat.

The knife fell from Curtis's hand. His knees gave way and he hit the floor. Then he was trying to put his hands over his heart, trying to stop that frantic blood flow as he toppled to the dirty floor.

Macey ran toward him. The little prick had been trying to kill her moments before but now she was putting her hands on his chest. Applying pressure. Being the doctor that she'd *always* be...and trying to save the confessed killer.

"Talk to me!" Macey thundered at him. "You were talking plenty a few minutes ago—tell me about the man who took you, tell me—"

His bloody hand reached up to touch her face. Blood smeared across her cheek.

Bowen stood behind her, his gun ready to fire again.

But he saw the life leave Curtis's eyes.

The man's hand fell back to the floor. His eyes—

Nothing is there now.

They closed.

NIGHT HAD FALLEN, but the old cabin in the woods was illuminated by what seemed like a thousand lights. The place was swarming with cops, feds, crime scene techs and even EMTs.

Cadaver dogs barked, still on the scene, though they'd done their work hours ago.

Bowen stood behind the cabin, his hands crossed over his chest and his eyes on the graves. They'd already dug up four bodies. Four skeletons, because that was pretty much all that had been left of the missing. But there were more graves out there. Curtis Zale had buried his victims right behind the cabin.

A cadaver dog whined.

He said more than ten. They'd found thirteen victims so far. They'd gotten an expert to come out— Dr. Amelia Lang—a forensic geophysicist from the University of Tennessee who'd brought ground penetrating radar. As soon as the cadaver dogs had pawed at the earth, marking their spot, she'd used her equipment.

And they'd found the dead.

"This is…this is the most I've ever found," Dr. Lang

said, her voice soft and sad. Bowen glanced to the left and saw that she was also staring at the graves. Her long hair was pulled back but tendrils had escaped to blow in the breeze. "How long was he doing this?"

"Several years." At first, he'd thought that Curtis had only been hunting for the last two years, but to know the time frame for certain, they'd have to figure out who the other three missing—*dead*—victims were. Maybe there would be dental records that could provide a match for them. Or DNA that—

"I heard you shot him." She turned to look up at him. She was small, probably only around five feet tall, so her head tipped back as she met his stare.

"Yes." *He was going to kill Macey.*

I could have aimed for his leg. I could have blown the bastard's knee out. But I didn't. "I killed him," Bowen said flatly.

"Did he say anything, before he died? About why—"

Bowen gave a rough laugh. "There wasn't a why. But he was bragging. Telling us about how easy it was to make the kills."

Dr. Lang drove her hands into the pockets of her jacket. "You work with serials all the time, right?"

Too much of the time, but it was a job he'd chosen. He inclined his head in response, but his gaze passed over her shoulder and toward the cabin. Where was Macey?

"Why do you think he did it? Why do they all do it?"

"Every monster has a different story." He looked

back at the graves. "Sometimes they were hurt when they were younger. Their minds get bent. Twisted. Sometimes they were just always twisted."

Dr. Lang took a step back. "Born bad."

"Something like that. I've seen killers who just like the pain they give others. They get off on the torture because they're wired wrong." He could be using fancier terms, but screw it. He'd killed a man that day. Macey had been hurt. He was long past the point of politeness. "And I've seen killers strike because they were abused so much as kids that they don't understand right and wrong any longer. They're in pain and they want others to suffer, too."

"What about the ones who have no empathy at all?"

He considered that. "Those are the most dangerous ones. When you can't feel, there's nothing to hold you back."

Dr. Lang tucked her hair behind her ear. "I see what the monsters leave behind. That's what I find. And that's what scares me."

There was plenty to be scared of out in the world. Plenty that most people never saw, but because of his job, Bowen had an up-close view of it day in and day out.

He'd surrendered his gun to the local FBI agents after the shooting. There were always procedures to follow after an agent-involved fatality. But he'd fucking hated giving up that gun.

The other perp is still out there. The guy who

took Curtis and kept him in that cabin is still running loose.

It was a good thing Bowen had a backup weapon. He didn't intend to be caught unaware.

And where was Macey? His hands had fisted at his sides. "Excuse me," he said to Dr. Lang. "I need to find my partner."

"Oh, right, yeah, I think I saw her with the ranger a few minutes ago." She pointed to the right. "They were over there."

He nodded and then he was stalking off to the right. After Curtis had died, things had moved fucking fast. Backup had flown in on a chopper, the scene had been swarmed and Macey—she hadn't spoken to him.

He rounded the corner of the cabin and saw her standing near an ATV. As Dr. Lang had said, Zack was at her side. Bowen's steps became faster as he closed in. She turned at his approach, and he swore that she tensed.

Bowen lifted his hand and curled his fingers very carefully under her chin.

Hands off... The warning whispered through his mind.

Fuck that.

He tilted her head back so that he could better study the white bandage on her neck. "Does it hurt?"

She took a step away from him.

Bowen's hand fell to his side and fisted once more.

"It's only a scratch," she said softly. "I've had worse."

His gaze flew to hers. *I don't like thinking of that, baby. I don't like remembering that this is the second time a twisted killer has put his knife on you.*

He didn't like that shit at all.

"You shot him," Zack said.

Slowly, Bowen's head turned so that he stared at the other man.

"I've never seen…" Zack blew out a hard breath. "I've never seen someone kill before."

"Curtis Zale *was* a killer," Bowen said. "There's a line of bodies behind the cabin to prove that fact. And he held a knife to my partner's throat. What did you expect me to do?"

Zack shook his head. "I—"

Macey moved again, only this time, she put herself right beside Bowen. Her arm brushed against his. "Bowen was acting in self-defense. Curtis Zale was coming at us with the knife. He wasn't going to stop. If he'd been able to do so, he would have killed me, killed Bowen, and then…then he would have come after you, Zack."

Zack ran a hand over his face. "Guess you two deal with this shit every day, huh?"

"We deal with killers every day," Macey said while Bowen remained silent. "And it doesn't get easier." She glanced at Bowen from the corner of her eye. "Sometimes, you have to make the hard decisions. You have to make decisions that rip you apart."

Someone called out for the ranger. "Excuse me," he mumbled, but before he left, the guy paused and squeezed Macey's shoulder. "I'm glad you're okay." Zack's voice had deepened, taken on a personal note. "I didn't like seeing him with that knife at your throat."

Like that moment had been a fucking cakewalk for Bowen. He clenched his teeth and bit back the angry retort he wanted to throw at Zack. Bowen remained silent until the ranger had walked away.

Then…he focused on Macey. His breath expelled in a soft rush. Her eyes were on him, her body still close. "Does it hurt?" His fingers skimmed along her throat.

Macey shivered. "I told you, it's barely a scratch."

He stepped even closer to her. "The ranger isn't the only one who didn't like that bastard having his knife at your throat." His hand was still against her throat.

Hands off. Once more, that warning slipped through his head. But, just like before, he ignored it. He wanted his hands on her.

"Bowen, there are a lot of eyes here," she cautioned him. "They're watching us."

"No, they're looking at a crime scene. Thirteen dead, Mace. Thirteen." All killed by that little prick who'd been in the cabin.

"I shouldn't have seen a victim." Now her voice was subdued. "That was what I wanted to see. If I'd been more careful—"

"We both saw the same thing." She wasn't going to carry that guilt, not when he'd been the one to pull the trigger. "The guy was good at making people see things. How else did he get all those hikers to trust him?" To trust him, then to die. "I'm the one who left you alone in there with him."

"I thought he was getting water out of his bag." She stepped away, damn it, and ran a hand through her hair. "I didn't realize he was going for a weapon, not until it was too late."

He shoved his hands into his pockets. "Because I was involved in a fatal shooting, you know I'm about to get benched."

"No, you don't—"

"Protocol." He smiled, but he knew it was mocking. "There always has to be an investigation. You know the drill. You'll be working in the field with someone else, probably Tucker, and I'll be playing bench."

"The perp contacted *you*, Bowen. You're in this thing, and I don't think you'll be able to step back. Protocol or not."

He didn't want to step back. If anything, he wanted to step closer to her and hold her as tight as he could. But Bowen didn't move toward her. He locked his muscles down and he stared at her, drinking her in. *She's alive. She's safe.*

But this was the second time, the second fucking time, that she'd come close to dying on his watch. "I'm sorry."

"For what? Saving us both?"

"For not doing a better job of keeping you safe."

Macey shook her head. "Don't give me that line of bull, Bowen. You're the reason we're both walking around right now. And you're the reason Curtis won't ever hurt anyone else."

His lashes flickered. "The perp found him first." He rocked back on his heels and considered the scene around him. "He found them all first. We're dragging behind him, and the guy knows it."

"Bowen—"

"Thirteen men died, and we didn't even realize a serial was hunting here. Curtis Zale had the perfect killing grounds up here. But someone, this perp— he figured out what was happening. He found Curtis Zale." And that just begged the question… "Who the hell will he find next?"

WHEN THEY FINALLY got back to town, Bowen and Macey stopped by the police station. A weary-eyed Henry Harwell stood on the front steps, staring into the night. When he saw them, he motioned them forward. Captain Harwell had been out at the crime scene, but the guy had been running around like mad. They hadn't exactly had time for a chat.

Harwell took them back to his office and shut the door. "You were right."

Macey sat in one of the chairs near the captain's desk. Bowen stood. "Right about what, exactly?" Bowen asked the guy.

"A serial was hunting here. Right under my nose. And I did nothing." His face was pale. "Now I have to live with that shit. *I didn't know.*"

"Serials can often go undetected," Macey murmured. Dark shadows were under her beautiful eyes.

"Especially the organized ones. Curtis Zale had a very distinct MO, and a very specialized hunting ground. He planned his attacks. There was never a reason to suspect foul play. Just that—"

"That amateur hikers got lost on a trail." Harwell's smile was humorless. "I should have investigated more. I should have seen this."

"You aren't the only one," Bowen muttered. He was still wondering just how the perp had found Curtis. The guy's knowledge of profiling was damn good. *He's showing us the killers he's found. The ones we've missed. He's showing us that he's the better hunter.*

Bowen's phone rang, and he pulled it from his pocket, frowning. He figured it would be a call from Samantha Dark, telling him to take a back seat in this investigation because of his involvement in the shooting.

But Samantha wasn't calling him. It was the same number that had called him before. A number routed from within the police station. His gaze shot to Macey. "It's him." In the next breath, he growled, "Search this fucking station… The call is from the *same* number." They'd thought the number had just been routed through the station before, a trick, but they couldn't overlook any possibility.

His fingers slid over the screen and he tapped to receive the call. "Murphy—"

"I beat you to him." It was the same robotic voice as before.

"The guy had been there for days—of course, you fucking beat us."

The captain had rushed out of the office, no doubt going to get his staff to search the building, but when Macey moved to follow him, Bowen's hand flew out and curled around her arm. *Stay*, he mouthed to her. He wanted her to hear exactly what the guy had to say.

"You stacked the deck," Bowen continued grimly. The FBI was monitoring his phone. After the last call, he'd made sure they would be keeping tabs on his callers. The longer he kept the guy on the phone, the better. *The captain can search the building and the FBI can wade through your tech tricks to find you.* "You had Curtis Zale all along. Trapped up in that cabin, hungry, dehydrated…"

The perp's laughter came again. "I thought that was fair, considering what he'd done to his victims. I mean, you know he starved them for days, right? Denied them food, made them piss themselves. Until they were so desperate at the end that they were ready to slit their own throats." He paused. "Not that they did, Curtis was the one to use his knife on them. He told me all about it…when I had him tied up in the cabin."

"You could have just called the police and told them about the guy."

"Not my fault the police were too blind to see what was happening. The dead are on them. On the inept captain who couldn't get shit done."

Bowen forced his teeth to unclench. "You keep calling me—why not just *tell* me what's happening—"

"You liked killing him, didn't you?" the distorted voice demanded. "Come on, it's me. You can be honest with me." More laughter. "Was it just like old times for you?"

Bowen's hand fell away from Macey's arm.

"Bet you loved pulling that trigger. I've got to know...was it a head shot? No, no, I'm guessing heart. You shot that bastard right in the heart, didn't you?"

Macey was texting on her phone. Contacting Samantha? The others at the FBI so they could give them the trace?

"Did it feel good, seeing him die in front of you? Did it make you feel...like the monster I know you are?"

Macey's head whipped up. Her eyes locked on Bowen.

He stared straight at her. *What does she see when she looks at me?* "I don't like your games," he snarled.

"No, what you don't like is that I'm better at profiling than you are." Even though the voice was robotic, smugness still rang through those words. "Daniel was 'the Doctor,' Patrick was 'the Pyro' and...dumbass Curtis didn't have a fun name, but I think I deserve one, don't you? How about you tell the press to call me 'The Profiler'? Because that's what I fucking am."

"No, you're a killer," Macey said, stepping forward. "You're a man who enjoys the terror he causes, but you want to justify what you're doing. You want to make your murders right so you're targeting the people you think are dangerous, expendable, you—"

"I wasn't the one who murdered Curtis. In fact, I fed him. I gave him water. I even kept him tied up so he wouldn't hurt anyone. What the fuck more did you want from me? For me to put a red bow on his forehead?" There was a crackle of static and what sounded like...was that a train horn in the distance? There were no train tracks near the station. "I'm guessing he pissed you off, huh, Bowen? What did he do? Did he use that knife of his on your pretty partner?"

Macey's eyes had narrowed. Had she heard that train, too?

"Not the first time a knife has cut into her skin," the caller mused. "Won't be the last, either."

Bowen nearly crushed the damn phone. "You aren't threatening her."

Laughter.

And then—

The line went dead.

The door flew open. "Searched...searched the whole station," Harwell panted. His chest rose and fell as he sucked in deep breaths. "Had my men... span out. He's *not* here."

Bowen hadn't really thought he was, but he'd still needed that checked.

Macey had her phone at her ear. "The FBI is tracking him... They say..." She listened for a moment. Then her lips thinned. "He's tapped into the phone lines here, but they caught him this time... He *isn't* here. Routing his call, pinging towers, jumping all over. He's—" Her eyes widened as she listened. "*Got him!* Five miles away. They have the address. *Come on!*"

And then they were racing out of the office and out of the police station. Bowen jumped into the SUV with Macey while Harwell and two of his men rushed into their patrol cars. Macey gave him directions and Bowen hauled ass to get to the scene. And as he approached...he saw the train tracks.

You bastard. You think you're so smart, don't you?

"Here," Macey said. "Stop here!"

He slammed on the brakes and jumped out. In the distance, he could see the light from the train as it chugged away. They were at an old building, a closed gas station that appeared to have been boarded up for years. Bowen and Macey pulled out flashlights as they began to search the scene. And there, right next to the filling pump, he found the phone on the ground.

He picked it up and ice filled his veins. There was a picture on that phone's screen.

The picture was of Macey.

Not the first time a knife has cut into her skin. Won't be the last, either.

CHAPTER NINE

MACEY STARED OUT at the night. She was back in her rented cabin, back in the loft, and the place was snug and warm, but she couldn't seem to shake the chill from her bones.

She'd showered. Changed. Gotten the blood off her skin. When she'd put her hands on Curtis's chest, his blood had pumped between her fingers so fast. She'd known she couldn't save him, but she'd still tried.

She always had to try.

She skirted around the pool table and her hand lightly pushed a few of the balls. They rolled across the table and she watched them, oddly soothed by their movements. Bowen was downstairs. Sleeping?

Maybe. He'd been silent when they came back to the cabin, but she'd felt his fury all around her. The picture…the picture of her had sent him into a cold rage. It had been a picture taken recently—taken of her when she'd been coming out of the ME's office in North Carolina.

The perp had been watching her there. She had the feeling that he'd been watching them for a very long time.

There had been other pictures on the phone. Shots of her and Bowen arriving in Hiddlewood. Images of Daniel…after he'd been killed. Photos of the ME in North Carolina, Sofia Lopez. Shots of Sheriff Burt Morris.

The perp had been watching them all. Keeping close tabs on their investigation.

Another component that made him an organized killer. Killers of his type often liked to get up close to the investigation; sometimes, they would even try to insert themselves *into* the investigation. They'd go back to the scene of the crime, hang around the police station, lurking in the shadows…

Exactly what he's doing.

Macey heard the groan of the stairs and her shoulders tensed. A faint creak came a moment later and then she saw Bowen's head at the top of the stairs.

So he hadn't just gone to sleep.

He'd come to her.

It's night now. We're alone. Does he remember the deal?

She turned toward him, letting the back of her body brush against the pool table. The ball slipped from her hand and rolled across the table.

Bowen had showered, too, and his hair was still wet. He wore a pair of jogging pants that hung low on his hips. He paused at the top of the stairs and his gaze seemed to drink her in. The lights were on in the loft, burning so brightly, because maybe…maybe she'd had enough darkness for that day.

His hand was holding on to the wooden banister

and as she stared at him, Macey saw his grip tighten around the wood. "I should stay away."

She shook her head. His staying away was the last thing she wanted.

"We know what's going to happen if I touch you."

Yes, exactly what she wanted to happen.

Bowen took a step away from the stairs. Another. Then he was reaching for the light switch. The loft plunged into the darkness she'd dreaded—only, the dark didn't seem so bad, not right then. There was no sound as he crossed to her side, but her eyes adjusted to the darkness and she could just make out his form.

Broad shoulders. Strong chest. Dangerous. Powerful.

Bowen.

His hand lifted and once more his fingers slid against her throat. A shiver worked over her at his touch. He bent his head toward her. His mouth replaced his hand as he pressed a soft, openmouthed kiss to her throat. One, two…

Her head tipped back so he could have better access.

"Didn't like him touching you… Wanted to fucking destroy him when he put the knife to your throat." His hands slid around her waist and he lifted her up, moving her easily, and set her on the edge of the pool table. Her legs were spread and he stepped between them. His hands stayed at her waist, seeming to burn right through the cotton T-shirt that she wore.

"He was right about me," Bowen said. "The damn

perp on the phone… You shouldn't let me touch you, Macey. You shouldn't want me near you."

He started to back away. Her hands flew out and held tight to his shoulders. "You're the only man I do want close." Didn't he get that? "I feel better when I'm with you." Not scared, not weak. She could just let go when she was with Bowen, and Macey knew that he'd catch her long before she could ever fall. "I trust you." That confession was whispered. She didn't trust many people. Wouldn't let herself, not with her past.

"Maybe you shouldn't. I killed a man today."

"In self-defense."

He didn't speak, and tension stretched between them. The kind that made a knot form in her stomach. "Bowen?"

"He was a dead man when he put the knife to your throat."

She shook her head. No, no, that wasn't the way the FBI worked. That wasn't Bowen—

"You don't know all my past, Mace. It's twisted and bloody, and I never wanted you to know it all."

She didn't understand. "Bowen—"

He kissed her. A deep, hot, hard kiss that was just what she wanted. Macey met him with equal need—equal fury. Wanting everything from him. Pleasure. Oblivion.

"Tell me to back away," he groaned against her mouth.

Her hands slid down his back. "Come closer."

He kissed her again. His hands rose to cover

her breasts. Her nipples were tight, aching, and she arched toward him. He squeezed her, stroked her, and then—

"Tell me not to touch you."

"Touch me *everywhere*."

He yanked her shirt out of the way. She wasn't wearing a bra, hadn't bothered with one after the shower. He took her breast into his mouth and Macey's hands flew back to brace on top of the pool table. He sucked her, licked her. The stubble on his jaw scraped against her skin.

"Tell me... Mace, tell me to get the fuck away from you."

Macey kept one hand braced on the pool table. Her other hand sank into the thickness of his hair and she pulled his head up. "Get the fuck...*in* me." Then she kissed him, stroking with her tongue, tasting him, seducing, showing him that she wanted him, that she wasn't holding back and that he shouldn't, either.

Bowen gave a low, animalistic growl in his throat, and then his hands were yanking at her shorts. He stepped back and pulled the shorts and her panties off her legs, tossing them aside.

"Tell me you have a condom on you," she said, her voice hitching a bit.

Instead of speaking, his hands pushed her thighs even farther apart, and then his fingers were sliding up against her sex. Sliding into her. Thrusting and stroking and making her squirm and arch against him. His thumb pressed to her clit, right there, just the way that made her whole body go bow tight. His mouth came toward her and he licked the lobe of her ear. "Yes, sweetheart, I have a condom… I just need you ready."

"Now." She was past ready. She wasn't afraid. Didn't doubt him. She just wanted Bowen.

He pulled the condom from his pocket. Had it on, and then he tossed his sweatpants who the hell knew where. He thrust into her, sinking deep, just the way she wanted. He took her while he was standing up, while she was arching against him on the pool table. Her nails raked down his back. She bit his shoulder. She held on tight. She pushed the demons of the day out of her mind and she only thought about him.

She came fast, exploding around him, and her cry was muffled against his shoulder. When she climaxed, he picked her up and held her tight against him. Her hands clung to his shoulders, holding tight as he began to move her, up and down. She'd always known he was strong, but Macey hadn't fully realized just how strong. Not until that moment. Not until right *then*.

Her release kept going, pulsing through her on waves that wouldn't end. She couldn't draw in a deep breath. Her heart was about to burst out of her chest and nothing, *nothing* had ever felt so good.

Then his release hit and the surge of his body in hers sent off more explosions of pleasure deep inside of her. She held him tight, holding on with all her strength. When the pleasure ended, when her body was so wrung out that she could barely lift her head, she drew in a gasping breath and her eyes opened.

His stare was locked on her. She could feel the hot weight of it in the dark.

"You're mine, Macey." His words had never seemed rougher or more possessive.

She wasn't his, of course. They were just…friends. Doing the whole with-benefits thing. *Partners with benefits.* But she didn't say anything because maybe right then she was thinking the same thing.

You're mine, Bowen.

If only it were true.

He carried her to the bed. Went to the bathroom. Ditched his condom. She pulled the covers up to her chin as she glanced at the light streaming from the bathroom. He'd leave now. Go back to his bed.

Or maybe…maybe he'd stay. Until dawn came. And then the barriers would be put in place again.

The light in the bathroom turned off. Darkness surrounded her again. His shadowy form moved toward the bed and Macey found herself tensing.

He slid into the bed with her and his arms reached out to pull her close. He was warm and strong in the dark, and she slid against him. It was strange, but she could have sworn she *fit* against him.

Silly.

He didn't speak and the silence stretched between them. Finally, she had to say, "I'm sorry you had to kill him."

His fingers were stroking her arm, a light caress that she wasn't even sure he knew that he was making.

"Taking a life is never easy."

He kept stroking her. "You've never killed, Macey."

No, actually, she hadn't. She'd shot a suspect once in the line of duty, but he hadn't died. And as for Daniel...

I wanted to kill him. "I could have aimed for his knee. I could have aimed for his hand. I could have shot the knife right out of his fingers."

She shifted her body. "Bowen?"

"When you pull the trigger, time doesn't go faster. It goes slower. A million thoughts fill your head. All of those thoughts were there, crowding in on me. Where to shoot, where to hit him."

"He was coming at you with a knife. You didn't have a choice."

"There's always a choice, we just don't want to admit it."

No, no, he was wrong. She sat up in bed, pulling the sheet with her. "You're letting him get in your head." *Him.* The twisted perp who seemed to get off on taunting Bowen.

His fingers slid down her arm.

"You're letting the perp get to you, Bowen. That's not the way it works. We get to him. We break *him.* We don't let him play mind games with us." And she knew that guy out there was fixating on Bowen. The way he kept calling him, taunting him.

"He knows about us, Macey."

Her lips parted.

"He left that picture of you there on the screen deliberately. Sending a message to me. Just like when he said you'd be cut by a knife again."

And she realized—he wasn't just stroking her arm. She'd been so lost *in* him that she hadn't even noticed… A shudder slid over her.

Bowen was stroking her scars. Lightly caressing them.

"It's not going to happen, though," he promised her. "I'll do better next time. My guard won't lower. He *won't* hurt you."

"I'm a federal agent. I know how to shoot to kill, too." Just because she hadn't done it yet…that didn't mean she *wouldn't*. "For the record, I don't plan to let him hurt *you*, either. In case you missed it, you're the one the guy is taunting. You're the one he's challenging. The focus is on you, not me. You're the one in this guy's sights."

He brought her wrist to his mouth and pressed a kiss to the raised skin. "He wants someone to appreciate what he's doing. He thinks I will. He thinks I'll understand."

"You're not like him," she whispered.

"Don't be too sure…"

HE HAD A murder board in his conference room. A freaking *murder* board. Police Captain Henry Harwell stared at the images that had been tacked to that board. The missing…the remains that had already been dug up. *Fucking hell.* The FBI agents had set up that board.

Bowen Murphy had first hung up the board earlier in the day, when he'd been digging into the missing persons' reports. When he'd started to put together the puzzle pieces and realized that a hunter had been hiding in Gatlinburg for a very long time.

And I never saw him coming.

"Um, Captain?"

He exhaled on a long sigh. It was close to three a.m., and he still had people coming to him. What did a guy have to do in order to just get quiet? To get peace? But he rolled back his shoulders and turned toward the open door.

Amelia Lang stood there, her hair tucked behind her right ear, her expression hesitant. The FBI had brought her in—a forensic geophysicist who'd found bodies buried beneath the dirt with some kind of technical shit that he didn't fully understand.

"I wanted to let you know that I'll be back at the cabin with the team at eight." Her voice was crisp and her golden gaze was direct. "I just finished up a few files here and I'm leaving for the night."

He should leave, too. But even if he left, he'd carry the guilt with him. "You found thirteen of them."

She nodded once, and sadness chased across her face. "So far."

For a moment, his eyes closed, and he found himself shooting up a quick prayer. *Don't let there be more. Don't let more men have been murdered on my watch.*

"Captain?"

His eyes opened. "Do you believe there are more out there?"

"I'm…I'm not an expert on killers. I just—I just find the victims."

And there were plenty of victims for her to find.

"I would think, though," Dr. Lang continued softly as she bit her lower lip, "that it would depend on just how long Curtis Zale was killing in the mountains. If he's been at this for a very long time, then yes…there could be more."

"He was born in Pigeon Forge." Because he'd already dug up everything he could find on Curtis. "The guy grew up here. His dad was a factory worker, his mom a schoolteacher. He was a *normal* kid."

"Then something happened that made him stop being normal."

Henry wanted a drink. Actually, he wanted a lot more than just one. "Thanks for your work on this case," he said, making his voice brisk. "Why don't you get one of the uniforms out front to drive you to your hotel?"

She nodded and turned away. He waited a few moments and then, shit, he had to get out of there, too. He walked down the hallway and wasn't surprised that the place was mostly deserted. At that time of night, he normally only kept a skeleton staff in place. He'd used so many officers that day—most of them had finally called it quits and were home sleeping things off.

This is the most excitement we've ever had up here.

Henry headed to his office. He grabbed his coat and his fingers slid over his desk. He didn't have any alcohol stashed in his desk. His life wasn't some damn TV show. He tried hard to do things right. To be by the book. Fair.

He'd tried…

And those men—at least thirteen—had still died on his watch. The mayor had called him that day, over and over again, wanting an explanation. He had no explanation. No justification. He had nothing.

Henry knew he'd be the one to blame for the deaths. There was always someone to blame. *The mayor won't go down for this. I'm the low man on the totem pole up here.* Henry left through the back exit of the station, heading for his Jeep. He was almost there when the keys slipped from his fingers. He'd been tossing them, not paying attention, and they fell right to the ground, sliding near the edge of his tire. He bent down, scooped them up and that was when he was hit.

A hard slam right into the back of his head. Felt like a hammer came at him, and Henry's head lurched toward the vehicle. He hit the driver's-side door, but he didn't black out. Henry fumbled, twisting his body, even as his hand went for his gun.

"Can't have that." And he was hit again. He had a fast impression of a jackass in a ski mask, and then…

Then Henry was hit hard again in the head. So hard that *everything* went dark.

CHAPTER TEN

THE DARKNESS SURROUNDED THEM. Bowen was still caressing her arm, moving his fingers lightly along her scar, and he didn't want to move. He didn't want to think about what would come tomorrow or the next fucking day.

He didn't want to think about the life he'd taken. Didn't want to keep seeing Curtis's eyes as death had claimed the man.

He wanted to see Macey. To touch Macey. To *feel* her.

While there was still time. *Because she shouldn't want me near her. I've been living a lie. Hiding so much of myself from her. From everyone around me.*

"Will you tell me about Arnold Shaw?"

He'd known this question would come. "Arnold Shaw raped and murdered four women in the Tampa, Florida, area. He abducted them, he kept them trapped for days and, when he was done with them, he slit their throats." His voice was devoid of all emotion, and as much as he had enjoyed stroking Macey's skin, he pulled his hand away from her. He rolled away from her and left the bed.

The simple fact was, he couldn't touch Macey,

not while he was talking about Arnold Shaw. Because if he did, then it was almost like that nightmare would touch her.

He didn't want that to happen.

"He...he killed your fiancée."

Bowen rolled back his shoulders. "That's what all the papers said, but actually Cadi and I weren't engaged. We'd been dating for a while, and yeah, I planned to ask her to marry me. Even had the ring picked out." But he'd held back. Held the fuck back. Why?

Because I wasn't sure she was the one?

Because I had doubts?

Or because I was a fucking coward?

"You...you loved her."

On that, there was no doubt. "Cadi was my best friend from the time I was ten years old. I loved her then, and I loved her the day she died."

Macey sucked in a quick breath. "I didn't realize..."

"Cadi and I lived next door to each other when we were growing up. We were friends, we dated in high school, and after college, everyone just expected for us to get married." But sometimes lines could blur. Sometimes, people made for better friends than lovers.

And sometimes, even the oldest of friends—and the truest of lovers—could keep secrets. "She met him online. That was how he found all of his victims. He pretended to be whatever they needed him to be.

A friend to listen. A lover to want. A fucking prince charming if their lives were going to hell."

He heard the rustle of covers and could see that she'd pulled them around her body in the dark.

"I'm not…easy." He lifted his chin. "I've never been a fucking easy guy to live with. I did a stint in the military, and Cadi hated that. She didn't want to be alone." He raked a hand over his face. "She never liked that…and he used her loneliness against her. He had her convinced that she could trust him. She went to meet him, and she never came back."

"I'm sorry."

"If I'd been there for her, if I'd been the friend I should have been, been the lover she deserved, Cadi never would have been taken. The police found her body five days after she'd gone missing. I was the one to ID her." He swallowed, remembering. "She looked like a broken doll. Covered in bruises, cuts. He hurt her for so long…and when I asked the cops what they were doing, they had *nothing* for me. They didn't know who he was. Didn't know how to track him. They didn't know any damn thing about him. He was still out there, waiting for someone else. Waiting for the chance to attack again."

"You didn't give him that chance."

"No."

"You hunted him."

He'd been relentless. "I hunted him, and I found him…right before the asshole was going to take another woman. Because I learned he used the same MO, you see. The women—they thought they were playing it safe. Meeting in a public bar. But something kept happening. They *left* the bar with him each time, and they were never seen again. I figured he might be slipping them roofies, and I was right. I caught the bastard while he was trying to force a woman into the back of his car. His next victim."

Macey was still on the bed. He was staring down at her, knowing he should stop the story before he went too far. While he could still pretend to be the good guy.

"His victim was barely conscious. I drove my fist into his face, and I heard the bones snap." He'd liked that sound. As he'd pounded Arnold's face, an image of Cadi's battered body had flashed through Bowen's mind. "I hit him until he wasn't fighting back. Until he was nothing but a ball on the ground, bleeding and crying. *He* was crying, after what he'd done to Cadi."

She rose from the bed, wrapping the sheet around her body. "You gave her justice."

"He died in that alley."

She reached for his hand. Damn it, no, she wasn't supposed to touch him now. He tried to pull away, but she just held him tighter. "Bowen, I *read* this part in the police report. You were comforting the victim. He came at you both, still attacking. You had no choice but to shoot him."

He looked down at her hand.

"You were licensed to carry a concealed weapon. You were defending yourself. Just like you did tonight. You were stopping a killer."

His lips pressed together. Her fingers were so soft against his skin.

"To hunt him, I became like him." The words came out, the words he *could* give to her. "I knew the sites he used online. I went there, and I thought like him, I tried to find the victims he'd want. The victims—they led me to him. I could predict his moves. What he was going to do." *Because I knew how he'd want to kill them.* "I knew what he was going to do to that girl in the alley."

"But he didn't do it. You saved her. You stopped him!"

I killed him.

"You stopped him, you joined the FBI and you've been fighting killers ever since."

She was talking as if he were a hero. But then, wasn't that the story he'd let others believe for far too long? He wished she wasn't touching him, not then. Not... "I was never going to let him out of that alley." His voice had turned into a growl. "I knew that, long before I ever threw the first punch at him."

"Bowen?"

"To me, he was a dead man the minute I saw what he'd done to Cadi."

Her hands pulled from his. "But you stopped...in the alley...you stopped. You were punching him, but you backed away to get to the victim."

I backed away because my gun was in the sad-dlebags of my motorcycle. "He lunged at me and grabbed me from behind. I'd just gotten my gun, and I whirled back. The woman was screaming, begging me to stop him, and I pulled the trigger." He blew out a slow breath. "And when the cops searched his car, they found handcuffs, rope, duct tape and knives. They also found his phone—and all of the videos he'd taken of the women he'd tortured." Bowen shook his head. "They didn't exactly question me much after that. A killer was off the streets. A victim was safe, and hey, the press got a hero for a day."

"You...don't think you're a hero."

He wasn't sure what the hell he was. But a hero? *No.* Not even close. And maybe that was why he'd joined the FBI. Because he'd hunted Arnold Shaw for the wrong reason. *To kill him.* Not to get justice. Just because at the last moment, Arnold had attacked and he'd fired in self-defense...*that doesn't really change what I intended.*

"Why did you join the FBI?" Macey asked him softly.

"Because I was good at hunting monsters."

"You...you fought your way onto Samantha's team."

He had, because his name hadn't been on the initial, very short list of agents that Samantha Dark had hand selected. She'd wanted agents who'd all been linked—personally—with serial killers. People who'd been lovers, friends or even siblings of serial killers. Samantha had a theory that that link wasn't a weakness. Instead, it was a strength, one that allowed the agents to have an insight into the mind of a serial killer that others lacked.

To put it simply, Samantha had wanted agents with a killer instinct.

And, at first, she hadn't picked him. Just as she hadn't picked Jonah Loxley.

But I didn't give up. I kept busting my ass to prove that I could belong there.

Her phone vibrated before he could answer her. Before he could tell her that he'd joined the FBI because he *wanted* to be the kind of guy who hunted for justice. Because Cadi's death had changed everything for him—torn off his blinders and made him see the world for exactly what it truly was.

She walked away from him, heading to scoop up her phone from the bedside table. The sheet trailed behind her, like a bride's train sliding on the floor. When she picked up the phone, the screen illuminated her face as she read the text. "Tucker said he's here. He and Jonah arrived a bit earlier and the FBI got them a cabin just down the road. He says he'll meet us at the police station at 0700 hours."

Not so far away. "We should get some sleep." He'd bared enough of his past. Tried to make her see him for what he really was.

He didn't care if others bought the lie he tried to sell, but for some reason, Bowen wanted Macey to know the truth about him. He wanted her to know everything. *And to still want me, despite all of that.*

Macey's fingers typed across the screen. "Tucker wants to know if you're all right."

Tucker Frost. Bowen counted the man as one of the few friends he had. "Never better." A friend, but

Bowen still lied to him. Tucker's brother had been a serial killer, and Tucker—hell, he'd had to kill the guy. Had to make a choice: the woman Tucker loved or his brother.

He'd chosen the woman. And Tucker was planning to marry her.

But sometimes Bowen wondered… Just how badly did that choice gut the other man?

"Why do you have to bullshit?"

He blinked.

She dropped the phone back onto the nightstand. "You think I don't see your pain? You think I don't hate that I caused you to shoot that man today?"

She was blaming herself? Fuck, no. He grabbed her shoulders and pulled her closer. "Let's be clear on one thing." His voice had roughened. "None of this is on you."

But once more, Macey said, "Bullshit. I made a rookie mistake. I bought the story being sold in front of me. I saw a victim because *I* have been a victim. I tend to think from that perspective. I want to help. I want to comfort, and I've got to stop. Samantha warned me about this weakness before. My past can help me, but it can hurt me, too. And tonight, it hurt. I looked at that man, tied in the chair, so desperate, and I saw myself. I wanted to help him, I wanted to get him out of those binds as fast as possible and get him to safety. Because *I* didn't look deep enough, he caught me unaware."

His fingers slid up her shoulders and skimmed

over her throat, sliding against the small bandage there.

"It won't happen again." It sounded as if she were making a vow.

"*I* left you in there alone."

"Then we both screwed up. There can't be *any* more screwups, not with this perp still out there. Because one thing I know with absolute certainty... this guy isn't done."

No, he wasn't.

"He's not done killing, and, Bowen, I don't think he's done with you."

It WAS THE phone call he'd known would come. Bowen stood on the back deck of the cabin, watching the sun slowly rise. Fog circled the mountains, giving them the smoky appearance that had led to the name Smoky Mountains.

"You understand, don't you, Bowen?" Samantha Dark said, her voice firm but sympathetic. "Anytime there is an officer-involved shooting—"

"I knew I would get benched. Yeah, I saw this coming." He kept his voice mild even as anger stirred through him. The second he'd pulled that trigger, he'd known what would be coming. *Internal investigation.* "Just get me cleared as soon as you can, because I need to be back working at Macey's side."

The better to keep her safe...like I fucking promised I would.

"Tucker is already in town. I've instructed him

to partner with Macey during the course of the investigation."

His left hand curled around the wooden railing.

"But I need you to stay close, Bowen." Intensity sharpened her words. "I'm not pulling you, and I told the brass at the FBI the same thing. You're not in the field, but you *are* on this case. The perp is talking to you—and every instinct I have says that he will keep contacting you. You're the key we can use against him."

Bowen released a slow breath and a fog appeared near his mouth. It was crisp out that morning, but he liked the cold. "He knows about my past."

"I think it's safe to assume this killer knows about your past, Macey's past and everyone's past on our team."

His shoulders stiffened.

"He went after Daniel Haddox, a deliberate tie to Macey. He contacted you—and, yes, I agree, he does know what you did to Arnold Shaw. But the way the guy is setting himself up, almost challenging you in these instances, to me, it seems as if he has something to prove."

Bowen saw the same thing. "The guy wants to prove that he's better at profiling than we are."

"Yes." Her sigh carried over the line. "Our team has gotten a lot of press recently. We've taken down some of the worst serial killers and predators out there—and this fellow, he doesn't like that. He thinks he's smarter than we are, and an organized killer like this, he would leave nothing to chance."

"Know your enemy," Bowen muttered. *And we're the enemy.*

"Exactly," she said. "He knew he was going to battle us. So he's learned every secret we have. Every strength and every weakness. I think this is less about the victims themselves and more about… well, you. Macey. Our team. *Us.*"

He considered that as the fog drifted in the distance. "Maybe because we're his real victims?"

She'd gone silent and he knew she was considering what he'd just said.

"The perp set the fire at the cabin with Patrick inside…set the fire *after* Macey and I went in." He forced his back teeth to unclench. "And Curtis Zale had his knife to Macey's throat. As soon as Curtis realized we were FBI, he lost all control. Curtis meant he wasn't being taken in. Curtis never saw us as his rescuers. He just saw us as the enemy."

"And you think that's what the perp we're after wanted? That he wanted Curtis to attack you and Macey all along?"

"Yes." He'd considered this, again and again.

"Then more attacks will come." Her voice was soft but certain. "And you have to be ready for them. He's proven that appearances are deceptive on this case. I need you and the other agents to be ready for anything." There was a pause. "One other thing you should know…"

He waited, knowing it wasn't going to be good. With this case? Good wasn't exactly an option.

"I'm launching an internal investigation here at the FBI."

What? Shock rippled through him.

"I'm concerned the perp has received access to our confidential files. Files about the Doctor's crimes, his victims…access to the material we had on Patrick Remus."

His breath rushed out. "Because the guy we're after knows too much for a civilian."

"I want to make certain our case files haven't been hacked. At first, I thought we might just be looking at a crime addict—someone who'd studied the cases carefully, but then when he contacted you specifically… your personal line…well, a hack at the Bureau is a possibility I can't, *won't*, overlook."

"The guy is good at what he's doing, Samantha. He spotted a killer who'd gone undetected for years."

"He looked for patterns," she said. "Disappearances and abductions. Pattern analysis is a potential gold mine for criminal investigators. That's one of the reasons I brought Jonah Loxley on board. His background in cyber investigations can help us."

Something was bothering him. "There's no cooling-off period with this guy." Serial killers, well, if there was one particular pattern, they usually built up to their crimes. Planned and plotted and let the need to kill all but overwhelm them. But after they'd made their kill, they had what some termed an emotional cooling-off period—the killers had satisfied their dark desires, and they could almost go back to leading a normal life, for a while. Until the urge to kill became overwhelming for them again. "The timing…it's more like a spree killing." Because time was of the most importance with a spree killer—the short time frame was one of the key elements for that type of predator.

"This killer isn't going to be easily classifiable," Samantha said, and he knew she'd been thinking the same thing. "It seems like it's less about the timing of the murders, and more about having a captive audience." A quick beat of silence, and then she added, "Specifically, I think the audience is you and Macey. He maneuvered you both where he wanted you, and now the crimes are occurring around you."

He was pulling them into his web. *Are we the flies and he's the big, fat fucking spider?*

"Stay vigilant, Bowen. Watch your back and—watch Macey's."

Always.

"I know the shooting will come up clean and we'll get you back in the field with her soon. In the meantime, I am *not* pulling you in to DC. I need you exactly where you are."

Because that was where the killer wanted him to be? "Wouldn't be using me as bait, would you, Samantha?"

"Better to use a trained FBI agent than some innocent civilian who gets caught in this guy's crosshairs."

That was the thing, though. "He hasn't gone after any innocents yet."

"No," Samantha said softly. "Not yet…"

WHEN MACEY AND Bowen entered the police station at 0700 hours, the area was oddly quiet. Macey
glanced at the officer stationed behind the desk, Tanner O'Neil, and he gave her a nod. "Your FBI friends
are already in the conference room, Agent Night."

Macey wasn't particularly surprised that Tucker
was already at it—he'd worked other cases with her
and she knew how dedicated he could be.

"Is Captain Harwell here or is he at the crime
scene?" Macey asked because she wanted to talk
with Harwell about their perp ASAP.

The officer frowned a bit and glanced down the
hallway. "His door was locked this morning and had
a message telling me that he had a few things to run
down this morning."

"Thanks, Officer O'Neil," Bowen said.

Macey nodded to the officer and then she hurried
toward the conference room. When she opened the
door, Tucker was inside and staring at the photos they'd
tacked to the wall—photos of their victims. He turned
his dark head and his blue eyes—piercing, bright
blue—skimmed over Macey and Bowen. "Morning,
Macey. Bowen."

"Tucker." Then Macey's gaze slid to the right, to
the other agent in the room.

"Good to see you again, Macey," Jonah said as
he came toward her and offered his hand in a brisk
shake. His hair was a dark brown, his eyes a pale
green. His jaw was freshly shaven and a pair of wire-
rimmed glasses perched on his nose. He'd always reminded her a bit of Clark Kent. He gave her a quick

half smile, one that flashed the dimple in his right cheek. "Guess I finally made it to the big leagues, huh?"

She shook his hand. "Glad to have you on board."

His smile slipped away. "I'm here because of you. I know you went to bat for me with Samantha, and I appreciate that."

She withdrew her hand from his. Yes, she had gone to bat for the guy, but it had been because she legitimately thought they could use him on Samantha's team. His computer expertise would be invaluable. Especially since she already thought they were dealing with a tech savvy perpetrator. The way he'd gotten his phone calls to appear as if they'd come from the police station…

This guy is good. And we all will be needed to bring him down.

Macey glanced back at Bowen. He'd been quiet that morning. Back to their rules. Lovers in private, partners in public. "Jonah, I believe you and Bowen have worked together before, right?"

Jonah headed toward Bowen and, once more, offered his head. "Briefly, but yes." He didn't flash a smile. His face was very serious. "Heard about what happened last night. I know it wasn't easy for you."

Bowen inclined his head as he shook the other man's hand. "Before I left the cabin this morning," he said as he pulled his hand back, "I spoke with Samantha." His face was grim and anger gleamed in his eyes. "Because of the shooting, I'm being asked to take a back seat on the investigation. Tucker, I believe you and Macey are now partners." His arms crossed over his chest. "This perp is pulling us into the line of fire. I need to know that you've got her back."

"I won't let Macey down," Tucker said quietly.

"And I won't let him down," Macey retorted briskly. "Now, look, we should get started. We can divide up—we need to get back at the crime scene and we also need to talk with the ME here in town. And there's an oddities museum I want us to check out ASAP." As she spoke, Macey headed toward the lone window in the conference room. "Tucker, did you talk with Dr. Sofia Lopez before you left North Carolina? Did she discover anything else about Gale Collins or about Daniel Haddox's death?"

While she waited on his reply, Macey stared out of the window. The view showed the back of the station. She saw Captain Harwell's personal vehicle— she knew the Jeep belonged to him because she'd seen him in it the day before. And…the sunlight was glinting off something near the Jeep. Macey pressed a bit closer to the window to get a better view.

"Dr. Lopez didn't have anything new for me, not when I left, but she's going to fax over more files to us today," Tucker assured her.

But Macey wasn't quite focusing on him. That object out there… Her eyes narrowed. "Excuse me, okay?" She turned back and saw the three men staring at her in surprise. "Sorry. There's just something I need to check." She hurried out of the conference room and rushed down the small hallway that would take her to the back of the station. Macey threw open the door and was outside in moments. She quickly approached the object she'd seen moments before, and realized she was staring down at a police badge. Crouching, Macey went for a better look at it.

Was that a smear of blood on the badge?

"Macey?" Bowen's footsteps padded behind her.

Macey looked up at the white Jeep that was right next to her. "Are we sure that Captain Harwell is out running down a lead?" Because she was looking at a captain's badge. Macey didn't touch the badge, not yet, but the ice in her gut told her that, yes, that *was* blood on the badge.

Macey heard Bowen's low curse and knew that he'd spotted the badge, too. "Let's make fucking sure." Then he was pulling her back to her feet and they were running into the station once more. Bowen was shouting for Officer O'Neil at the front desk and everyone in the station seemed to whirl toward them.

Jonah stood in the conference room doorway. "What's going on?" he asked Macey.

"We need to get inside Captain Harwell's office," Macey said, her words directed at Officer O'Neil. *"Now."*

He blinked. "It's… I told you, the door is locked."

"Then *unlock* it," Bowen ordered. "Now."

More officers came forward, their expressions tense.

"I don't have the key!" Officer O'Neil said, his eyes wide. "There's…there's usually a backup for all of the offices at the front desk, but that key ring wasn't there this morning when I came in—"

Bowen shoved through the crowd and stopped in front of the locked door.

"Bowen?" Tucker called out. "What are you doing?"

Bowen didn't reply because he was too busy kicking in the door.

"You can't do that!" Officer O'Neil yelled. "This is police—"

The door flew inward and Macey saw that Captain Henry Harwell was inside, sitting at his desk. He was in his chair—his body *tied* to the chair—and blood soaked the front of his shirt. Blood from the giant slash that went from one ear…to the other.

CHAPTER ELEVEN

"So...ARE WE supposed to think that the police captain was some kind of killer?" Jonah asked hours later as they stood inside Harwell's office. An office that was now an active crime scene.

The body had been taken away. Macey was currently with the ME. Bowen had been left with Jonah and Tucker, and he grimly stared around the room. The crime scene team had come and gone, and they'd found *nothing* to help their investigation.

Because this bastard knows what he's doing.

"I mean, that is the MO we're looking at with this perp, right?" Jonah said as he carefully skirted the desk. "He goes after killers that he's profiled. And the last guy—Curtis Zale—you hadn't even realized he was hunting, not until our perp contacted you." His gaze trekked around the room. "Maybe it's the same thing with the dead captain. Maybe he was a killer, too. One who hid in plain sight."

Just like with the other victims, a nail had been found in Harwell's body—two nails, actually. His hands had been nailed to his desk. Bowen moved behind the desk, trying to figure out just why the killer had set the scene in such a manner.

"Could be possible, I suppose," Tucker mused from the right, "that Henry Harwell was working with Curtis Zale. I mean, perhaps all those murders occurred in the mountains because Harwell was making sure no one investigated the disappearances?" His voice roughened as he added, "Wouldn't be the first time a law enforcement officer went bad and, though it's uncommon, serial killing teams *do* work together."

Bowen wasn't ready to buy that the captain had been a killer. "The perp is ballsy as hell. He's throwing his crimes in our faces. The guy came into a police station." The whole fucking place was a crime scene. "Based on the blood spatter we found outside, we can assume that the killer attacked Harwell next to his Jeep, and then the killer brought the captain back *in* here." Because the blood had pooled on the chair, on the floor. "The amount of blood here tells us this is where he died. He brought Harwell back in here specifically to set the scene for us. If the perp attacked Harwell outside, in that back parking lot, he could have easily killed him there." His head lifted from the marks on the desk and he met Tucker's stare. "But he didn't. The perp brought Harwell back in here to deliver a message to us."

"What message is that?" Jonah wanted to know.

"He thought the captain was guilty, all right." Once more, he stared at the marks left on the desk. "Did you see the files that were beneath Harwell's hands? The hands that were fucking nailed to the desk? They were the files on Curtis Zale's victims. Our killer was blaming Harwell for those crimes."

That was easy enough to see. But when Curtis had been making his grand confession at the end, he'd never implicated anyone else. He'd taken all of the credit himself.

"Because Harwell was guilty?" Jonah said.

Maybe. Or maybe something else was at play. "Dig into his personal life," Bowen said. He knew Jonah could hack into the guy's life far too easily. "See if there isn't something that stands out to you. Missing money. Absences. Property that wasn't listed on official records. Trouble with a current lover or even an ex. If Henry Harwell had skeletons in his closet, we'll find them."

A knock sounded on the open door.

Bowen looked up. Officer O'Neil stood there. His face was pale and the lines near his mouth appeared deeper. His gaze studiously avoided staring at the desk. "Dr. Amelia Lang is in interrogation room one. She's waiting for you."

The police station had security cameras in place— cameras that had stopped working right after Amelia Lang left the night before. As far as they knew, she was the last person to speak with Harwell before he'd been murdered.

Other than the killer, of course.

The video footage had showed Dr. Lang walking out of the front door. A few moments later, Captain Harwell had gone out the back.

Then the security feed had just stopped.

"Jonah, let us know what you find," Tucker ordered as he led the way to the door. He cast a quick glance at Bowen. "You're standing in for this one, right?"

Standing in, but not leading the investigation. FBI orders. Jaw locking, Bowen snarled, "Yes."

Tanner hurried out, not looking back, and Bowen knew the guy was glad to get away from that scene. The station had been like a grave site all day long. The officers had been lost to shock, grief...and a growing rage.

"He's ballsy as fuck," Tucker groused when they stopped right in front of the interrogation room. "How much more in-your-face can you get than this kill?"

"He didn't call me," Bowen said. That nagged at him. "Didn't challenge me on this one. Didn't do his routine like he did with Curtis."

Tucker's stare turned measured. "You mean he hasn't called...*yet*. Because my money says he will. I think the guy was going for shock value. He knew you'd be back at the station today. He locked that door, left his twisted prize inside and he waited for you to find the captain. He was sending a message to you—to the FBI."

Bowen shoved open the door.

Dr. Lang jumped. Her face was tense and her hands were fisted on the table in front of her. "I—I was told that I needed to come in and speak with you two." She hurried to her feet and walked toward them. "The captain is really dead?" Her voice was weak.

Bowen nodded. "Yes."

"I was talking to him last night. He seemed...he seemed like a good guy. He was worried about me getting back to my motel for the night. Tried to get me to take a uniform with me." Her lips twisted. "I never—not even for a second—worried about his safety. It was nearly three a.m., I was dead on my feet and I—" The phrasing seemed to hit her and a dark flush stained her cheeks. "Oh, God, that's terrible, isn't it? I didn't mean—"

"It's okay," Tucker said softly. "We know what you meant. Why don't you just sit back down and we'll talk? Bowen and I have a few questions for you."

She seemed to collapse in the chair.

THE BODY WAS on the exam table. Police Captain Henry Harwell had been given top priority at the ME's office. One of their own had been taken.

And the mayor, the governor, everyone was demanding immediate action.

"I found a contusion on the back of Henry—the victim's head," Shamus McKinley corrected quickly, his Adam's apple bobbing as he swallowed. "I believe he was struck from behind, and, based on blood recovered in the parking lot, I think he fell forward, his head hitting the side of the driver's door, and the impact caused this contusion." His gloved fingers hovered over Harwell's forehead. "But then...then I think his assailant came at him with another power-ful strike here—"

Macey realized his fingers were shaking. "Dr. McKinley." She spoke his name quietly.

Once more, his Adam's apple bobbed, and he looked up at her.

"Are you all right doing this investigation?" Because she did *not* believe that he was. "I think it might be for the best if another ME led this exam."

Before they went too far.

"You're too close," Macey added.

He licked his lips. "I'm the leading ME in Gatlin-burg, and I'm the only one who can do this exam the *right* way—"

"No, you aren't. Because you're too close to the victim," Macey said again. "Look, I get that you're being pushed by the mayor and the governor and who the hell knows who else, but you need to back away." She nodded. "I know another ME who can take your place. Dr. Sofia Lopez," Macey said, throwing out the name quickly. "She's already familiar with this perp, and she can be here very soon. I spoke with her not five minutes before I walked into this lab, and she volunteered her services."

He was staring down at the body, as if unable to look away. "I know Sofia's work. She's top-notch. We've even done some workshops together at con-ferences. She's someone I would trust completely." He sucked in a deep breath. "I think, yes." He pulled off his gloves and tossed them into the trash. "I think it would be best if Sofia came for the full exam."

He looked up at her. "I've done exams on police officers before. Men and women who've come into my office as they ran their investigations and I got to know them, but Henry…" Dr. McKinley turned away from the table. "I've known him for the last ten years. He was a good man. And I called him a friend. You don't…you don't cut into your friend."

No. "I'll have Dr. Lopez come immediately." Because Dr. Lopez had finished her exams in Hiddlewood. If there was any red tape to cut through, Macey was confident that the FBI could do it. She'd leave that matter in Samantha's capable hands.

Sofia Lopez was familiar with the cases, and she didn't have any personal ties to the victims. She'd be the ideal ME to have on hand.

"Excuse me," the ME said. "I need some air."

He hurried out, and Macey pretended not to see the moisture filling his eyes.

She glanced back at the body—at Henry Harwell. For an instant, she saw him as he'd been in the office last night. The shadows lining beneath his eyes, the haggard tiredness…and the guilt that had shone in his stare.

"WHAT DID YOU talk about with Henry Harwell last night?" Tucker asked as he took the seat across from Dr. Amelia Lang.

She crossed her hands over her chest and slanted a quick glance at Bowen.

"Sorry," Bowen said, "should have made the introductions sooner. Dr. Lang, this is Special Agent

Tucker Frost. He just needs to ask you a few questions."

"Just…just Amelia, okay? I kind of think we're past the formal phase." Her gaze slid down to Bowen's side. "You don't have your weapon." She bit her lip.

"I won't have it, not until the official investigation into Curtis Zale's shooting is over." He pressed his shoulders to the wall. "I've briefed Tucker about your work."

"You're the forensic geophysicist," Tucker added. "And you found the bodies behind the cabin."

"Thirteen of them," she said softly. "So far. That's what I was talking about with Captain Harwell. I was finishing up my notes—he'd let me use an office here at the station. Before I left, I found him in the conference room." Her lips formed a tight line. "He was staring at all of the photos on the board. The pictures of the victims."

"Did he say anything to you about those victims?" Tucker questioned.

"He…he wanted to know if I thought there were more out there." Amelia shook her head. Her hair was in a loose bun. "But I told him I didn't know yet. That my job was just to find the victims, not to understand the killers. I wouldn't know more until I'd done more searching with my equipment." She started to say more, then hesitated.

"Amelia?" Tucker prompted her.

"He…he started talking about Curtis Zale. He said that Curtis had grown up here. That he lived over in Pigeon Forge. He even told me that Curtis *had* been a normal kid, once upon a time." She licked her lips. "He almost sounded as if…as if he knew Curtis."

Tucker slanted a quick glance toward Bowen.

Bowen inclined his head.

"Anything else?" Tucker asked her. His voice was low and easy, a deliberate technique that he utilized when he wanted to keep his witnesses talking without intimidating them.

"Then he just said I could get one of the officers out front to drive me to my motel. That was it. When I left him, he was still in that conference room, staring at the pictures."

Tucker's fingers tapped along the table. "And did you see anyone when you went outside?"

"No, the lot was empty."

Bowen pushed away from the wall. "Why didn't you get an officer to take you to the motel?"

"I had my own car. A rental. There wasn't a need for anyone to see me to my motel. I was perfectly safe." Her shoulder lifted in a shrug.

I'm sure Henry thought he was perfectly safe, too.

"He seemed sad," Amelia blurted. Then she winced. "Sorry. You probably don't care about how I *think* the guy felt—"

"On the contrary." Tucker's attention was completely on her. "I'd love to know what you thought about him."

"He seemed…" Her breath rushed out again. "Guilty, okay? That was my first thought when he turned to me. He was in front of those pictures, asking if I thought there were more victims, and the tone of his voice… I felt as if he were blaming himself. I wanted to say something to make him feel better." Her shoulders lifted once more. "Only I'm not very good at that sort of thing. I was afraid I'd make things worse, so I left him. I thought he might want to be alone."

"And who was here when you left?" Bowen asked, though he'd already gotten a list of staff members. Not many at all had been there.

"I don't know. There was an officer at the front desk. Maybe one…one on his phone in the bull pen? It was empty. So late. And I was just trying to get out." Her eyes were wide and stark. "I'm sorry that I'm not more help. Do you think the killer was here when I left?" Her hand rose and fluttered near her throat. It was a move he'd seen witnesses and victims make hundreds of times—an absolutely primal response to danger. When threatened, humans always covered their most vulnerable spots…like the jugular.

Tucker smiled at her. Instead of answering, he said, "Thanks for your time, Amelia. I know you have to get back out to the cabin and finish work at the Curtis Zale crime scene, so I don't want to hold you up any longer." He rose, and she did, too. "Actually, I'm sure I'll be seeing you out at the cabin. I want to come and take a look around myself."

She nodded. "Okay, um, thanks. I'll be heading out there—I actually called in my assistant because there is so much work there. Carlisle is a grad student at the university. Very capable, and I could definitely use him right now." Her head dropped a bit as she turned for the door. "There are just so many more bodies there than I've ever found before."

Bowen opened the door for her. "Thanks again."

She stopped and glanced up at him. "Is Agent Night all right?"

Bowen frowned.

"You seemed quite worried about her last night at the cabin." Her hand lifted and her fingers fluttered near her throat. "She's not here today and I was concerned about her wound—"

"Agent Night is fine. She's assisting the ME right now."

"Oh." She gave a weak smile. "Glad she's all right." Then she slipped through the doorway.

Bowen didn't speak until the lady had disappeared. "So Captain Harwell had a guilty conscience…" He craned his head to look at Tucker.

"Because he was involved in the crimes?" Tucker asked. "Or because they happened right under his nose and he didn't see them?"

"Let's talk to Harwell's family. Find out if there was any connection between Curtis and the captain."

Tucker nodded. "I'll take care of it." But his gaze was considering as he stared at Bowen.

Bowen frowned at him. "What?"

"I saw it, man."

Bowen turned to face him fully. "Excuse me?"

"Heard it, too. So you'd better watch it."

Bowen shut the door to the conference room.

"Okay, you need to clue me in on what it is that you're talking about."

"I saw the way you looked at Macey this morning." His lips twisted. "I know the look, man."

Bowen shook his head. "You're mistaken."

"You often stare too long and too hard at Macey, especially when you think she isn't watching."

Bowen made sure his expression was schooled to give nothing away. "Tucker, you might know killers, but you have no freaking idea what you're going on about right now."

Tucker gazed at him, straight in the eye. "When you say her name, your voice changes. When you talk about her, your face changes. You need to watch those giveaways."

Fucking hell.

"I'm guessing Samantha doesn't know?" Then before Bowen could answer, Tucker shook his head. "Course not, she wouldn't have paired you two together in the field. Although…" Now his brow scrunched. "Come to think of it, Samantha is engaged to her ex-partner, so maybe it's another one of her experiments. The way she thinks all of us can hunt killers better because of our pasts. Maybe Samantha saw this shit between you and Macey coming, and she thought it might make you even better in the field."

"You know the FBI doesn't allow agents to become—"

But Tucker waved that away. "We've both seen Samantha say screw off to the FBI rules when they don't match what she wants." He flashed a cold smile. "One of the things I admire about the woman. So maybe she *does* know you and Macey are in a relationship."

"We're not." Flat, cold.

Tucker cocked one brow.

"We are *not* in a relationship, so don't go spreading that shit around." They were just...meeting in the dark. "We were partners, that's it." *But we're not even partners right now.*

That one eyebrow of Tucker's slowly lowered. "Are you lying to me—or yourself?"

The guy could go fuck off—

Bowen's phone vibrated in his pocket. He pulled it out, and glanced down at the screen. "Unknown caller."

Tucker swore. "I'll alert the team. Keep him on the line, got it?"

"I know the drill." *Just when I thought the jerk wasn't going to call anymore.*

Tucker pulled out his own phone and hunched his shoulders as he made his call.

Bowen let his phone ring again. Once more.

Tucker motioned to him. *We're set.*

Bowen slid his finger across the screen, then tapped to accept the call. "Agent Murphy."

"Sorry you lost a member of your task force." The same robotic voice filled the room. Bowen had made sure the phone was on speaker so that Tucker could hear what the killer had to say. "But the guilty have to pay."

"Guilty?" Bowen repeated. "Just what crime do you think Henry Harwell committed? The guy was a cop, he dedicated his life to—"

"He didn't stop the crimes. He didn't even *see* them. Those men died on his watch, so that made him guilty."

"The fuck it did. He never lifted a hand to anyone."

"Sometimes, the guilty aren't the ones holding a weapon in their hands. They're the ones who do nothing." Static crackled. "But you think the same thing, don't you? That's why you went after Arnold Shaw yourself. The cops weren't doing anything to help you. They knew women were dying. You blamed them. I know you did."

"You don't know jack shit about me."

"I know you're fucking your partner."

Every muscle in his body locked down. His gaze jerked toward Tucker.

"And here I thought you'd love precious Cadi until the day you died. I'm disappointed in you, Bowen."

"Yeah? Well, I'm disappointed that I'm standing here talking to some psychopath who murdered a cop. Who thinks he's the freaking hand of justice when he's just some delusional killer who needs to be put in a cage."

"That's not what you really think. You think Henry Harwell was a blind fool who was too worried about the tourist business and not worried enough about the people in his mountains. You think that Daniel Haddox deserved a painful death and that Patrick Remus had the send-off to hell that he had coming." Robotic laughter. "You're welcome, Bowen."

"That's not what I think. You don't know me. You know—"

"You went into that alley intending to kill Shaw. You went there knowing he wouldn't make it out. You even see yourself as a killer."

Bowen's back teeth clenched.

"Don't deny what we both know."

"Where are you?" Bowen wanted to find that bastard and rip him apart. "You want to punish someone? How about punishing your damn self? Because you're the one killing. You're the one—"

"My work isn't done."

A chill slipped over Bowen.

"Maybe the FBI should clean house. Because I think…I think the guilty are there, too, Bowen."

The line went dead. Bowen looked up at Tucker. "Tell me that you got that location."

Tucker had his phone to his ear. "They're triangulating and they think…" His eyes widened. "They say the call came from within a one-mile radius of this station. The killer is right *here*."

Bowen yanked open the door and raced down the hallway. As he passed the conference room, Jonah called out to him. Bowen paused long enough to snarl, "Bastard just called again—he's close. So fucking close."

Jonah ran after him. Tucker was barking orders, trying to organize the officers there, and Bowen was searching for the caller. He ran outside. *One-mile radius. One mile.*

He hurried toward his SUV. Bowen yanked open the door. And he saw the phone lying on his front seat.

"Bowen?" a female voice called out. He glanced over his shoulder. Amelia Lang stood uncertainly near a pickup truck. "Everything okay?"

No, it damn well wasn't. He knew he'd found the phone the killer had just used. "Did you see anyone here?"

"Um, yes, actually, there was a uniformed cop by that vehicle just a moment ago." Now she glanced around, as if she were confused. "I don't know where he went." A furrow appeared between her brows. "Why? Is something wrong?"

Not something. A whole lot of fucking things.

THE MUSEUM WAS closed to the public. It was dark and quiet, cavernous. When Macey walked inside, with Bowen just steps behind her, she couldn't quite shake the chill from her bones.

The perp had called him again. Bowen's voice had been flat and his face expressionless as he told her about the call. They hadn't found the guy. Their team had interviewed every cop at the precinct and even those *not* on duty, but they'd turned up nothing.

Dr. Lang had said she'd seen a white male, maybe around six feet, with dark hair. She hadn't gotten a good look at his face, and Macey figured that had been deliberate on the guy's part.

No prints had been found on the phone, and Dr. Lang had *thought* she remembered the guy wearing gloves. The phone had been a burner, one picked up at some gas station. Used and dropped.

Bowen had been pissed, a quiet fury that seemed to roll off him. Tucker had gone to investigate the cabin and the remains of Curtis's victims that were still being unearthed, and Jonah had stayed to try to determine just how their perp had disabled the security footage at the station. Bowen wasn't supposed to be at the crime scene, and when Macey had said that she was checking out the museum, he'd insisted on accompanying her.

Were they breaking the rules about him being in the field? Not exactly. She'd taken the lead and would be doing the bulk of the questioning. Bowen had promised to stay silent.

She wasn't so sure he'd be able to keep that promise.

"You're... You really think hate nails could be connected to a crime you're investigating?" the museum's manager asked. Peter Carter. Midthirties, with light brown hair, dark eyes and tats that circled his wrists and lower arms. "That's crazy. Like, seriously crazy." He turned away from them and led the way to the exhibits upstairs. The stairs creaked beneath their feet. "It's just a display, you know. Nothing for people to get worked up about. The kids come in, they see it and they get a little creeped out..."

Macey glanced around at some of the displays in the museum. She was noticing a definite trend.

"That's what you do, right, you creep people out here?"

"Well, yeah." Peter turned back to look at her. "People like to be scared, you know? It gets their adrenaline flowing. Makes 'em feel more alive."

Macey considered him a bit more. "How long have you been working here, Peter?"

"Last five years." His smile stretched, revealing not dimples, but deep slashes on either side of his face. "Never would have thought a guy with a degree in criminal justice would wind up in this place, huh?"

Bowen was silent. So far, he was keeping up his end of the deal.

Macey replied, "I've learned you can never judge a book by its cover."

Peter's gaze slid down to her right hand. Her hand was against the banister, and her sleeve had slid up a bit, revealing part of her scar. "No," Peter murmured. "You can't."

She pulled down her sleeve.

"Show us the damn skull," Bowen growled.

Peter straightened. "Right. This way." He led them into another room. This room was dim, deliberately so, Macey knew. A glance around showed her that the room was supposed to appear menacing. There were lots of scary props in that room. Mummies, vampire relics, and, in the back, next to a strobing light, she saw the skull.

And the nails.

"Interesting, isn't it?" Peter mused. "Families tend to stare the longest at it. Some just can't look away."

Macey was having a bit of trouble looking away
herself. She crouched next to the glass. She could
see the old, rusty nails that had been driven into the
skull. And the sign right next to the skull told about
the "hate nails" on display. "Every nail is a wish for
bad luck, for a grievance." She read the description
and then glanced back at Bowen. The lights were
strobing, flashing right on him, and he appeared sinister as light and darkness shadowed over him.

"How long has this display been here?" Bowen
asked quietly.

"Only a few months. It's a new addition. We try
to keep things fresh here at the museum."

Macey's gaze slid back to the skull. "This isn't a
reproduction." Macey knew she was staring at a real
human skull. The tourists who came in the museum
might not understand that fact, but she did.

"Of course it's not fake!" Now Peter sounded of-
fended. "We are an oddities museum, not some trick
shop. Our materials are all authentic."

Macey glanced over at the mummy. "That's not
real."

"*That's* for scene setting, not an actual display."

Her head tilted as she studied the skull once more.
"How many people have been to see this skull since
it was put on display?"

Bowen had stepped closer to her and the skull.
Macey could almost feel him behind her.

"Thousands," was Peter's instant reply. "I'd have
to check my receipts for an exact number. See, um,
summer is actually one of our busiest seasons…and

then fall…oh, man, we get so many people here because they come to the mountains to see the leaves change colors. You would not *believe* how many people visit this little town each year."

She'd seen the bumper-to-bumper traffic on the little roads in Gatlinburg. Macey definitely believed.

"You remember anyone showing too much interest in the skull?" Bowen asked.

"I don't…I don't watch the guests, man. They can come in and wander around as much as they want. Not like I police them."

Macey rose to her full height. "We're going to need a list of all your employees."

Peter gave a weak laugh. "Look, I, um, I've heard the tales about what's happening in town. The story about that Pyro guy, Remus? It made the news. But I mean, you two coming in here and asking all of these questions…you don't seriously think murders are related to the skull here, do you?"

So far, they'd managed to keep much of their investigation under wraps. But Macey knew that wouldn't last much longer. The bodies were piling up—and, as evidenced by Peter's words, gossip was spreading. With the police captain's death, the whole case was going to explode soon. She knew that as soon as he got back from the Zale scene, Tucker was supposed to be organizing a press conference with the mayor. They were trying to get on top of the story, trying to control the flow of information before things got out of hand.

If it's not too late already.

"I think we are investigating all possibilities." And the manager definitely wasn't going to like what she had to say next. "I'm afraid we're also going to be confiscating the skull for the time being."

"What?" Peter demanded. He took a lunging step toward her. "No way, no *way*. You can't just take part of my exhibit."

Bowen put his body in front of Peter's, blocking the guy from reaching Macey. "Yes way. We can. This is a criminal investigation and you have material that may be pertinent to the investigation. So we'll be taking that skull. We'll be checking it for fingerprints and DNA and anything that could possibly be useful to us. And when we're done—" his voice was flat "—the FBI will thank you for your assistance and we'll return the skull."

The strobe light kept flashing.

"Now, we'd really appreciate that list of your employees. Because we're going to need to speak with them."

Macey thought Peter might argue again. Instead, he let out a frustrated sigh. "I'll get the list," Peter muttered. "Excuse me." He hurried out, leaving them near the exhibit.

Macey waited until he was gone, and then, voice deliberately void of emotion, she said, "I thought you were going to keep quiet."

He growled. "The jerk was invading your fucking personal space, Macey."

"I could handle him." Her head tilted. "You're usually a bit more tactful."

Bowen swung toward her. "My tact is running low because the bodies are piling up."

And because the killer was taunting him. She took a step closer to him as the lights flashed. "What did he say, Bowen?" Because he hadn't told her. She just knew another call had come through, and then the team had leaped to action.

And Bowen…she'd seen the dark rage gathering in his eyes.

"He thinks he knows me." Bowen's words were low, angry. "And that he knows you."

Her heart jerked in her chest. "I don't understand." Macey glanced down and saw that his hands had clenched.

"He realizes we're lovers, Mace." His words were a deep, hard rumble. "He said that."

Her heart wasn't jerking now. It was racing. "He's trying to get into your head. He doesn't know anything. No one does but us—"

"He talked about Shaw. About how when I went into that alley, I intended to kill the bastard all along." His words were softer, but still tight with anger, and she found herself leaning toward him so that she could catch each word. "He knows what I was doing. He thinks he understands me." Bowen shook his head. "He doesn't. I'm not going to play some game with your life on the line."

But Macey was considering exactly what he'd just said. Or rather…what the killer had told him.

"Samantha was worried there could be a leak

at the FBI. I think she's right," Bowen continued grimly. "I think the bastard has hacked into our files. Our psych reports. I think he's using what he knows against us. Hell, access to the FBI files would also explain how he knows so much about these victims."

"But it wouldn't explain how he knows about us." She eased even closer to him. "And I'm betting you haven't told any FBI shrink what you told me last night." Because he'd bared his soul to her.

He shook his head, and once more, she couldn't help but think Bowen looked particularly dangerous— sinister—in that flashing light.

"Then he found out another way." A way that had her worried. "Bowen, I believe he's still watching us."

She saw his shoulders stiffen. The perp had taken their pictures in North Carolina; of course he'd continue his stalking in Tennessee. But maybe, maybe he'd gone past just the picture-taking phase of things. "If he truly knows we're lovers, if he knows what you said to me last night…" There could only be one explanation. "He has surveillance at our cabin. He's literally seen us together. He's heard our secrets."

"Son of a—" Bowen began.

"Got them!" Peter announced as he hurried back into the room. "Here are the names of our staff members, though I assure you, we have thoroughly checked the background of every person here. We are a top-notch facility. You will not find any criminals working at our museum—"

"That's the thing, buddy." Bowen took the files from him. "Sometimes, you just don't know who people really are. Not until it's too late."

CHAPTER TWELVE

THEY FOUND THE video camera and the listening devices in their cabin. Three of them. One in the loft. One in the downstairs bedroom. One on the back porch.

Bowen watched with fury as the crime scene team tagged and bagged each item. The bastard had been watching and listening. Every single moment. He'd known what Bowen was doing. Known just what steps they were taking with the investigation.

He'd been watching. Everything.

"Jonah said there wasn't a long-range feed on the devices," Tucker murmured as he came toward Bowen. "The guy had to be within a five-mile radius to get the feeds, and with these mountains—" he gestured around to the peaks that surrounded them "—Jonah said it would have been even harder to transmit. So he thinks the perp was close. Very close."

Bowen marched outside and studied the cabins on the street. Tucker followed him. They were in a rental subdivision, of sorts. A whole mountainside that was full of open cabins for tourists. "He was right here."

"He could *still* be here," Tucker argued. "We need

to search these cabins. Because my money says the guy isn't leaving anything to chance. He didn't want to be too far away and risk not getting his feeds. He wanted to know everything that you did. Everything that Macey did—"

"We're lovers." The words came out hard but he knew he couldn't cover this. Not now. "Macey and I. He knows."

The guy had been two steps ahead of them during this entire investigation, and Bowen was tired of that shit. *You were hunting us all along, weren't you? Well, the game is about to change.*

"I'll tell Samantha," Bowen continued gruffly. "Because to answer your question from before... she didn't know." *No one did.* He didn't know what Macey was going to think about the team suddenly knowing their personal story. Would she withdraw from him? Fuck, he didn't want that. The last thing he wanted was for Macey to pull away. He'd worked too hard for too long in order to get her close.

"And the rest?" Tucker asked him. Tucker's hands were loose at his sides and his face was expressionless. "The things the guy said about Arnold Shaw? You want to tell me about that?"

Not particularly. But if there was a recording somewhere—and he feared there would be—Bowen knew he didn't have a choice. "I wanted the bastard dead. I went into that alley knowing I'd shoot him."

"But you didn't attack him with the gun first." Tucker's voice was low. "I read the police files, man. You went at him unarmed first."

Because I wanted to hurt him with my bare hands.

"With my past, do you think I'm going to judge you?" Now anger broke free, cracking the mask of Tucker's expression. "I want to help you. I want to have your back. But if you're keeping secrets, if Macey is, I can't do that. You both have to be honest with the team."

"There aren't more secrets. The perp out there has found them all."

"You sure about that?" Tucker asked, tilting his head. "Because I think this guy gets off on secrets. I think he likes to find them, and exploit them. If your secret is dark enough, then he judges you…and he punishes you." His eyes narrowed as he seemed to consider the situation. "Fuck. It could be part of his MO…"

Bowen shook his head. "What are you talking about?"

Tucker's jaw had clenched. "The videos. The bugs. He's learning his prey. Learning the secrets out there. What if…what if he did the same thing with Daniel Haddox? With Patrick Remus? He watched, he listened…and he learned their secrets, one by one, before he decided it was time for them to die."

"We didn't find any surveillance equipment at Haddox's place…"

"Was the crime scene team even looking? We almost missed them here! They were so small, we had to do three sweeps to find them." He nodded. "What if the crime team didn't see them the first time? Or maybe the perp took them after he killed Daniel? He could have cleaned up after himself. We know that's what he does—he's so good at leaving a clean crime scene. He could have taken the devices with him."

Bowen considered the idea. "He had the bugs there, so he knew when Haddox killed Gale Collins."

"Yes...he was watching, listening. He'd found Haddox and he wanted to watch his prey."

Bowen hissed out a hard breath. "If that's the case, then the guy would have needed to be watching Haddox for a while. He would have known who the guy truly was...and the woman the Doctor sliced and tortured... Our perp *let* Gale die."

Tucker's hard gaze held his. "Yes."

Bowen's mind was spinning. "We need a team to sweep the captain's office again. This bastard...he could have his eyes everywhere." But then Bowen shook his head. "Not everywhere. There's no way he could have gotten a signal transmitted from Curtis Zale's cabin. The place is too remote. I didn't even have cell service up there. We needed the ranger's radio to get backup."

"Then maybe he used the apartment Zale had in town. A team is there now." Tucker pulled out his phone. "I'll tell them what to search for. If we get a hit on a listening device at even one more location, then that's another piece of the puzzle for us."

It meant their killer watched his prey first. Watched and learned.

It also meant...

He hasn't just been calling me to jerk me around. The guy is after me. I could be his next target.

MACEY WAS BACK in the ME's office. Goose bumps rose on her arms as she hurried into the lab. The place was cold as ice—always was. And the scent of antiseptic was strong. "Dr. McKinley!" Macey called out. She rounded the corner and saw him at his desk. He'd been leaning forward, his head slumped into his hands, but at her call, he straightened quickly.

She went closer to him and could have sworn that over the heavy odor of antiseptic that clung to the air, she caught the scent of...

"Have you been drinking?" Macey asked him quietly.

Shamus McKinley swallowed, and then he rose to his feet. He was a bit unsteady, and his gaze darted to her, then away. "I think...I think Dr. Lopez will be arriving any moment. I'm just waiting for her."

Macey paced closer. She saw the open drawer of his desk and the scent of alcohol grew stronger. Her lips thinned. "I need you sharp on this case. We can't afford screwups."

He raked his hand over his face. "My friend is on a slab in the back. He is right there—"

Macey touched his shoulder. "You need to go home for the day, Dr. McKinley."

His lower lip trembled. "I need to help him. Some bastard put nails into his hands. Some bastard—"

"I can't have you working on this case when you're compromised." She kept her voice soft. Sympathy pushed through her. She could see his pain. "I need you to go home. Go home, grieve, take some time and just...get yourself together."

His eyes closed. "I've been sober for ten years. Ten long years…and now this."

She squeezed his shoulder. "Do you have a sponsor you can call?"

He nodded once, grimly.

"Then do it. I'll stay here and meet Dr. Lopez. You come back tomorrow, and we'll hit the ground running, okay? But…go home now."

"I've fucked up."

"You're human," she told him. "And you're in pain. You need to get out of here." *And not stay with the dead.*

He nodded and Macey helped him collect his things. A few moments later, Shamus was gone, and she was left in the too cold and cavernous lab.

Macey reached for a pair of gloves. She slid them on and then headed over to the storage lockers. She pulled in a deep, steadying breath, and then she opened the second locker. Captain Henry Harwell's locker, according to the label. She pulled out the slab and then carefully unzipped the body bag.

His skin was dark, bruising near the top of his forehead. She leaned in closer, examining that bruise, and then she turned his head, studying the wound at the back of his head. A rough circle. She measured the diameter of it…and then the diameter of a similar wound on the side of his head.

A hammer. He used a hammer on your head. The same hammer he used to put those nails into you?

She straightened her shoulders.

And all of the lights went out in the lab. Macey was plunged into complete darkness.

What in the hell?

She paused a moment, thinking that a generator would kick back on. There had to be a generator in this place, right?

She could hear the hum from the storage lockers, so they were still getting power. But...

Macey fumbled in the dark. She zipped up the body bag. Pushed it back into the freezer so that it would stay safe and—

Had she just heard the shuffle of a footstep?

Macey straightened. "Is someone there?"

Maybe the ME had come back.

"Dr. McKinley?" Macey called. "Is that you? Do you know what happened to the lights?" *A short. Could have just been a short.* But her gut was tight, her muscles were battle ready and her instincts were screaming at her.

There was no answer to her call. Macey pulled out her weapon, not about to take chances. Her eyes had adjusted a bit to the darkness and she could make out the exam tables. She could see the desk up ahead. She could also see...

A man. A tall shadow. Blocking the door.

Her eyes narrowed as she tried to see better. And her gun aimed dead at him. "Identify yourself!" Macey yelled at him.

Instead of answering, he turned and ran out the doorway.

Shit. Macey lunged forward, but her feet hit a box

that was on the floor. She hit it hard and stumbled, but then she straightened and ran into the hallway.

The lights flashed on right then. Bright, and she blinked, momentarily blinded. But then…then she saw the man in the hallway.

Not some masked man. Not some killer.

Dr. McKinley was at the end of that hallway and his desperate eyes were on her. He had his hand to his throat, and he was trying to stop the blood that pumped out so quickly from the deep wound in his neck. He tried to call out to her, but no sound broke from his lips.

Macey raced to him even as her gaze swept the long hallway. There was no sign of the attacker. She knew he'd been there moments before. They were on the basement floor. Had he taken the elevator back up? Gone up the stairs?

She fell to her knees beside Dr. McKinley. He was bleeding—so badly. She put her hands to his throat, trying to staunch the blood flow.

The elevator dinged and the doors started to open.

Macey grabbed for her gun. She'd just put it down when she reached for the ME. Her hands curled around it, and she brought it up in one fast arc, aiming right at those opening doors.

Jonah stood there. Wearing a black shirt and dark jeans, and blinking nervously behind his glasses. "Macey?" Alarm flared in his eyes and he yanked out his own weapon as he took in the scene and saw the blood on her—and Dr. McKinley. "What happened?"

"The perp was just here," Macey snapped out. "He took the stairs or the elevator—"

"Not the elevator," Jonah immediately denied. "No one else was up there." He yanked out his phone and called for backup even as Macey struggled to tend the ME's wounds.

She was still wearing the white exam gloves. Macey realized that fact dimly. His blood was smeared all over the gloves.

"Keep him alive, Macey!" Jonah yelled, and then he was running for the stairs.

Macey stared into Dr. McKinley's pain-filled eyes. "Did you see the person who did this?"

Tears leaked from his eyes. He managed a weak nod.

"What did he look like?" Macey demanded. "Tell me, tell—"

Mask... His lips formed the word but no sound emerged.

Then his body slumped to the side. Macey grabbed him, holding tight. "No, you are *not* dying, do you hear me? I won't lose someone else. I *won't*!"

"WE NEED TO go door-to-door with these cabins," Tucker said as he stared at the cops and local FBI agents they'd just assembled for the search of the mountainside rental community. "We think our perp may have a base nearby—he's getting the signals from the devices he planted so he can't be that far away. We need you to look—"

Bowen's phone rang. Frowning, he looked down

at the scene, wondering if the perp was calling again for another of his taunts.

But, no, Macey's image was on his phone.

Bowen turned away from Tucker and the crowd, and he hurried a few feet away. He put the phone to his ear. "Macey? What's happening?"

"He struck again." Her voice was flat.

Bowen stiffened. "What?"

"I was at the ME's lab. He went after Dr. McKinley. Cut his throat—"

He was about to shatter the phone. "Is McKinley dead?"

"No, I don't know if the guy counted on me being here or what, but he didn't finish." Her voice was weary. "He didn't get a chance to finish. McKinley was just rushed to the hospital. Jonah is here. He tried to find the guy, but it was too late. The perp is like a shadow, he can just vanish as soon as you try to shine light on him."

There was something about her voice. "Macey, are you okay?"

"He was in the room with me, Bowen. The lights went out. I was in the lab, standing right over Harwell's body. And I—I heard a footstep. I turned around and he was there. He was just…watching me."

The way he's been watching for a while. "I'm on my way."

"No, you're supposed to stay with Tucker! Look, I have to secure the scene here, okay? I'll check the area. I'll find out how the guy got access to what should have been a monitored lab, and then I have to brief Dr. Lopez when she arrives." Her breath rushed over the line. "We need her now more than ever. And until we can figure out how the security failed at this place, we need to make sure a guard is here with her."

"Why did he go after McKinley?" Bowen demanded. "What could have sent him after the doctor?"

"Maybe we'll find out soon." Her voice still had that weary tone. "After all, he likes to call you after his kills, doesn't he? Update you. Share his story with you."

Share his story with you. "Because in his mind, I understand."

"Use that, Bowen. When he calls, *use* it."

He heard a voice in the background, and then Macey said, "I have to go. Jonah needs me. Watch your back, got it, Bowen?"

He was still holding the phone far too tightly. "And you watch yours, Macey." He cleared his throat. "I need you to make sure that Dr. McKinley's office is swept for listening devices. For video cameras."

There was a stark pause. "You found them at the cabin."

Yes. "You were right. He was watching us. And Tucker and I…we think he may have been watching the other victims, too."

"I'll check Dr. McKinley's lab and work space." Her voice was softer.

The call ended and he stood there a moment. He

fucking wanted to be with Macey right then. Wanted to make sure she was all right.

"Let's get started on the search," Tucker announced to the team he'd gathered. "Remember, this is a door-to-door trip. We don't have search warrants. We're doing a visual hunt. I want to know who is in these cabins. You see something suspicious, you report back immediately."

The group went to work. Tucker marched toward Bowen. "I can tell by the look on your face that that call was bad."

Bowen shook his head. "The ME just got his throat sliced."

"Fuck."

"He's alive, but the perp got away."

Tucker's eyes glittered. "The guy is ballsy. Going into a lab—"

"Macey thinks he's going to call me again. If he does, we have to get the bastard." Each time he'd called, the perp had been dicking around—playing his games and leading them astray when they tried to search him out. "The guy is screwing around with us. He knows tech. He can have his phone signal bouncing from tower to tower. He has us chase our own asses while he lines up his targets." Frustration boiled in his words.

That same frustration was mirrored in Tucker's bright blue gaze. "Who will he come after next? I thought he was focusing on you, but—"

"We have to make him come after me," Bowen said grimly.

Tucker's face tightened. "I don't think—"

"I have to push him. I have to get his focus totally on me. The bastard is already calling me. He wants to play some fucking game with me? Then we let him. We get him to come after me, not after anyone else, and when he does—" Bowen exhaled "—that's when we get him."

"Playing the hero—that gig can get you dead."

"I know how to fight back when a killer comes at me." He'd had plenty of practice. "Dr. McKinley? He didn't. The next target might not, either. The guy isn't stopping. He's getting bolder with his attacks. Macey was right the hell there. He could have gone after her!"

Tucker's gaze swept over him, lingering on the hands that Bowen had clenched in his rage. "Why do you think he didn't?"

"Because Macey isn't guilty of anything in his mind," Bowen immediately snapped back. "She's a victim, not a killer."

Tucker nodded. "By that logic, then Dr. McKinley was a killer."

Bowen had already thought the same thing. "He survived the attack. We'll find out what skeletons shake loose in his closet. If there *are* any. The killer murdered Captain Harwell because the poor bastard didn't stop Curtis Zale."

"Maybe there is something that McKinley didn't do, either."

Bowen forced his back teeth to unclench. "I'll get this killer to come after me."

Tucker threw up his hands. "Why? Because you have a death wish?"

No, because he didn't want anyone else dying on his watch.

"MACEY, ARE YOU all right?"

Jonah. He was back. Macey lowered her phone and glanced back at him. He stood at the end of the hallway, right near the spot that the crime scene techs were marking. The spot where she'd found Dr. McKinley.

Macey lifted her chin. "I've been better." On the days when she didn't let a killer get away.

He hurried toward her. His worried stare swept over her face, and the overhead light glinted off the lens in his glasses. "I checked the power grid. The guy made it go down—had a timer in place. He gave himself ten minutes without power. Seems there is a generator that feeds directly to the body storage unit, but everything else went down. The guy had his attack timed perfectly." Jonah almost seemed admiring. A dangerous thing.

"We need to check Dr. McKinley's office." Macey turned back toward the lab—and the office in question. "Tucker and Bowen found surveillance devices at our cabin. They think the perp we're after could be watching his victims." She made her way back into the lab. A cop in uniform was there, and Macey cast a suspicious glance his way.

Dr. Lang said she saw a cop near Bowen's vehicle.

Was she supposed to start suspecting every cop she saw now? *Maybe.*

Macey reached for a pair of gloves. "The whole place is a crime scene, so be very careful, okay?"

Jonah had already reached for his own gloves. "Always." His gaze slid to the corners of the room. "Tech can be so tiny these days, freaking microscopic. We need to get a sweeper in here so that we can detect any devices."

Macey sat down at McKinley's desk. She drew in a bracing breath, then opened the top desk drawer. A bottle of whiskey sat inside.

Jonah gave a low whistle. "Don't see that every day in an ME's office."

Her fingers bumped the mouse, and the computer woke up as the screen flashed.

"No." She gazed down at the bottle. A fourth of it had been consumed. "He said he had a sponsor. That he'd been sober for ten years."

Jonah paced closer to her. "You believe that? Or you think the ME has been hitting the bottle for a while now?"

He hadn't seemed drunk when she'd met him before. His eyes had been clear. His words hadn't shown any typical alcohol-use slurring. He'd spoken in a normal pattern, articulating well.

"Macey..." His fingers stroked over her shoulder. Jonah's voice had dropped to a whisper. "The camera is on."

What camera?

His head bent, and he whispered in her ear, "The computer, Macey. The camera is *on* right now."

Her gaze lifted, and sure enough, she saw the faint red light next to the camera—a camera that was perched on the top of the computer monitor.

"Don't stare at it. Just…act naturally, okay?" Again, Jonah had whispered in her ear. "Come with me."

She rose, moving with him, and a few moments later, they were in the hallway.

"Genius," Jonah announced. "Fucking genius."

Macey shook her head, wanting to make sure she understood. "He was watching McKinley…through the guy's own computer?"

He nodded quickly. "You can do it remotely. Hell, try a search on the internet—you'll get instant results, a freaking how-to guide. Anyone can do it. You hack into your victim's webcam and *boom*, you can always see what they're doing."

"The camera was on when I woke the computer up. Was he watching me? *How?*" He'd said, "hacking," but she wanted specifics.

Jonah waved his hand. "It's really easy to do. You get the vic to download a bad link on a website, you give a malicious document to the target—so many options."

Her stomach was dropping. "Can you figure out who did this? Can you figure out *where* the guy is?"

But his gaze had turned distant. "The perp could have taken still shots from the camera. Or even done a live viewing."

And if he caught McKinley drinking... Her eyes
squeezed closed. "He saw Dr. McKinley." *With the
whiskey?*

"Trojan malware," Jonah said, nodding hard. "The
malware found a way to activate the camera and from
that moment on, Dr. McKinley was *his*."

She stepped closer to him. "You can find out when
the malware was installed." He was their tech genius.
He'd better be able to find that out.

"I can find out when it was installed." His eyes
were bright. "Dr. McKinley wouldn't have noticed
it. I saw it because I knew to look for the LED light
flashing with the camera… When that happens, always a fucking sign."

She made herself take a deep breath. "You can
find the guy, right? You can trace this for me." He'd
gotten her out of that office fast, and he'd whispered
the whole time. *Trying not to alert anyone who is
watching?*

He smiled at her. "I can find the guy."

Yes. "Then let's get to work."

CHAPTER THIRTEEN

"WE'VE GOT HIM," Macey said, her voice catching with excitement as it filled Bowen's ear. He stood outside a cabin—another damn cabin that he'd been searching with Tucker. "Jonah just did a reverse DNS query and tracerouting and some pretty much computer voodoo magic—and he *found* the guy."

"What? Slow down, Macey."

"The perp was watching Dr. McKinley through his computer. Jonah found the email that was sent with the Trojan file attached. Jonah traced him—*we've got the bastard!* The guy is at the museum, Bowen. The file was emailed directly from the oddities museum!"

Fuck. "He was screwing with us."

"Jonah and I are going there now—I left a cop to stay with Dr. Lopez. She just arrived. Are you meeting us at the museum? I—I know you're supposed to stay back, but—"

"Tucker and I are on the way." He'd let the other agent take lead, but Bowen would be there for his team.

She disconnected the call, and he turned to Tucker. "They got him!"

Tucker bounded toward him.

"The ME's computer was being hacked. Jonah traced it back—he said the guy was at the oddities museum. The fucking place with the hate nails." And the museum director had been so calm and controlled during their meeting. Peter Carter.

But Tucker shook his head. "The signal from your cabin wouldn't transmit that far."

"Then keep the men here searching. Maybe he has a second base here." Tricky son of a bitch. "But Macey and Jonah are closing in and we're their backup."

Tucker barked orders to the local agents, and then they were rushing for Tucker's rented SUV. They jumped inside and sped down the mountain.

"Do I need to remind you that you don't have a fucking gun?" Tucker snapped at him. "You can't go running into that place—"

"Then I'll make sure he doesn't run out," he replied grimly. "You go in with Macey and Jonah. You watch her back."

They rounded another curve. As they went down the mountain, Tucker could feel his ears popping. The road was steep and small, and dotted with cabins to the left and to the right.

"We checked that list of employees," Tucker said as he held tight to the wheel. "No one came up as raising a red flag."

"Then our perp just doesn't have a record. He's been good at hiding in plain sight." But not good enough. "He didn't count on Jonah."

Tucker's hands tightened around the wheel. "Right, Jonah." But there was a note in his voice. A hesitation when he said the other agent's name.

Bowen's eyes narrowed. "Something you need to say?"

Tucker was silent.

"The guy is with Macey right now. She's about to confront a killer. I need to know that the man with her can be counted on." Wait, what was he even saying? Of course, Jonah could be counted on. The guy was FBI.

"I was the one who didn't want Jonah on the team." Tucker paused at the stop sign. Darkness was falling fast and his headlights flashed onto the road up ahead. "He doesn't have enough field experience."

Shit. Bowen had expressed that same worry—

"He's done the training, yes, but then the guy sat behind a computer for years. When he's confronted by a guy with a gun... I just wasn't sure what he'd do." He exhaled on a rough sigh. "Macey pulled for him," Tucker continued as the vehicle accelerated. They'd left the subdivision of rental cabins and were snaking down the twisting mountain roads that would take them to Gatlinburg. "She worked with him on a few cases."

And she got him to try to find Haddox.

"She knows more about his past than I do, and she convinced Samantha that the man would be an asset." They crossed a bumpy, wooden bridge. "I have no doubt that Jonah Loxley is smart as hell, but I wanted to know that his instincts in the field were good." Tucker slid him a quick glance. "You shot a man less than twenty-four hours ago. And it's like you have freaking ice in your veins."

No, that wasn't what was in his veins.

"I would trust you under any high-pressure situation, any day of the week. Because I know you'd get the job done. You'd do anything necessary to protect your teammates and to protect any victims out there."

Bowen cleared his throat. "You'd do the same."

"Yeah, because you and I...we're alike inside. We've seen the monsters, and we've both had to make the hardest fucking choice of all."

The choice to kill. Because Tucker had taken out his brother.

"What choice do you think Jonah would make?" Bowen asked quietly.

"I'm afraid that's what we will all have to find out."

Bowen stared into the darkness before them. Macey was out there. "Hurry the hell up, would you, man?"

"Is it always this busy here?" Jonah demanded as he pushed through the crowd in downtown Gatlinburg. The small town was at the bottom of the mountains. The streets were lined with stores—the buildings connected one after the other. Families strolled the streets. Bands played. Cars honked. Chaos reigned.

"I think so," Macey replied as she skirted a group of teenagers. Her holster was a reassuring weight at her side, hidden just beneath her coat. A chill was in the air, and the chill seemed to sink straight to her bones. She could see the oddities museum up ahead, but it was dark. She checked her watch. The sun had set just a few moments ago. Darkness came fast in the mountains, something she'd learned. Very, very fast.

"The sign says they shouldn't be closed yet," Jonah muttered.

No, they shouldn't be. But the place was pitch-black.

"Guess someone decided to go home early," he added darkly.

The police force in the area was stretched too thin. With their captain gone, with their mayor's office in chaos, the cops had been divided—half were still at the Curtis Zale crime scene, searching for bodies. Some were with Tucker and Bowen, checking the cabins there, while other officers were tending to the basic safety needs of the people in the area.

So Macey and Bowen didn't have a big backup force with them. They'd called the PD, but it was going to take time to marshal the officers, and time was a luxury they didn't have. So she and Jonah had come alone.

But Bowen and Tucker are en route.

A big Closed sign hung on the main entrance. Macey put her hand to the front door. She expected to feel resistance from the lock, but instead, the door swung right open. Her head turned toward Jonah.

"Like that's not suspicious." He'd pulled out his gun.

She had hers at the ready. If the door was open,

they'd be going in—especially with their intel pointing to this building.

"The guy could have just cleared the hell out," Jonah said. "Maybe he realized we were onto him at the ME's office."

"Maybe." She squared her shoulders. "I'm going in first. Cover me?"

"Right." He nodded briskly. "Let's do this."

Macey pushed the door open and she rushed inside.

"You stay out here," Tucker directed. They'd finally arrived at the museum, but the place was dark and quiet. Tons of people lined the streets but the museum… *It's like a grave.* "I'm going to check the back of the place."

"Macey and Jonah are inside." He knew it. They'd had a head start on him and Tucker. They *had* to be in there.

Tucker glanced at the building, and then he slid toward the front door. He put his fingers around the handle and he pushed it open.

Not locked.

"You cover the front," Tucker said again, "and I'll get the back."

The guy rushed around the building. And Bowen pulled out his backup weapon, more than ready to face any threat that came.

His gaze strayed to that unlocked door.

Was Macey okay in there?

He took a step toward the door.

THEY CREPT UP the stairs. The place was as quiet as a tomb. Macey remembered her way around, thanks to her previous trip, so she knew the business office was located on the second floor.

The displays were turned off. The mannequins and animatronics were all still. In the dark, they created big, hulking shadows. Creepy as hell.

At the top of the stairs, she turned to the right.

Then she heard the stairs creak behind her, beneath Jonah's feet.

He immediately stilled.

So did she.

"His office is to the left," she said, barely whispering the words. She had a flashlight in her hand, one that she used to sweep out around her. A few more feet and she was at his office. The door wasn't shut. Macey walked right in, with Jonah behind her. He pushed the door closed and then flipped on the lights.

Only they didn't turn on. She took a step forward and heard something crunch beneath her shoe.

Macey's flashlight swept the scene and she saw the destruction. Every computer there had been smashed. Glass and broken hard drives were scattered on the floor.

Her flashlight danced over the material once more. "Guess someone didn't want us to see what was on those drives." She hoped that Jonah could still recover the information. "We need to search this whole building," Macey said. "We have to make sure he's not still here." She pulled out her phone and called Bowen. His line rang once, twice.

"Macey, where the hell are you?"

"Inside," she told him, keeping her voice barely above a whisper. "Second floor—in the office. But the place is wrecked. Every computer here is smashed."

Bowen swore. "I'm right outside the building, in the front. Tucker is around back."

So they had the place surrounded. Good. "Jonah and I are going to search all the rooms."

"Macey…"

She could hear something nearby. A faint moan.

"Someone's here," she whispered to Bowen. "I have to go." She shoved the phone into her pocket and picked up her flashlight again. Jonah was already on the move. He'd left the office, following that low moan.

And, up ahead, she could see that a light was flashing. On, off, on, off. The strobe light. Everything else in the building was pitch-black, but the strobe light had power in that display room.

How the hell is it still working? And I swear…it wasn't on a few minutes ago.

Jonah entered first. The strobe light kept flashing, and the moaning was definitely coming from that room. Jonah's flashlight aimed to the right, catching the mummy there.

It was moaning.

She saw Jonah's shoulders sag.

"Just a special effect," he muttered. "Just—"

Someone lunged from the darkness, racing right at Jonah and slamming into him. Jonah lost his grip on his light and it went flying.

A man was screaming, yelling, and Jonah's gun went off. The thundering blast was deafening.

WHEN HE HEARD the gunshot, Bowen grabbed for the front door. He raced inside the darkened building, and he immediately saw the flash of lights coming from the second floor. He grabbed for the banister and rushed up, barely hearing the squeak of stairs beneath him. His heart raced in his chest, and he couldn't get up to the second floor fast enough.

"FBI!" Macey's voice called out.

She's all right. She's all right.

"Freeze!" Macey shouted. "Put down the weapon *now.*"

Bowen burst into the room behind her. The strobe light was flashing, and it made the scene before him appear to be in slow motion.

Macey stood with her body braced. Her gun was aimed and pointed at her prey.

Jonah was on the floor, but his weapon was still in his hand, and his gun was also locked dead center on his target.

Peter Carter.

Peter's shoulder was dark—was that blood? Bowen couldn't tell in the flickering light, but he *could* see the gun clutched in Peter's shaking hand.

"Ac-accident…" Peter stammered. "That's what it was… I don't care what you think… I never *meant* to kill her!"

"Peter, drop the gun," Macey demanded. "Now."

But he didn't. The weapon kept shaking in his hand as it swung between Macey and Jonah.

"I l-loved her." Peter took a stumbling step back. "That's why I couldn't let her go!" His words tumbled out too fast. He took another step back. The strobe kept flashing. "I wanted to keep her close, that's all. But when you took her…I knew I had to leave."

"You aren't leaving," Jonah snarled. "You aren't getting away. You killed too many people. You *hurt* too many—"

"No, no!" Peter yelled. The gun in his hand locked on Jonah. "I didn't! Trying to frame me! That's what's happening! I checked the computer—I saw! I saw what happened!"

"Did you destroy those computers?" Macey asked quietly. She edged closer to the museum manager. "Are you the reason they're smashed into bits?"

Peter nodded.

Bowen stalked up behind Macey.

Peter's frantic gaze immediately jerked to him—and so did his gun. Peter stared straight at Bowen. "I didn't do it… Just her. Just her… An accident."

The guy was making zero fucking sense. "Put down the gun," Bowen ordered him. "And you can tell us your story."

But Peter didn't. He shook his head. The gun kept trembling. "You'll lock me up. I'll never get out. I can't…I can't live that way."

"Then maybe," Jonah growled at him, his voice hard and cold, "you should have thought about that

shit before you killed the police captain. Before you
went after Daniel Haddox and Patrick Remus and—"

"I didn't! I never did that!" Peter's voice was a
screech.

A scared screech.

Peter's hand jerked. "Who else is here?" he called
out. "Who is here?" Now he was almost yelling.

"Calm down, Peter." Macey's voice was calm.
Soothing. She took another step toward him. "We all
need to be calm. I want you to lower your weapon,
and when you do, we'll lower ours, too. No one has
to get hurt today."

But Peter looked down at his shoulder. "I'm already hurt." The gun flew toward Jonah. "He shot
me."

"Because you ran out at me in the freaking dark,"
Jonah snapped back. His grip on his weapon had
never wavered.

Peter's body sagged. "I loved her," he said again.
"That's why... I was just... I was so mad at first. She
said she loved me, too, you know? But she was cheat-
ing on me. Screwing around with *him*. I couldn't
stand it. I couldn't let her go, not to him."

"Who?" Macey blasted.

"The cop," Peter said. "She was screwing around
with him."

"With Henry Harwell?" Bowen pushed as a puzzle piece slid into place.

Peter's gun rose. "Couldn't let her leave... It was
an accident but... So mad..." His eyes squeezed shut.

The strobe light flashed.

"Sorry...so fucking s-sorry."

And he whipped up the gun. Bowen knew what the guy was going to do. Peter had already told them he wouldn't go to jail.

So he'll go to the grave.

"No!" Jonah yelled.

A gun blasted.

Peter's body jerked, like a marionette who'd just had his string yanked hard, and he stumbled back. The gun was still in his hand.

But only for a moment...

The gun fell to the floor. Then Peter fell.

Bowen ran toward him. Jonah rushed to the left. Jonah kicked the gun away, and Bowen tried to find the wound as the strobe light flashed.

"Left side," Macey said quietly. "That's where I aimed because I didn't want to kill him."

And Bowen found the wound. He put pressure on it, and Peter screamed, "No! No! I won't go to jail!"

"Yes," Bowen told him grimly. "You fucking will."

THE POWER WAS back on at the museum—back on everywhere. Apparently, the power had been shut down to all the rooms, every room except the one that had been home to the skull and its hate nails.

Peter Carter had been taken away in an ambulance—one complete with an armed police guard. Macey and Jonah had been grilled about the shooting—and she knew the FBI brass would want official statements from her soon. Another officer-involved shooting. Only this time, the perp wasn't dead.

Because she'd made sure of it.

Lights flooded the area, and Macey stared at the destruction that had been left in the business office on the second floor. "Think you can save anything from those computers?" she asked as she motioned toward the wreckage.

"You'd be surprised by just how much damage one of the machines can take," Jonah muttered back. "But I can't make any promises, not yet."

"Do your best." She turned away and headed for the door. But Jonah placed a hand on her shoulder to stop her.

"Who was he talking about?" Jonah asked her. "Who is the mystery woman?"

Macey glanced back at him. "I don't know yet, but I *do* know how to find out."

Jonah's brows furrowed.

"I'm pretty sure we have her skull," Macey said softly.

His eyes widened.

"That's why he panicked. That's why Peter was trying to get away. We have him dead to rights, and he knew it." She gave a bitter laugh. "That's why he wanted death. Because we're going to have enough proof to lock the guy away for a very long time."

"I don't understand…"

Macey parted her lips to respond.

"It was the skull that put things into motion," Bowen answered before Macey could.

She glanced toward the door and saw him filling the space. His eyes were on her and Jonah.

Jonah's hand slipped from her shoulder.

"We're going to need to thoroughly examine the skull we took from this museum," Macey said. "Because I suspect it's not some ancient relic like the info card next to the exhibit said. I think it's the skull of Peter Carter's victim." A girlfriend, one who'd been involved with Captain Henry Harwell.

"You're telling me the guy kept his ex's skull on exhibit?" Jonah sounded disgusted. He shook his head. "That's some twisted shit."

"Some people are twisted," Macey replied as she pulled down the edge of her sleeve. "Some people just can't let go."

"So what…we think Peter Carter is good for the kills? That he offed the girlfriend, then also took out the captain?" A line appeared between Jonah's brows. "Why everyone else? Did the guy get a taste for killing?"

Macey shook her head. "I don't think he did kill the others."

"But the nails…" Jonah began. "He used them on the skull. *If* that is the dead girlfriend, he used them on her, and our perp has been using that same sick MO with every single kill."

Yes, he had.

"Get to work on the computers," Bowen said. "When you make some headway, let us know. Macey and I will be heading to the hospital."

"I want to check on Dr. McKinley." He should be

out of surgery by now. As for Peter Carter, she knew he'd be staying in the hospital—under guard—for the time being.

She turned and followed Bowen out of the office. The building was teeming with activity, hardly surprising considering everything that had gone down. No strobe light was flashing any longer. In fact, every light in the place was on, and as she walked past the exhibits, the whole scene almost felt surreal.

They slipped down the stairs, past the cops and investigators, and when they were finally outside, Macey wasn't the least bit surprised to see the crowd that had gathered there. Her gaze swept the scene, curious about the bystanders there.

So many people were avidly watching the scene unfold. Morbid curiosity was in full effect as the police lights flashed. Reporters were there, too. She figured they'd run out of time as far as the news was concerned. But Macey didn't stop to talk with the reporters. Tucker was handling them, and as they eased past the throng throwing questions at him, Macey heard Tucker say, "The FBI will be issuing a full statement soon. Again, I just want to reassure the public that the FBI has contained this crime scene, and one suspect has been placed under arrest."

For suspicion of murder. "I need to see that skull," Macey said as she and Bowen finally cleared the crowd. The identity of that victim was *key*. They climbed into Tucker's SUV—she knew Tucker would be hitching a ride back with Jonah.

She sat behind the steering wheel, her gaze darting around the parking lot. There was so much she wanted to do. So much she *needed* to do.

"You okay?" His deep voice rumbled in the quiet interior of the vehicle.

"Never better." She reached forward to turn the key.

His hand flew out and curled around her wrist. She could feel his fingertips brush over the scars on her wrist. "I thought we were past the bullshit point."

Her head turned toward him. "I'm okay, Bowen."

"He wanted to kill himself."

"Or he wanted *us* to kill him." Because she wasn't so convinced that he would have pulled the trigger. Peter had waved that gun at them again and again, so desperately, wanting them to fire. "He attacked Jonah. Came right at him. Peter wanted to die. He wanted an out because he didn't want to spend his life in prison."

"Too bad, because that's exactly where he's heading."

Right.

His fingers slid from hers.

She turned the key. The vehicle's engine immediately growled to life.

"You never thought about killing him, did you, Mace?"

She pulled out of the lot. "Our job isn't to kill the perps. We're supposed to arrest them. Give the victims justice." She swallowed and kept her grip tight on the steering wheel as she slowly navigated through the bumper-to-bumper traffic in downtown

Gatlinburg. "Every bit of evidence we have points to this guy as being our perp. McKinley's computer—Jonah traced the hack back to the museum. The fact that all of the victims had nails in them—just like that skull…" Her breath blew out. "Jonah is right—it does fit the MO. Peter is the right age, he's a local, so he knows the area. He had a personal vendetta against Henry Harwell. So much about him being the killer makes sense."

He shifted in his seat. "But there are things that still don't add up."

She kept her breath nice and easy. Her fingers wanted to tremble and that was why she had a death grip on the steering wheel. A shooting was never easy, and she kept seeing that moment again and again in her mind. She'd have reports to complete on the shooting, but Macey didn't think she'd be pulled off fieldwork. Not now—there was too much at stake. Things were moving too fast.

Bowen *should* have been completely benched after the Zale shooting, yet he'd been right in the thick of things with her, and she'd been grateful to have him there.

She always felt better when Bowen was closer. Safer. Stronger.

She'd made the decision to wound Peter, not kill him. But what if that had been the wrong decision? What if he'd fired back at her? Or at Bowen?

"Why go after Haddox?" Bowen wondered. "After Remus? If Peter is our perp, why would he go after such big game?"

"We'll be asking him that question," Macey said as she finally pulled free of the traffic and headed toward the giant, gaping tunnel that had been carved right through the mountain itself. The SUV shot into that tunnel. "We've got him in custody. He's not going anywhere. We'll find out the truth about him."

She risked a glance to her right and found Bowen staring straight at her. She shivered.

"You were supposed to stay outside," Macey said.

"Fuck that. I heard the gunshot blast. You were in there."

He said the words...*like I matter.* But then, they were partners. Partners mattered. "It's good to have a partner like you on my side."

The tension in the vehicle seemed to deepen. "Macey." Her name was a growl. "I think we need to get a few things straight."

He sounded angry.

"There's a pullover right after the tunnel. Park there," he said.

She knew the spot. There were plenty of places like it in the Smokies. Spots to stop and take pictures. To see the streams. The wildlife.

"Pull over, Macey."

She eased off the road. She shifted into Park and turned toward him. The light from the dashboard provided a bit of illumination so that she could see his face.

"We're not just partners."

Her breath slid out. "Right. Everyone knows now,

don't they? They have to know that we slept together because he was watching—"

His hand curled beneath her chin. "It's not just sleeping together. Not just fucking. At least, that's not what it has been to me."

Her heart slammed into her chest. "Bowen?"

"I've wanted you for a long time, Mace." Her nickname rolled off his tongue and seemed to chase some of the chill from her body. "But I didn't want to scare you. I know you were hurting."

Damaged. She stiffened.

"Don't." He seemed to bite the word off. "Don't tense up, not with me. Don't block me the way you do everyone else. I don't need your mask or your shield. I need *you.*"

Macey couldn't look away from him.

"You're not my secret. Having you in my bed isn't something I want to hide from the world. I want you, Macey. I want you at my side. With me. And I didn't fucking run into that building just because you were my *partner.* I did it because I can't stand the thought of anything happening to you."

He leaned toward her.

"I wish I could take all of your pain away, Macey. I wish that I could have been the one to stop Haddox. I wanted to make him pay for what he did to you. I never want you to hurt again, and if I have my way, you won't."

She wanted to kiss him. His mouth was close to hers and the adrenaline rode her hard. She wanted to throw her hands around him and hold on tight. *Don't let go. Don't.*

"*That's* how I feel," Bowen rasped. "Now you need to figure out how you feel. The case will end. We'll go back to our lives. What do you want that to be like?"

He was putting the choice in her hands.

Need and fear clawed within her. "Bowen…"

He kissed her. Her mouth was open and his tongue slid right past her lips. Her hands flew up and locked around his shoulders, holding him as tight as she'd wanted moments before. Holding him as if she would never let go.

There was desperation in the kiss. Passion. Raw need. She wanted to let go—to finally just let all of her emotions go and be with him.

Bowen pulled back. "Your choice, Mace."

Her breath was coming too fast and hard.

"In the end," he said, "it's always going to be about you."

THE MURDERING BASTARD wasn't dead.

The crowd was still thick in front of the museum. People twisting their necks and whispering about the crime that had happened. Or what they *thought* had occurred.

Peter Carter had been taken away. Not in a body bag.

In a freaking ambulance. He'd been moaning and spouting about his innocence the whole time.

Peter should have been dead. The feds should have

gone in there and shot him. The scene had been set. And Peter...the fool would have been armed. He'd found all of the evidence, all of the videos, everything on *his* computer. The guy should have panicked. He should have attacked.

And then the feds should have taken him out. Every move had been planned perfectly and he'd been *promised* this ending.

What went wrong? Because something had.

Now Peter Carter was alive. He was in a hospital, not on a slab in the morgue. And that wouldn't work.

Not at all.

CHAPTER FOURTEEN

THE LIGHTS GLEAMED in the hospital and Bowen's shoes squeaked as he strode over the freshly polished floor. A nurse glanced up at him and Bowen flashed his badge. "Agents Murphy and Night to see Dr. McKinley."

The nurse, a man in his early twenties, pointed down the hallway. "He's in Recovery, but you know he's not going to be able to really talk now, right?"

Bowen glanced down the hallway and nodded curtly. "Thanks." He and Macey made their way to Recovery.

"He needs a guard," Macey said. "After his attack, we can't be sure the killer won't come back to finish the job."

"That's if the killer *isn't* Peter Carter." Because Peter was also in that hospital. Under guard and in surgery.

They flashed their badges to the staff in the recovery area, and soon they were standing next to McKinley's bedside. Thick bandages covered his throat, and the doctor who'd accompanied them inside—Dr. Tracy White—leaned over her patient. "Dr. McKinley," she announced. "You have guests."

She looked up at Bowen, then Macey, her dark gaze stern. "My patient has been through quite an ordeal. I can only allow you to stay with him for a few moments, and I must ask that you do not stress him in any manner."

"We're not here to upset the doc," Bowen said. "We just need some answers."

McKinley's head slowly turned toward them. His gaze dipped toward Macey and he mouthed the words, *Thank you.*

"He isn't going to be able to talk normally for a few days. Here." The doctor put a small whiteboard in McKinley's hand. "He can use this, but keep things simple, okay? He's going to tire easily." After giving a brisk nod, Dr. White exited the room.

McKinley's fingers closed around a marker, and he scrawled a message on the board. "Saved. Me."

Bowen saw Macey read those words. She gave the ME a weak smile. "I was doing my job." She paused. "Can you help us understand what happened?"

He nodded and wrote "Try."

"Thank you." Macey's face was pale, and Bowen wanted to get her somewhere and just, hell, fucking protect her from the world.

But that wasn't the way things worked.

That wasn't the way Macey worked.

They had a job to do. They'd do it.

"Did you see the man who attacked you?" Macey asked McKinley.

He wrote "Mask."

"Right." Macey's gaze cut to Bowen's. "He was wearing a ski mask. I saw that, too. I just…" Her stare turned back to the ME. "Where was he? When he attacked you, where was he?"

The machines around him beeped. His body shuddered as he wrote "Behind me." His words were becoming harder to read. "Stairs."

"You think he came from the stairwell." Bowen nodded. That made sense. "He was waiting for you."

"Dr. McKinley." Macey squared her shoulders. "I have to ask you some questions, and they're going to be personal, but they are pertinent to the case."

The marker shook in his hand.

"We learned that the perp has been watching you," Bowen told him.

McKinley's eyes widened.

"He hacked into your webcam, and he was watching you while you worked." Macey's voice was soft and sympathetic. "Was there something he might have seen you do? Something that—"

McKinley shook his head.

Macey's lips pressed together, and then she said, "There was whiskey in your drawer. I know you told me that you'd been sober for ten years, but was that the truth?"

The machines beeped faster.

"We need you to be very honest with us, Dr. McKinley." Bowen's gaze was on the ME. "Because this perp? He would have jumped on anything that he thought you did wrong."

The marker slid across the whiteboard. "Ten years."

Dr. White came bustling back into the room. "My patient's vitals are going through the roof! I must insist that you leave." Her face was set in determined lines.

"Thank you, Dr. McKinley." Bowen inclined his head to the ME. "You rest now."

Macey squeezed McKinley's hand.

They turned to leave.

"Um, wait!" Dr. White called out. "I think he has one more message for you."

They turned back. McKinley had written again, barely legible. "Ten years since I lost her." Tears gleamed in his eyes.

Her. The emotion there was so strong. "Your wife?" Bowen guessed.

The marker shook as McKinley wrote "Daughter."

"I'm sorry," Macey told him quietly.

McKinley lowered his whiteboard.

"Thank you," Bowen said again. He and Macey slipped out of the room. As soon as they were out of Recovery and back in the general area of the hospital, Bowen turned to Macey. "We need to find out exactly what happened to his daughter."

"That will be easy enough. We just need to pull up old records or…" And she already had her phone out, tapping on the screen. "Or we can search the internet. You can find everything there these days." She scrolled through her search results and sadness flashed on her face. "Shannon McKinley...died at age twenty-one. She was...drinking and driving."

Hell.

Macey glanced up at him. "Our perp was watching the ME, but maybe it was less about what McKinley was doing. Not about punishment at all for him." She put the phone back in her pocket and her eyes narrowed in thought. "The skull from the museum had been delivered to the ME's office. Dr. McKinley was supposed to run tests on it. Maybe *that's* what the attack was about. If he'd run his tests, then he would have found out that skull wasn't some relic— but the skull of a recent crime victim."

That made sense. "If Peter Carter is the perp we're after, then, yeah, he would have wanted the skull back. He could have been keeping tabs on the investigation. Could have seen the skull arrive and knew that he had to act. But you were there, so that threw everything off for him."

She nodded. "And he had to flee the scene. He could have gone into the lab to retrieve the skull, but then he saw me and had to leave before he could get it."

One option. "We need Peter Carter talking."

She glanced at her watch. "That's not going to be happening anytime soon." Her lips twisted. "And my money says that Peter is going to lawyer up. Fast and hard."

"Then let's find evidence that talks for him." He marched toward the exit and Macey fell into step with him. "Dr. Sofia Lopez arrived earlier, right?"

"Yes, but it's nearly eleven p.m. She won't be at the ME's lab now."

"Let's get her there." The sooner they found out the identity of their Jane Doe, the better. He shoved open the door and the crisp night air hit them.

Macey grabbed his arm. "Bowen!"

He whirled back toward her. "He hasn't called anymore, Macey. No more taunts. No more games." Bowen pointed back to the hospital. "Is it because he's in there? Because you and Jonah put bullets in him?"

She swallowed. "Jonah is piecing those computers back together. If he can recover information from the hard drives—"

"Then we can have hard evidence. Fuck, yes, but we need that skull identified ASAP."

"It doesn't happen instantly, Bowen!" Frustration burst in her words. "If we can't make a DNA or dental match, then we're going to need facial reconstruction work. We're talking about a process that can take days. Weeks."

That was time they didn't have.

Macey pulled out her phone and fired off a text. "I haven't even talked to Dr. Lopez since she came to town. I made sure security was set up at the lab, but everything was happening so fast then, I didn't get to discuss much with her."

Her phone vibrated.

Macey read the text and then her head whipped up. "Dr. Lopez said she met with the mayor, and he set her up in a second lab at the ME's building." A

surprised breath escaped her. "She's at the lab now—
and working on the skull."

Fuck, yes. "Let's go," Bowen said.

"BE CAREFUL WITH THOSE!" Jonah barked as the officers picked up another hard drive. There had been
five computers in the office and they were all beaten
to hell and back.

At his sharp command, the two officers sent
him disbelieving looks. "They're already in pieces,
man."

"Yeah, but I don't want them in any *other* pieces.
No more damage. The more damage we have, the
more corrupt the material will be." *And the harder
it will be for me to recover anything.* "Be careful
with them," he ordered curtly once more. "I need
all of this equipment transferred to the police station." And he'd be spending all night trying to retrieve the data.

The officers filed out. Jonah put his hands on his
hips as he surveyed the area.

"You really think you'll be able to pull anything
off those machines?"

His shoulders stiffened at Tucker's drawling voice.
Jonah glanced over his shoulder. "I can try."

Tucker stepped into the office. A considering expression was on his face. "You're the computer whiz,
right? You're supposed to be able to do anything
with tech."

"*Almost* anything," Jonah qualified. He didn't

want expectations too high. "I can't work miracles."
He kept his hands loose at his sides.

Tucker's bright gaze swept over him. "You fired
the first shot tonight."

And he'd already given statement after statement
about that scene. There was always so much red tape
at the FBI. Sometimes he wondered how anything
got done. "Macey and I were under attack. I did what
was necessary."

"That your first shot in the field?"

"You know it was." Jonah inclined his head toward the guy—the agent he'd known had never
wanted him on the team. "Isn't that why you cam-
paigned to have Samantha keep me off the unit?
Because you didn't think I'd be able to handle the
pressure of the job?"

Tucker didn't deny the charges. He just raised one
brow. "How would you know that?" He tapped his
chin and took a step closer to Jonah. "You haven't
been using those tech skills to dip into confidential FBI files, have you? Peeking at files that you
shouldn't see?"

He wasn't going to bother answering that. "For
years, whispers followed you around." He knew all
about Tucker Frost. "Reports claimed that maybe,
just maybe, you'd been involved in the murders your
brother committed."

Tucker's jaw locked.

"But you were still first pick for Samantha Dark's
team. Why was that?" It was a question that had
nagged at him because he'd been busting his ass to

prove himself at the Bureau. He'd busted his ass, and Tucker Frost had basically flown to the top of the class.

"Samantha wanted me on the team because I stared at the monsters, and I didn't flinch."

The monster had been Tucker's own brother.

Tucker's eyes swept over him as the other agent said, "When it came down to making a choice, I made that choice. I pulled the trigger and I killed my own brother rather than let him hurt an innocent woman."

A woman that Tucker loved. Yes, Jonah knew all about that story. And about the fact that Tucker had recently reunited with that woman. Too bad that reunion had caused a wake of bloodshed in New Orleans.

"Then I turned my damn life around," Tucker added, voice tight. "I made it my mission to hunt others like my brother. The ones who hid behind charming smiles but were really the worst monsters of their kind. I hunted them, I stopped them and I never let emotion get in the way. You can't, not with this job. If the cases get to you, they will wreck you. They can't become personal. You can't let them. If you do, you'll find yourself with a fast trip to see the Bureau shrink."

Jonah swallowed. "You don't think I can handle the pressure of the job?"

"You shot a man tonight, and your hands are dead steady."

Jonah lifted his hands. They weren't shaking.

"That tells me that two things could be happening. One, you've got fucking ice in your veins. You've locked down your emotions and you *won't* let the job get to you because nothing gets to you."

"Is that a bad thing?" An agent should be clear-headed. An agent *should* get the job done. "I saw Agent Murphy—Bowen killed a man, and the guy is carrying on like it's business as usual."

"No, he's not."

"Could have fooled me," Jonah muttered.

"He has," Tucker assured him flatly. "I know Bowen. I've been in the field with him again and again. He shuts down when he has to make the bad choices but Bowen deals with the aftermath. He knows the aftermath is brutal and ugly and that the guilt and second-guessing don't stop. He shoulders that burden, and he only lets those close to him even see that he's carrying it."

His inner circle. Right. Jonah knew that was a circle that he wasn't a part of, not yet. "Let me get this straight, you're riding my ass right now because my hands aren't shaking? But it's totally cool with you that Bowen fired and never hesitated?" Such bullshit.

A faint half smile curved Tucker's lips. Jonah didn't like that smile. To be honest, he didn't much like Tucker, either. *He fought to keep me off this team.* "Maybe I'm not being fair. Could be that I don't know you well enough yet. Maybe you *are* like Bowen. You lock down tight and only let the ones closest to you see your pain."

Bowen felt pain? That was news to him.

"It's so important in this job...to be able to fucking *empathize*. With the victims. With the families. You have to be able to understand pain."

The guy thought he didn't know about pain? *Bullshit.*

"But perhaps there is another option at play with you. Maybe the crash just hasn't hit you yet. It hasn't fully settled into your head that you were seconds away from dying tonight. You fired wildly when he came at you, and that's why you only clipped him in the shoulder. If Peter Carter hadn't been desperate and frantic with fear, the scene could have gone down different, and that truth hasn't really struck you yet. You don't realize that death was breathing down your neck, but it was. And if Macey Night hadn't fired her shot to take *down* Carter—that's *down* and not *out*, because Macey, she's the kind that always tries to save people, even when they don't deserve it—if she hadn't fired, you would have just stood there and watched Carter blow his own brains out."

Jonah flinched. "You don't know..."

"Isn't that what you did before?" Tucker pushed.

It was just the two of them in that office, and the tension that he'd always felt when Tucker was around, it was boiling to the surface.

"Because I know the stories about *you*, too," Tucker said quietly as his watchful gaze swept over Jonah. "I know that your father used a gun on your brother and your sister. I know that he turned that gun on your mother."

Jonah's hands clenched into fists.

"And then I know that you were in the room the whole time. You watched while he finally turned that gun on himself."

The sound of Jonah's pounding heartbeat filled his own ears.

"The only one to survive," Tucker murmured. "That was you, right? You made it out, but the rest of your family didn't. You stood there, and they all died."

"I was…*eleven*. What did you want me to do?" His voice was too rough. Too ragged. He needed to fix that. He needed to control that. *Control*.

"You're not eleven anymore. Yet you just watched a man nearly kill himself, the same way your father did, and you have no reaction?" Tucker's hard gaze swept over him. "That shit worries me. That shit is the reason I'm—how did you put it?—'riding your ass' right now. Because your reaction isn't adding up for me."

"You don't need to worry about me." Jonah forced his hands to unclench, but he couldn't stop his heart from racing. "You've doubted me the entire time." Maybe the gloves needed to come off. No more lying. *Clear the damn air.*

Again, Tucker didn't deny the accusation. He wasn't the type to deny. Or to lie. But he was sure as fuck apparently the type to judge.

"I'm not some ex-SEAL like you are," Jonah snarled. "I haven't spent my life running into battle." *Or killing.* "I lost my whole family on the worst night of my life. And I wondered why. Why did it happen?

Why did everything go so horribly wrong? Why did I lose them and why—why the fucking hell—was I left standing? I asked myself that every day. I asked myself that every single time I went to see a shrink. Because when I was a kid, being bumped from foster home to foster home because everyone thought I must be tainted, they made me see a shrink. Made me talk about that night over and over until it was burning in my head."

Tucker just watched him.

"I don't judge you because of what your brother did. How the fuck *dare* you stand there and judge me?"

But Tucker shook his head. "Not judging you. Never said you were guilty of anything. But I did say you're acting as if nothing happened. And that's not good. I need to know that my agents are sound—that their pasts won't wreck them on a case."

"I'm not wrecked," he gritted out. "I'm doing my job, and you need to stop pushing me." Was the guy just testing him? Jonah thought Tucker was, and he was going to pass this test, just like he'd passed all of the others thrown into his path over the years. "I deserve to be here."

Tucker moved to stand right in front of him. "You were closer to the perp than Macey. I saw the crime scene. You *should* have shot first. You hesitated. You can't do that again. Not when another agent's life is on the line."

Jonah swallowed. "You have to get past this grudge you have against me."

"You've spent the last five years behind a computer. You haven't gotten enough fieldwork experience. I might sound like a grade-A bastard, but it's because I'm putting the team first. You have to be able to count on the man or woman at your side. Hesitations cost lives. Simple fact."

Jonah's spine was so stiff and straight that it hurt. "I can contribute to this team. Macey knows that—Macey trusts me."

"I get that Macey went to bat for you, but I also know why. You were helping her track Haddox, weren't you?"

He had to tread carefully. "I was helping her look for patterns. Patterns are the key, you see. You might not even know that a killer was hunting, not until you looked at the patterns in an area."

Tucker blinked and then his whole expression seemed to lock down. "That's how you find where serials are hunting."

"Yes!" Maybe the guy did get it. "You don't even need all the boots on the ground." That was old-school thinking. "We can analyze from missing persons' reports. NamUS. We can look at the times of the year when the disappearances occur. I've even made a program that can predict victim-type based on previous disappearances and—"

"Have you used this program of yours on any serials out there now?" Tucker's voice was too flat. His face was blank, and no emotion showed in his eyes.

And he was talking about me not responding the right way.

"Just practice runs, nothing substantial, not yet."
But he planned to take his program to Samantha
Dark as soon as this case was tied up. Now that he
was on the team, Jonah knew it was time to take
things to the next level—

"Because I can't help but notice, we have a perp
here who has been hunting serials. He took out Daniel Haddox. He took out Patrick Remus. He found
Curtis Zale. He used profiling tricks and he predicted
where they would be. Sounds a whole fucking lot
like the program you're discussing." His head tilted.
"We already thought the guy had a background in
law enforcement."

"Wait! Wait!" Jonah laughed and the sound was
raw to his own ears. "You aren't serious." Anger
began to stir in him when Tucker just stared back
at him. "You think I'm involved in this? That I'm a
killer?" He'd gone from not having the right reaction after a shooting to being a *killer*? Was that jerk
for real?

"I think I'm not exactly sure when you arrived in
Gatlinburg. We came separately, and all I know is
that you got to the cabin that had been booked for
us sometime before dawn."

"I was in the area," he snapped. "I drove over myself because I'd just finished some vacation time. I
was in Asheville—"

"That's damn close. So close that you could have
gone to Daniel Haddox's home on a quick trip from
Asheville. So close that you could have come here
and taken Patrick Remus. So close—"

Jonah surged toward him, standing toe to toe. "This is bullshit. I'm a fucking FBI agent! I'm on your team, and you're going to throw this crap at me?" He shook his head in disgust. "I wanted to prove myself to you. Wanted to show you that I could do the job, and now you're suspecting me...because what? Because I have a shitty past and you think I might fit your profile? I was in Asheville because that's where my family's home is—not my real family, because as you pointed out, they're all dead. But the last foster family I wound up with? I stayed with them...my foster mother is still in Asheville and I try to visit her every now and then."

"So that would make you very familiar with this area."

Yes, he was familiar with it. So what? "I created my program because I wanted to stop predators. I wanted to hunt the killers, not be one of them." He shouldered around the other agent. "Now, I'm going back to the police station with the cops out there. I'll be finding material on the computers that connects us to the real killer." In the doorway, he stopped, and his hands flew up to grab the door frame.

"They're shaking now," Tucker said.

Jonah fired a glance over his shoulder. "Because I'm pissed off. I thought you were going to accept me. I thought the whole team would. Isn't that the point of our unit? We've all got ties to killers. I'm freaking FBI. And you dare to suspect one of your own?" He was done. *Done.* He marched away without giving Tucker a chance to respond.

Tucker Frost could go screw himself. Jonah had a job to do. He'd do it. He'd prove exactly who was guilty.

TUCKER WAITED UNTIL Jonah had stormed away. Then he pulled out his phone and called Samantha Dark. He knew it was the middle of the night, but that didn't matter. Samantha would be waiting for his call. After all, she was the one who'd tipped him off about Jonah moments before he'd walked into that office. If it hadn't been for her call, he never would have pursued his line of questioning with the other agent.

She answered on the second ring. "Well?"

"You're sure the leaks in the office go back to him?"

"I've got five techs working on this." Her voice was weary but firm. "He's been slipping into personnel files here. He wanted to know more about our team. That raises every red flag I've got."

Especially since their perp knew so much about Bowen's life.

"Jonah said he made a program to track serials," Tucker told her. "But he told me that he'd only used it on practice runs." He wanted to be fucking wrong. He wanted Samantha to be wrong. *What practice runs? Who was his guinea pig? Was it Daniel Haddox? Patrick Remus?* Why hadn't Jonah told him?

There was a moment of silence on the line, and then Samantha announced, "We need to notify

Macey and Bowen about the discovery of the personnel leaks at the FBI. And I'm getting on the jet and coming to Gatlinburg tonight." Tension crackled in every word. "I want you to stay close to Jonah, understand? We could be wrong, but it's not adding up."

"No, it isn't."

"Maybe he's not involved in the crimes," Samantha said. "I still need to know why he thinks he can sneak into confidential records for other agents. He has *no* business doing that."

No, he didn't. And that was a huge problem. "Jonah just left to get a ride with the cops downstairs. Said he was heading back to the police station."

"Stay with him, Tucker. Every step of the way, got it?"

"Got it." He hung up and hurried downstairs. He threw open the door. The crowd had dispersed— people were finally going home for the night. *About time. It's nearing midnight.* He saw the two officers he'd passed earlier, and they were still loading the confiscated computer equipment into their van. He jogged toward them. "Where's Agent Loxley?"

They turned and frowned at him.

"The agent who told you to pack up all of this equipment," he clarified because there had been a ton of local agents running around earlier. "Where is he?"

"Don't know," one of the officers replied. "Haven't seen him."

No, that didn't make any sense. Jonah had just

gone that way. Tucker yanked out his phone. He dialed Jonah. It rang once, twice—

I hear the phone. He turned away from the cops. Went to the side of the building, and right there, with its screen cracked, lay Jonah's phone. It was still ringing, but Jonah was nowhere to be found.

Just the broken phone.

Tucker's heart lurched in his chest.

We have a big fucking problem.

CHAPTER FIFTEEN

"THE VICTIM IS a woman," Dr. Sofia Lopez said as she pointed toward the skull with a gloved hand. She bit her lower lip. "But, um, you both already know that, right?"

Right.

"Men tend to have heavier skulls," Dr. Lopez added. "Thicker ones. They're also generally bigger than female skulls." Her gloved finger moved toward the eye socket. "And you can see the sex here, too. Women have an, um, the ridge here is sharper than for a man."

"Any idea how old she was?" Bowen asked. He was right beside Macey, and his arm brushed against her.

"Oh, yeah, that was something else easy to see. It's all in the teeth, you know." Dr. Lopez flashed them a vague smile. "All of the teeth have erupted. Usually teeth finish erupting by around a person's twenty-first birthday. This skull—I mean, this victim—she had a lot of dental work. She even still has her bar in place." She indicated the bar that was attached just behind the bottom teeth.

Macey stared at the skull. The nails had been removed, and now gaping holes were left in the skull. It wasn't white and gleaming, but brown. Almost stained? "Did he paint the skull?"

"Yeah, I think so, I chipped off some samples and I sent them in for testing," the ME replied. Her face turned considering. "I think he did it to give the appearance of it being an old skull."

"How did she die?" Bowen asked.

Dr. Lopez lifted the skull. "See this hole here?" She tapped it with her finger. "This didn't come from a nail. Her skull was cracked."

"Blow to the head," Macey concluded.

The ME nodded. "That would have done it. That would have killed our vic."

Macey glanced at Bowen. "Peter kept saying it was an accident."

"What? You think the vic fell and hit her head?" His lips twisted. "Don't buy it. He *kept* the skull. He was covering up his crime. He killed her."

"And he might have killed more, right?" the doctor blurted.

Macey and Bowen both glanced back at her.

She swallowed. "I, um, I went ahead and got to work on Captain Henry Harwell. And I noticed something really interesting. Something you've got to see." She put the skull back down on the exam table and hurried toward the line of storage lockers.

They weren't in McKinley's lab, but instead were in another space just down the hallway. When Macey had walked in, she'd seen the uniformed police of-

ficer standing in the hallway. He'd demanded to review their ID before allowing them inside.

Dr. Lopez opened the locker and pulled out the
slab. She unzipped the body bag, and Macey saw
Henry Harwell's still face.

"I had him transferred in," Dr. Lopez said. "Now
look at this." She turned his head sideways and
Macey realized that the ME had shaved the hair
around his wound.

"It's exactly the same size," Dr. Lopez said. "His
wound matches the wound in the skull you gave
me! Both are the exact same diameter. Both caused
the exact same kind of damage, and I believe," she
added, eyes gleaming, "they were made with the
exact same type of weapon."

"A hammer," Macey said.

The doctor nodded. "Damn straight." She rolled
back her shoulders. "So maybe you do have your
killer. Your Peter Carter killed this mystery woman
and Captain Harwell. He could have killed them all!"
Dr. Lopez added, as her voice hitched. "Maybe Harwell was his intended target all along, but he killed
the others to throw you off his scent. He wanted
you to think the murders were for another reason,
when all along he was just working his way up to
Harwell—"

"No." Macey's quiet voice cut through the other
woman's tumble of words.

The ME blinked.

Macey eased out a slow breath. "I know you followed Haddox's crimes, Dr. Lopez."

"I studied them extensively," she said, her eyelids flickering. "I knew about Haddox, and I've studied other big serials, too. There's so much to learn from them—"

"You don't hunt down some of the most infamous serial killers in the US because you want their deaths to be cover for you." No, there was much more at play. Macey shared a quick look with Bowen.

He cleared his throat. "These serial killers were hidden, well hidden. They were predators at their core. It would have been very hard to catch them unaware, and Peter Carter…to go and kill them just so that he could work his way up to Henry Harwell? That would have created unnecessary risk for him."

The ME's gaze dropped to Harwell's body.

And Macey's phone rang. The shrill cry caused Dr. Lopez to jump.

"Excuse me," Macey murmured. She backed away as she saw that Tucker's number appeared on the screen of her phone. She exited the lab space and nodded toward the uniformed officer who still stood guard. Macey put the phone to her ear. "Tucker? Is there news?"

"Jonah Loxley is missing."

Those were the last words she'd expected. "What?"

"There are some things…shit, there's some stuff you need to know, okay? Listen, where are you and Bowen right now?"

"We're at the ME's building with Dr. Lopez."

"Get to the police station. I'm on my way there now."

"Tucker, what happened?"

"Jonah walked out of the museum and vanished. All I found was his busted cell phone."

Her heart lurched in her chest. "You think he was taken by our perp?"

She heard voices in the background.

"I've got an APB out for him now," Tucker said. "I'll tell you more at the station, okay? Meet me there in twenty minutes."

He hung up.

She heard the lab door open. Her gaze swung to find Bowen standing in the doorway. She could see the concern in his gaze. "I—I need to talk with you." Dr. Lopez was peeking over his shoulder. Macey cleared her throat. "Dr. Lopez, please update us right away when you learn new information." But the ME couldn't possibly stay there all night. "Did you get your room in town settled?"

"I did. I'm heading there now." Wearily, the doctor rubbed at the back of her neck. "I just need to crash for a while, and then I'll be back at it. Count on me calling you the minute I have news." She eased around Bowen, then nodded to both him and Macey. "Thank you for bringing me onto this case. Thank you for trusting me with the job."

Macey's hand flew out and touched the other woman's shoulder. "No, thank you for helping us. I know that you and Dr. McKinley are friends—"

"He's been a mentor to me," the ME replied, and for a moment, tears gleamed in her eyes. "He's…he's going to be okay, right?"

"Yes." She was certain of this. He would recover. "He spoke highly of you, Dr. Lopez. He said he trusted you to get this job done."

Her shoulders straightened. "I *will* get it done."

A few moments later, the cop escorted Dr. Lopez out of the lab and toward the waiting elevator. Macey and Bowen were left in the hallway. She walked over the tiled floor, her gaze drawn helplessly to the spot that had been marked by McKinley's blood. Someone had done a very good job of cleaning the scene.

As soon as the elevator doors closed and Dr. Lopez was gone with her cop, Macey turned toward Bowen. "Jonah Loxley is missing."

He shook his head, even as surprise had his eyes flaring.

"That was Tucker on the phone. He said Jonah left the museum and vanished. The only thing he found at the scene was Jonah's cell phone."

"Fuck."

"Tucker wants us at the police station, right now."

"He thinks the perp took Jonah?"

"He didn't say, but what else could he think? This killer went after a cop, he went after the ME and now he's taken an FBI agent." He'd been taunting Bowen all along, and she'd feared he'd be the one attacked by the killer. Her hands were clammy. "He took one of our own." The fact that Jonah was missing—that proved that Peter Carter couldn't be the perp they were after. Had he killed his girlfriend? Yes, she believed he had.

But the man they were after...

He was still hunting.

He wasn't in some hospital bed, under police guard.

He was somewhere in Gatlinburg, and he had new prey.

MACEY FELT AS if she were running on empty. She and Bowen rushed into the police station, and they found Tucker waiting on them. He gave a jerking motion of his hand and they filed into the conference room. As soon as the door closed behind them...

"Samantha Dark is on her way to Gatlinburg," he announced flatly. "She's going to be joining us for this investigation, but she's actually been working on the case all along." His gaze swept between them. "Samantha found...glitches, I guess you could say, in the FBI's personnel files."

"Glitches?" Bowen repeated as his brows shot up. "What kind of glitches?"

Tucker crossed his arms over his chest. "It was your file that was the red flag. Someone accessed it illegally. Dug into the reports on your talks with the FBI shrink, revealed the case history you had with Arnold Shaw—"

"In other words, someone ripped into my life."

Bowen inclined his head. "Not just someone... The hack has been traced back to Jonah Loxley."

Macey took a quick step back, shocked to her core. "What?" But then, before he could respond, Macey shook her head in denial. "There's a mistake here. He wouldn't do that—"

"No mistake. She thought he might be the patsy for someone else—that was her first suspicion, so Samantha pulled in a whole team of cyber analysts. They traced the hacks back to Jonah Loxley's home. And these hacks? They've been going on for months. Ever since Samantha created her team."

She could hear a dull ringing in her ears. *But I trusted him. He was my friend.*

She'd trusted him, the same way she'd trusted Daniel Haddox.

"Jonah hacked into the files of everyone on Samantha's team," Tucker said grimly. "And by the guy's own confession to me, he's been developing a program that will help him to track and identify serial killers, to find them when they're hiding."

Bowen swore. "Hiding…just like the Doctor. Like the Pyro."

"They could have been test runs," Tucker said.

Macey could only stare at them both, in shock. "You're not serious." Hacking into computer files at the Bureau was one thing, but what they seemed to be suggesting… "This is bullshit! He's one of us! He's missing now—"

"He's missing." Tucker nodded. "He went missing *right* after I threw my suspicions at him. Less than five minutes later, the guy went AWOL. That timing, it's a little too convenient for me."

It might be convenient, but that didn't mean Jonah was a killer. "He is one of us," she snapped. "I've been friends with him for a long time. He busted his ass to get on this team. He wanted to prove—" But she broke off because she realized her words weren't going to help Jonah.

They'd only be another nail in his coffin.

But Bowen knew exactly what she'd planned to say. "He wanted to prove that he was a good profiler, right? That he could find the killers better than the rest of us. Us being the ones who'd originally been picked for Samantha's team."

Macey swallowed. "We need to find him. That's our priority. We find him. We make sure he's safe, then we can get answers to our questions."

"You were the closest one to him, Macey." Tucker began to pace. "You didn't see any red flags? Anything that might make you think—"

"Think what?" she snapped back. "That he's some kind of killer? No, no, I didn't think that. I've never thought that." She still couldn't. They were just talking about suspicions, not facts. *Not yet.* "He wants to help people, same as we do."

"He hacked into our files, Macey. He did that. The evidence is conclusive."

"And we can question him about that, *after* we find him." She shook her head. "Look, let's focus here. We need security footage. I saw cameras all around the oddities museum. Let's tap into them and see what happened."

"Already working on that," Tucker assured her. "But Jonah's phone was found on the side of the building. The sides and the back—there are no cameras there."

Her nails were biting into her palms.

A knock sounded at the door. "Come in," Tucker called.

Officer Tanner O'Neil—with dark circles beneath his eyes and stubble grazing his cheeks—appeared in the doorway. "I—I heard about the skull you found today." His Adam's apple bobbed. "I think I may know who your mystery woman is."

They all surged toward him.

He licked his lips. "I saw Henry with her once. The guy acted like he was wild for her, but said she wanted to keep things secret."

"What's her name?" Bowen demanded.

"Susannah. Susannah Kaiser. She looked like she was in her early twenties. Blond hair. Pretty smile." He swallowed. "She left town...or, I thought she did...back before summer started. Henry didn't talk about her after that. Said she hadn't chosen him and that was all there was to it."

Maybe she had, though. Maybe she'd chosen him and Peter Carter hadn't been able to live with that choice.

"We need every bit of intel we can get on Susannah," Bowen said. His body was tight with tension. "Her family, her friends. Anyone who was close to her—we need to know who those people are."

Tanner nodded. "I can get that for you." But he hesitated. "I heard the cops talking... Was Henry killed because of her? Did that guy at the museum kill him?"

"We need to talk with Susannah's family," Bowen

said again. "The more information we learn about her, the more we'll understand her killer."

Tanner nodded and hurried away.

"We need to take a step back here," Macey said, striving to keep her voice flat. "Look, I get that the hacks at the FBI look bad—they *are* bad. But we can't overlook the possibility that the perp we're after here has taken Jonah. I mean, doesn't Jonah fit this guy's MO perfectly? What if he knows Jonah broke the rules at the FBI? You said Jonah disappeared *after* you confronted him, right?"

Tucker nodded.

"Maybe our perp thinks Jonah did something wrong. He loves guilt so much." She rocked forward onto the balls of her feet. "Are we sure there wasn't any surveillance equipment at the museum? If this guy was after Peter Carter, if he knew what Peter Carter had done, then it only stands to reason that he was watching him, too."

Bowen moved closer. "If he was watching Carter, then the surveillance equipment could still have been operating. He could have heard your accusations against Jonah. Maybe he thought the guy was guilty—or hell, maybe he just thought Jonah would make for a good fall guy."

"Crime scene techs are still searching the museum," Tucker said. "If they find anything…"

Then they'd know the killer had been watching.

"The techs swept Henry's office," Tucker added. "They didn't find anything. And we don't have any report of equipment being found at Haddox's place, either. Could be that the guy removed the devices after his kills."

Because the guy was very good at covering his ass. "He isn't just going to let Jonah go. If our perp took him, it's just another game," Macey said. "He *will* kill him."

HE WAS SURROUNDED by darkness. And his head fucking *hurt*.

Jonah twisted his body. His hands were bound behind his back. He was trapped, fucking tied up like an animal. His knees rapped into metal and he felt the rope bite into his ankles.

He was…moving. He could feel it. A steady roll beneath him and the crunch of gravel?

I'm in the trunk. In the fucking trunk.

He'd been at the museum, pissed and scared because he'd realized his hacks had been found at the FBI. That was the only explanation for Tucker being in his face all of a sudden. Samantha Dark must have found out what he'd done, and she'd sent her bulldog agent to interrogate him. Everything he'd wanted had been exploding in his face. Then—

Then I don't remember. But my head fucking hurts.

The car stopped moving. He heard a door slam. Were those footsteps, walking on the gravel? He tensed and then he heard the groan of the trunk as it opened.

Light didn't pour in. It was too dark outside for

light but he strained anyway, trying to see the face of the bastard who'd taken him.

"I admired your work, Agent Loxley."

He blinked, surprise shoving through him.

"It's such a pity…that I'm going to have to kill you now."

DAWN HAD FINALLY COME. They'd searched for hours, they'd scoured security footage from every business near the museum, but they hadn't found Jonah.

He'd vanished.

Macey stretched slowly as she stood in the conference room at the police station. She'd pulled an all-nighter and she wanted to crash but…how could she just go and sleep when Jonah was out there? With every hour that had passed, the tension and the fear she'd felt had deepened.

They all knew the drill in their business. The more time that passed, the greater the likelihood that they *wouldn't* find their victim. Not alive.

"You need to rest." Bowen's voice. He'd just entered the room behind her. She turned at his approach, her eyes sweeping over him. He looked tired, too, the faint lines around his mouth deeper, his gaze weary. He'd been out with the search teams, running through the town.

But they were in the Smokies…too much ground to cover. Too many places for a person to vanish.

"The perp stopped calling you," she said.

Bowen's lips thinned. "Yeah, no more fucking taunts."

"But why? Why stop? He was pulling you in constantly, and now you've got nothing but radio silence."

He moved toward their board—their victims were on that tactical board. Daniel Haddox. God, it was still hard for her to think of him as a victim. When she saw his face, she just remembered what a cold, sadistic bastard he'd been.

"I wanted him dead," Macey whispered as she stared at Daniel. "I wanted that for so long." And she'd gotten what she wanted. Time for her confession. "I went to Jonah. I knew he was working on a program to predict the behavior and identify the location of serials. I wanted Daniel Haddox to be his test dummy. I gave him every bit of information I had on Daniel. Everything I knew…" She turned to look at Bowen. "And he turned up nothing."

Bowen's face was hard. "Macey…"

"He turned up nothing because Daniel had vanished so completely. I even began to wonder if he was dead. There weren't any victims who fit his profiles. I mean, I know that Daniel liked to hide the bodies, so Jonah and I were focused on the missing. On people who'd had recent surgeries or any genetic abnormalities—the things that used to make prey stick out for Daniel. But we weren't turning up any hits. We couldn't find missing individuals to fit our profile. We knew Daniel wouldn't have turned away from medicine. He had to be practicing off the grid, so we figured he'd gone to a rural area or maybe… maybe he'd fled the country." That had been her suspicion. "If he'd gone to Mexico and set up shop, we weren't ever going to find him and we wouldn't be able to find his victims, either."

"But he hadn't gone to Mexico."

"No." Her lips pressed together, and then she said, "And Jonah's program—it didn't predict where he was. We only found Daniel because Dr. Lopez recognized the wounds on Gale's body. Dr. Lopez is the one who notified the FBI. She put the wheels into motion for us." She reached out and curled her hand around his arm. "Do you see what I'm saying? The whole program that makes Jonah a suspect...*it doesn't work*. That's why he didn't go to Samantha with it sooner. He wasn't able to find the serials."

But a serial had found him.

"The hacking, Mace," Bowen murmured, his voice gruff. "It went back to his personal computer. Not his work computer, but the laptop he kept at home. The guy was prying into all of our files."

"That doesn't make him a killer. We need to look at him as a victim."

"Right now, I think we're looking at him as both."

But they weren't finding him. "He's in these mountains, somewhere," she added. "And we know the perp we're after doesn't keep his prey alive for long."

Bowen shook his head. "No, he doesn't."

"He was calling you," Macey said again. "Each time. But something changed. Something made him stop. *What? What was it?*"

He glanced down at his watch. "Peter Carter

should be awake now. The guy hasn't asked for any lawyer yet—"

Mostly because he'd been unconscious and in surgery.

"—so this is our chance. We can go to that hospital and grill the bastard."

Right. She nodded abruptly. Her hand slid away from his arm, but *his* hand flew up, and his fingers curled under her chin.

"This is going to get even worse before it gets better."

They both knew that.

"I will have your back. I will stand with you no matter what comes our way. You can always count on me."

Her chest seemed to burn. "And you can count on me." Didn't he see that? With them, the trust cut both ways. She trusted him more than she'd ever trusted anyone.

She turned for the door and she'd only taken a few steps when her gaze met the golden stare of Samantha Dark. Macey stopped short.

"Agents," Samantha said, but her voice was weary. "We need to talk." She shut the conference room door behind her. "Clear the air a bit."

"Jonah—" Macey began.

Samantha held up one hand. "There is no doubt that he accessed confidential FBI files. And that he's been accessing them for some time." Samantha's eyes were lined with dark shadows. "I spent two hours at his home last night. He'd been keeping journals on all of the agents in my unit. He was profiling you all."

Shock pushed through Macey.

"I don't think he took well to not making the original cut for the team," Samantha continued with a tired shake of her head. "So it seemed he wanted to find out just why you all were deemed to be better agents than he was." She rubbed a hand over the back of her neck. "I *hate* to say this—God, I hate it—but everything I turn up on Jonah seems to indicate that *he* fits the profile for the perp that we're after in Gatlinburg. Even the way this killer has been *competing* with the FBI, the way he's so zealously hunted down serials…it's like he was trying to show us he was better."

"That he should have made the fucking team," Bowen said grimly.

Samantha inclined her head. "Yes. Damn it, yes." She began to pace. "I have a crack team of computer analysts going through his files now, and that infamous program of his? Turns out he was trying to use it to locate Patrick Remus."

Bowen rolled back his shoulders. "We need to talk with Patrick's girlfriend again. Find out just what Patrick may have been doing for the last two years. No way he quit cold turkey."

"Lydia Chasing didn't know who he was!" Macey fired back. "She's not going to have any clue about what he did."

Samantha seemed to consider this. "Let me take a run at her."

Macey's head tilted toward her and her eyes widened in surprise.

"I've got a bit of experience," Samantha continued as her lips twisted into a humorless smile, "with being too close to a lover who turned out to be a killer. I can understand exactly what she's going through."

Because Samantha's ex-lover had turned out to be one of the worst killers out there.

"As for you two... I hear that Peter Carter is out of surgery and that he's conscious—for the moment." She looked pointedly at them. "Find out what you can from him. Push hard on the dead vic, I think her name is—"

"Susannah Kaiser," Bowen supplied. "We already tried to dig, but it seems her family is gone. Her mom passed away when Susannah was a teen. Her dad died a few months back. She has a brother, but the guy cut out when he was seventeen. No one seems to know where he is."

"Then he doesn't even know his sister is dead." Sadness flashed in Samantha's eyes. "I'll make sure the FBI is using all resources to locate him." Then her gaze dipped between Macey and Bowen. "Is there anything else I need to be aware of regarding this case?"

"When do I officially get my gun back?" Bowen demanded.

"Consider yourself cleared," Samantha told him. "The shooting was justified, we're in the middle of a clusterfuck, and I want *you* in the field. If there is any pushback from brass, I'll handle them." Her eyes gleamed. "I'm pretty good at getting Executive Assistant Director Bass to see things my way these days."

Bowen's head inclined toward her. "Thank you."

"Before you two go, don't you think you need to update me on your...personal situation?"

Macey tensed.

"There's nothing you—" Bowen began.

"We're lovers," Macey said as she stepped forward. "I'm the one who went to Bowen. I'm the one who pushed for the relationship."

But it wasn't a relationship, not really. It had just started...

As a way to stop the pain.

Only, being with Bowen had become so much more. *A lifeline.*

At Macey's blurted words, Samantha merely raised one perfectly arched brow.

"Did you know?" Macey asked, taken aback.

"Let's just say that I knew this could be coming." Her gaze slid to Bowen, then back to Macey. "FBI brass won't approve of you two continuing to be partners in the field, so we'll be dealing with that firestorm *after* we close this case."

"Do you truly think Jonah is the killer?" Macey didn't want to be wrong about a friend again. No, damn it, not again.

"I think that's a possibility that can't be ignored. He's either involved or he's a victim. Either way, he's one of us, and we will be bringing him in."

A SHORT TIME LATER, Samantha Dark paused just outside the interrogation room. She squared her shoulders. She tucked her hair behind her ears. She eased out a slow breath.

Lydia Chasing was in that room. Samantha had gotten an officer to bring the other woman back to the station. Lydia was grieving, hurting for the lover who'd been brutally taken from her.

She was also a woman trying to come to grips with the fact that she'd never known that lover at all, not really. *I understand. Believe me, I do.* Samantha reached for the doorknob, and then she walked briskly inside, her high heels clicking on the floor.

At her approach, Lydia glanced up. She wore no makeup. Her nose was red, her eyes were bloodshot and her lips were trembling. "Who are you?" Lydia's voice was weak and rasping, probably because she'd broken it with too much crying.

"My name is Samantha Dark, and I'm with the FBI."

Lydia's gaze fell. "Patrick wasn't a killer." Her scratchy voice was almost painful to hear. "He…he was a good man. He loved me." And her hand fell to her stomach.

Oh, sweet hell. That one gesture pierced right through Samantha. The way the woman cradled her stomach. "Are you pregnant?" Slowly, Samantha sat down in the chair across from Lydia.

A tear leaked down Lydia's cheek. "The other agents…they had my blood checked. They said they thought I might have been drugged while Patrick was taken. They don't have the results yet on the drugs. I—I hope I'm okay."

"Did you tell the nurse who took the blood sample about the baby?" Because she was convinced now.

Lydia shook her head. "Patrick...he wasn't a monster."

Samantha's gut was in knots. "As a precaution, I'm going to call the local hospital. I want you to go in and have a full evaluation, okay?" She started to rise.

Lydia's hand flew out and curled around her wrist. "He wasn't a monster."

She knew that Lydia desperately wanted her to agree, but Samantha couldn't speak because she'd seen the victims left in Patrick's brutal wake. A lie wouldn't come to her lips.

"He didn't start all those fires." But now doubt had crept into Lydia's words.

Samantha swallowed. "How long were you with Patrick?"

"Over a year," she whispered in her broken voice. "And I would have known. I would have known if..." But she didn't finish that sentence.

It didn't matter. Samantha knew what the woman had been about to say. *I would have known if he was a killer.* "*I* didn't know."

Lydia trembled.

"I didn't know that the man I'd given my trust to, the man I'd shared my bed with...I didn't know he was a murderer."

Lydia's trembles grew worse.

"I didn't know until he came for me."

More tears slid down Lydia's cheeks. "Patrick never hurt me."

"Did he hurt anyone else?" She kept her voice as soft as possible. "Think about it, Lydia. Was there ever anyone who may have…" God, how to say this delicately? "Were there any unexplained fires during your time with Patrick?"

Lydia's eyes squeezed closed and a low, keening sound emerged from her.

"I have to ask, I'm sorry. But Patrick Remus had a schedule, of sorts. He took a victim every six months. You said you were with him for over a year. I want you to think about that time. Think about it really hard. Was there ever a suspicious fire in the area where you lived? Ever anything that—"

A sob broke from Lydia.

Samantha wanted to reach out and comfort her. She wanted to pull her close and tell the other woman she wasn't alone—

"My stepmom." Lydia was rocking her body back and forth now, still cradling her belly. "There was a fire at her house. Thought it was just… God! God! She was always so mean to me. Never letting me see my dad, and I told Patrick, I told him…" She nearly choked as she said, "That I wished she was out of the way." Her tears came harder.

"Did she die in the fire?" Samantha asked her.

Lydia nodded. "I didn't mean it…when I told him… I was just mad… I didn't mean it…"

And Samantha knew that Patrick had been up to his old tricks.

She rose.

"Will the baby be like him?" Lydia asked her.

Samantha's heart seemed to freeze in her chest.

"I don't… Will the baby be like him?" she asked again. "Is she gonna be…wrong?"

Samantha went to her then, and she wrapped her arms around Lydia. Samantha held the other woman as Lydia cried.

CHAPTER SIXTEEN

"YOU'RE THE...ONE who shot me..." Peter Carter rasped. He was strapped to the hospital bed, and an armed police officer was at his side. Machines beeped near him and his skin was almost as pale as the sheets.

"Guilty." Macey gave him a cold smile. She stood to the right of his bed and a very watchful Bowen waited at the foot of the bed.

"Don't got...nothin' to say..." Peter began.

"Really?" Bowen drawled. "Because we've got plenty to say. We'd actually like to start by telling you that we know what you did to Susannah Kaiser."

Peter flinched.

"She didn't choose you, did she?" Bowen demanded. His tone dripped with disgust. "You were fucking insane for her, but she was walking away. She wanted the cop, not you."

Peter swallowed. "D-don't have to talk...to you..."

"I don't think you quite understand what's happening here, Peter." Macey kept her voice as cold as her smile had been. "We're not just looking at you for Susannah's death. Right now, there are at least four other murders that we are investigating. Daniel Haddox. Patrick Remus. Curtis Zale. Henry Harwell—"

"Didn't k-kill that cop!" Peter cast a frantic glance at the uniformed officer beside him, an officer that looked *pissed.* "Didn't kill any of them—"

"But you *did* kill Susannah," Macey pushed. "I mean, you confessed that already. Right before I shot you."

He swallowed and eased out a ragged breath. "Ac-accident..."

Keeping her skull at your museum was no accident, you freak. "Why don't you tell me about it?" Macey invited. "Tell us your side of the story before it's too late." *It's already too late. There is no going back from what you've done.*

"Should have let me f-fucking die."

Macey just stared at him.

"I was...working my shop. Just working." His eyes squeezed shut. "Susannah came in there, told me we had to talk." His eyes snapped open. "I knew she'd been screwing Henry. I *knew* but I thought it was over. That she'd come back to me."

"She didn't," Bowen said.

Peter's head moved in a *no* motion against the pillow. "She...said we were done. That she was going with him. That she wanted to...*marry* him." Anger rattled in his voice. "Fuck, fuck, fuck! I don't know what happened! I swear, I just—I was so mad. So fucking mad. The hammer was in my hand, and the next thing I knew...the next thing..."

Macey thought of the skull. "She was walking away from you, and you hit her in the back of the head."

He licked his lips. "I think she was dead...even before she fell to the floor. I grabbed her, I told her I was sorry, over and over, but it was too late. Her blood was everywhere. I— Jesus, she was *gone*." His breath panted out. "An accident. See? That's... what it was."

No, that wasn't an accident. At best, he was describing manslaughter. A crime of passion. *Gone so wrong*. But he hadn't stopped with killing her. "You took her skull." Macey couldn't get past that. Neither would a jury. "You kept it."

His lashes lowered. "I couldn't...let her go. The hate nail exhibit had just opened and I—I switched the skulls. I just wanted her close."

No, she didn't believe that. "You still wanted to punish her. *That's* what the nails were for. Even in death, the hate you felt for her betrayal wasn't easing. You kept the skull and you kept the nails in it because you enjoyed hurting her. Even. In. Death," Macey said again.

The uniformed cop's hand slid toward his weapon.

The machines beeped.

Peter cast her a quick glance from beneath his lashes. "I think I need my lawyer."

She'd wondered just how long it would be before he lawyered up. "Four bodies. Four other crimes are being linked back to you."

"Didn't kill them," he mumbled back. "Only Susannah, only—"

"Where is her body?" Bowen cut in.

Peter's lips parted.

"You kept her head. But what about her body? Where did you put her body?"

Peter's gaze shifted to Bowen. "We had this place in the mountains that we liked. Not too far from Rainbow Falls."

Every muscle in Macey's body locked down at the mention of Rainbow Falls. *Not a coincidence, can't be.*

"There's an old cabin up there," Peter continued. "You just…you divert off the Rainbow Falls Trail and head over to Bullhead Trail."

Macey's gaze met Bowen's. *Oh, hell.*

"Most folks don't ever see that cabin because you have to go off the path in order to find it, but Susannah showed it to me. Said when she was younger, she and her brother would go up there all the time. It was their place… Their parents fought a lot, so they went up there to get away."

Macey knew he was talking about the cabin that Curtis Zale had used with his victims. She *knew* it.

"I buried her there, because she liked the place so much."

"Tell us exactly *where*," Bowen snarled.

"There's a…a yellow birch, about twenty feet from the front of the cabin. I—I put her under its branches. She always said that tree was so beautiful. That it was her favorite."

This is all related. Everything. Susannah. The nails. The cabin. Curtis.

"Would you…um… Can you tell her brother I'm sorry?"

Macey turned to stare at Peter once more. "No one knows where Susannah's brother is. We heard that he'd been gone from her life since he was seventeen."

His eyes widened. "But he was in town, about two months ago. Wesley was looking for her. God, I had to stand right there, with her skull right behind him, and tell the guy that I hadn't seen her. One of the hardest fucking things I've ever done."

Peter Carter was a serious piece of work. "Even harder than *killing* his sister?" Macey snapped, pushed to her limit.

A muscle jerked in Peter's jaw. "You know… Wesley was always so smart."

No, I don't know. Because I haven't found Wesley.

"Susannah bragged about him all the time. Said even when he was a kid, Wesley could do amazing things. That's why she hated so much that he left when he was seventeen. She'd wanted him to be something, wanted him to use his skills to be—" Peter's eyes widened. "It was him!"

"What?"

"Wesley! It was him! He's the one who put all that shit on the computers at the museum! Susannah told me he was a fucking computer genius, but I didn't even think about him. *Shit!* I just saw everything and I panicked and—" He tried to lunge up in the bed, but the restraints wouldn't let him go far.

The uniformed cop tensed. "Easy."

But Peter wasn't being easy. He was thrashing against the restraints. "Son of a bitch! He knew! All along, he knew! And he's fucking trying to frame me!" He twisted his body and Macey saw the blood begin to seep through his paper-thin hospital gown.

"You're reopening your wounds," she said quietly.

"It was him!" He struggled harder. A doctor and nurse rushed into the room. "When I find that prick, I'm gonna *kill* him!"

The nurse injected something into Peter's IV line.

"Just like you killed his sister?" Bowen said.

Peter stilled. "I want my lawyer."

"Yeah." Bowen turned away. "Good luck with that shit. Probably should have asked for him *before* you made a full confession regarding Susannah's death." He headed for the door.

Macey moved to follow him.

"Agent Night!" Peter bellowed her name.

She looked back at him.

"That little prick…you find him! He… Shit, the last time I saw him, he'd dyed his blond hair black. He'd put on about twenty pounds, wasn't so scrawny anymore, not like in those old pictures of Susannah's. The guy even told me that he was in school, at college. Don't remember which fucking one."

No, because he'd been too busy trying to cover up the murder of the man's sister. Once more, Macey turned away—

"Agent Night. Why didn't you kill me?"

Her shoulders stiffened. Bowen had turned to stare at her. He was holding the door and his eyes were on her. "Because I'm an FBI agent," Macey said without looking back at Peter Carter. "And death would have been too easy for you."

He'd murdered a woman. He deserved a lifetime of punishment. She'd make sure he got it.

THEY DROVE HELL-FAST toward the helipad. The SUV slid into the twisting, snaking curves of the mountain roads. Macey was in the passenger seat, her hand gripping the phone at her ear. "Right, yes, Samantha, the guy said Susannah's remains are at the Curtis Zale crime scene. No, no, I have no idea why Dr. Lang didn't find them. I thought she was using her equipment on the entire area there. I tried to reach her on her phone, but didn't connect." There was a brief pause. "She's supposed to be out at the crime scene today. That's where we're headed now. We're going to find Susannah. Absolutely. I'll call you again when I have more news."

Bowen waited a beat. "Any updates on the brother's location?"

"No, not yet. Samantha did confirm that a Wesley Kaiser had enrolled at the University of Tennessee, but that was a year ago. The school is going to fax over his student ID picture. But, apparently, he never showed up for his fall classes."

"Because the poor bastard realized his sister was dead." *And he went looking for some vengeance?*

"Samantha said he had a history of drug and alcohol abuse. I'm sure the fact that his sister vanished wouldn't have sat well with him."

"What about the fact that Dr. Lang didn't find the body that *should* be at the scene?" Bowen demanded as his hands tightened around the steering wheel. *Be-*

cause that shit isn't sitting well with me. He braked the vehicle and they jumped out.

"I don't know," Macey said. "I'm not sure how she missed that."

We're about to find out.

It would take far too long to hike to the cabin, and he'd secured transportation on the chopper. He and Macey slid inside and buckled up, and a few moments later, the pilot was lifting them into the air. They rose fast, and the ground seemed to shrink beneath them. The pilot had been ferrying law enforcement personnel back and forth to that particular crime scene, so he knew exactly where they were headed.

Bowen's gaze slipped from the scene below him and rose to look at Macey's profile. She was staring out the window, seeming to be a million miles away, even though if he just reached out his hand, he could touch her. Her words to Peter Carter kept ringing in his ears.

Death would have been too easy for you.

Macey was right. Sometimes, death was too easy. Far too fucking easy.

The chopper skirted through the mountains. The trees were a bright sheen of colors. Those trees just stretched and stretched as far as the eye could see. A thousand places to hide. A million.

It was—

Macey's hand curled around his.

Surprised, his hold jerked in her grasp. She stared straight at him now. "You." She spoke into her microphone and he heard her perfectly in his headphones. "When this is done, know that I choose you."

His heart lurched in his chest. He wanted to pull her into his arms. To hold her fucking tight, but he couldn't move.

Not then.

Did Macey understand how much her words meant to him? He needed her to know. "You've always been the one I chose." *Always.*

Her lips lifted in a faint smile.

The blades of the chopper carried them away.

AS SOON AS the chopper touched down, Bowen and Macey leaped out. The wind beat at Bowen's back as he took Macey's arm and made sure she was blocked by his body. He hurried forward and saw the small group of law enforcement and crime scene analyst workers still there. Most wore their white uniforms, with gloves on their hands, moving carefully to make sure they didn't contaminate the scene.

The chopper began to rise again, leaving as fast as it had arrived. Bowen and Macey hurried to the back of the cabin.

"Be careful!" Dr. Lang was saying. "Absolutely careful! Those remains are fragile. We have to make sure everyone here understands that you can't remove the bones too quickly." She was leaning over a yawning grave as she talked to the man at her side. The guy was stooped on the ground, and a baseball cap covered his head.

"Dr. Lang," Bowen called.

She glanced back.

"We need to talk."

Her eyes had widened. "I didn't realize you two would be at the scene today." Her gaze skirted to Macey, then back to Bowen. "But, right, of course. Let's talk." She patted the shoulders of the man in the cap. "Carlisle, I'd like to introduce you to the FBI agents I mentioned before."

The man in the cap glanced back. The fellow was younger than Bowen had first suspected. A dark beard covered his face.

"This is my assistant, Carlisle," Dr. Lang said. "Carlisle, this is Agent Bowen Murphy and Agent Macey Night."

Carlisle inclined his head toward them. He didn't offer his hand, probably because the guy was wearing his gloves, and his gaze jumped between Bowen and Macey.

"Thanks for the work you're doing here, Carlisle," Macey said.

His shoulders jerked a bit. "I just… I want to help, you know?" His voice was a low rumble. "They had families. All of them. People who cared about them—people who wanted them back." There was grief there, flickering in his gaze.

Dr. Lang squeezed his shoulder. "You are helping," she assured her assistant. Then she exhaled and straightened her shoulders. "Keep supervising things here for me, would you? I'm going to talk with the agents for a moment."

Carlisle nodded. He turned back toward the grave.

"Why don't you walk this way with us, Dr. Lang?" Bowen invited as he motioned to the side of the cabin.

But as they started to pass around the side of the cabin, they nearly collided with Ranger Zack Douglas. The ranger staggered to a quick stop. "I was just coming to look for you, Dr. Lang." But his gaze darted to Macey and Bowen. "I wanted to see if there was anything I could help with today." Then he squared his shoulders. "The rangers have been helping to secure the scene. Not our normal type of work, but it seemed like an all-hands-on-deck situation, and these mountains? They are *ours*."

But Bowen could see the guilt on the guy's face. He still blamed himself.

"Give us just a moment, Ranger," Macey murmured. "We really need to speak privately with Dr. Lang."

"Oh, right. Sorry." And then he was hurrying back toward the rear of the cabin.

Toward the graves.

Bowen led them about twenty feet away. He stopped when he was beneath the colorful branches of a yellow birch tree. "How many bodies have you found?"

Dr. Lang frowned. "So far…just thirteen. I've been checking the area all around the cabin, spanning out more and more as a precaution—"

"Have you checked here?" Bowen asked her. "And I mean, specifically…right here? Beneath us?"

She blinked and looked down at the ground. "Um, yes. My assistant reviewed this entire area. It's clear."

Macey and Bowen shared a hard look.

Then Macey cleared her throat. "We'd like for you to review it again."

Dr. Lang seemed hesitant but she nodded. "All right. If that's what you want, but it will take a little time."

And it did.

But by the time Dr. Lang had finished using her equipment, they'd found another body. A body that was exactly where Peter Carter had said it would be.

Susannah Kaiser was resting beneath the birch tree.

"How did your assistant miss this?" Bowen demanded.

"I—I don't know…" Amelia was obviously flustered. "I'll find Carlisle. We'll ask. Maybe the equipment malfunctioned…"

But they soon realized they couldn't ask him. Because when they searched the area, Carlisle had vanished.

"IT'S HIM."

Macey stared at the picture of Dr. Lang's assistant Carlisle Adams…and the picture they'd recovered of Wesley Kaiser.

The hair was different…because, as Peter had told them, Wesley had dyed his blond hair.

The face shape was a bit different…because, as Peter had said, Wesley had put on weight.

He'd grown a beard, making his jaw appear stronger. He'd even dyed the beard black, too. He'd used contacts but... *That is him.*

Carlisle *was* Wesley Kaiser.

"We have an all-points bulletin out for him now," Bowen said. He stood to her right, his gaze on Wesley/Carlisle.

"He knew we were going to dig up Susannah." That was why he'd disappeared in the mountains. "He knew, all along, exactly what Peter had done." She shook her head. "The hate nails—that's exactly what they were. With every death, it was about his sister. He was trying to show her to us."

Bowen raked a hand over his face.

"He doesn't fit our profile." That was Tucker speaking. His low voice seemed to hang in the air. He was seated at the conference table, right next to Samantha. "Not exactly. This kid was a mess. Substance abuse, in and out of rehab. The last thing this guy seems to be is organized."

"We thought we were looking for an older, more seasoned killer. A practiced hunter." Now Samantha spoke. "But this fellow...he's young. He's angry."

Macey turned to face them. "He actually *does* fit the profile, in certain ways, at least. He knows the area. Wesley grew up here. He has a desire for vengeance, I think that's obvious. He's highly intelligent."

"I swear," Tucker muttered, "it's like we're looking at a perp with a split personality."

Yes, Macey could see what he meant. Organized at crime scenes, so very careful, but...

Vengeance driven? Shadowed by addiction?

"And the guy is currently AWOL," Bowen added grimly. "And that fact alone tells me that we have big fucking trouble. Jonah is still missing, and now Wesley is in the wind."

Samantha tapped her fingers on the conference table. "Dr. Lang is in interrogation. Macey, I want you to have a run at her."

Macey nodded as she turned for the door. Exhaustion pulled at her, but, determinedly, Macey pushed it back. She had a job to do. She couldn't afford weakness. Not right then.

JONAH TWISTED AGAINST the ropes that bound him. This should *never* have happened to him. He'd been tied up all damn day. He could barely feel his fingers. Were the FBI agents looking for him? Were they still searching?

Shit, shit, shit. This screwed everything to hell. When he vanished, they would have immediately started digging into his life. And that meant...

They went to my house. They'd know that he'd been hacking at the FBI. But they didn't understand... he'd just wanted to see what made the other agents so special. He'd wanted to find out what he was doing wrong in his sessions with the shrink. How could he fix things if he didn't understand the problem first?

It was dark again. The light had vanished from the

window. His stomach growled, reminding him that he'd been without food and water all day.

But the ropes…they were starting to give. He could feel it. He'd worked on them long enough. Hard enough. He'd be able to break away soon.

Soon.

The door to his room opened. His prison. A low, long squeak, and his head lifted. He couldn't see the face of the man before him, there was too much darkness, but he knew he was looking at the bastard who'd ruined everything for him.

"They found my sister today," the guy told him. And he sounded…happy. "Susannah is finally coming home."

"I DIDN'T KNOW!" Dr. Amelia Lang jumped to her feet as soon as Macey stepped into the interrogation room. "I swear, I didn't know he'd…he'd taken someone else's name! He came to me as Carlisle. Carlisle Adams *was* the graduate assistant that had been approved to help me. I never had any reason to suspect otherwise—"

"We can't locate the real Carlisle," Macey told her. "At this point, we fear he may be dead. It's possible that Wesley murdered him so that he could take the other man's identity."

Dr. Lang shook her head. "No, no, no…" Her body seemed to hunch in on itself.

"When did Wesley start working with you?"

Dr. Lang wrapped her arms around her midsection. "About…a month ago? Two? I needed help desperately for a project. He was like a godsend." She rocked onto her toes. "You think he was involved in…all of this mess, don't you? Curtis Zale, the police captain—"

"About that," Macey interrupted smoothly. "You told me before that you saw a man in a police uniform near Agent Murphy's SUV. You told us that you only saw the back of that individual's head."

Dr. Lang quickly nodded. "Yes, yes, he had dark hair and broad shoulders and—" Her eyes became saucers. "It could have been Carlisle—I mean, Wesley. I didn't even realize…" She hurried back to the table and sat down, hard. She appeared shell-shocked. "The…the night that Captain Harwell died, Car—Wesley wasn't at the motel. I went there, and I knocked on his door, but he didn't answer. I just assumed he was sleeping, but now I have to think… *he wasn't there*."

Because he'd been killing Henry Harwell? "Where was he when Daniel Haddox was killed?"

Dr. Lang just blinked at her.

Macey unclenched her back teeth and gave Dr. Lang the specific date of the crime.

"I don't know. We were on a small fall break at the university. I thought he was taking some time to relax, maybe he'd gone hiking in the mountains…" Her words trailed away. "When I got the call to come to Gatlinburg, I texted him. Told him that I needed him." Her voice dropped. "And he was here within the hour."

Because he'd already been there? All along? "You know that FBI Agent Jonah Loxley is missing."

Dr. Lang's hands twisted in her lap.

"Where was Wesley last night? When Jonah went missing, *where was he*?"

Dr. Lang could only shake her head. "I don't know. I was dead tired. I passed out at the motel, and I don't remember anything else."

Not helpful.

"He could have been gone the whole night," Dr. Lang whispered, "and I didn't know." She stared into Macey's eyes and then said once more, as if ashamed, "I didn't know."

I didn't know that I was working side by side with a killer.

Macey nodded and she slipped out of the room. She closed the door behind her, and then stood there for a moment, her shoulders slumping.

"You need rest."

Samantha.

Macey's head whipped up.

"How long has it been since you slept, Agent Night?"

Macey stared at her, honestly not sure. It had been twenty-four hours since Jonah went missing and she had been awake at least—

"I booked you a room at a lodge on the edge of town. A place that I've made sure is completely secure." Samantha waved toward her. "Go there. Get some sleep. Because you are no good when you're dead on your feet."

Bowen slipped into the hallway. He'd been in the room next to the interrogation area, and she knew he'd watched her interview with Dr. Lang through the one-way mirror on the right wall.

"You, too, Bowen," Samantha ordered him. "Go get some rest. Tucker and I will take the night shift. If anything happens, if we get any news, I'll call you both right away."

Since Macey could feel herself bottoming out, she nodded. Walking away from the case wasn't easy, but it was either walk or, if she didn't get some sleep soon…

Fall.

SAMANTHA WATCHED AS Macey and Bowen filed out of the police station. Dr. Amelia Lang was still in the interrogation room, and Samantha knew she would be sending a patrol with the forensic geophysicist when Lang left the station.

"You think Wesley will come after Dr. Lang?" Tucker asked as he drew near to her.

"Not going to take any chances on that." Dr. Lang had worked side by side with the missing man. Would he view her cooperation with the feds as some sort of betrayal? This guy seemed to judge everyone—and everything. *And he finds us all lacking.*

"If this kid is the one we're after—" Tucker exhaled and his voice dropped, carrying only to her ears "—then I was wrong about Jonah."

Her head turned and she met his gaze. "You were always against him joining our unit."

"He avoided the field like the plague. I talked to other agents. They all warned me of the same thing. He wasn't the type to have your back." A muscle jerked in his jaw. "With our group, I couldn't take the chance on having a weak link. We battle some of the most vicious criminals out there. A single hesitation is a death sentence."

Yes, it was.

"But now I'm fucking second-guessing myself. With this news about Wesley Kaiser..." He exhaled. "I could see the kid wanting revenge. But hell, why not just go after Peter Carter directly? Why all of this other stuff? It doesn't *fit*."

"No, it doesn't." She began to tap her right foot. "Your instincts have always been good. You know I respect them, and you."

"So did Jonah run?" Tucker demanded. "Does he know his ass is in the fire and he just vanished? I mean, maybe the perp didn't take him. Maybe that's why Bowen hasn't gotten a call."

"Is that what your instincts say?"

Slowly, he shook his head.

"Mine, too," she told him. Samantha exhaled on a slow sigh. "You know, I think you had a point earlier. When you said it was almost like our killer had a split personality."

His brow furrowed.

"A split personality, or maybe we're just looking at two distinct personalities. Maybe we always were." She hurried toward the conference room. "Make sure that Dr. Lang has an escort tonight—and that the cop *stays* at her motel to keep watch. Then come with me. We need to go over those files again. Every one. Because we've missed something."

Or maybe not something, she realized, but someone.

CHAPTER SEVENTEEN

THEY HAD CONNECTING rooms at the lodge. Bowen's
gaze slid to that connecting door—and he wondered if Macey had already crashed. She'd looked
exhausted, and hell, he understood. They'd been running on fumes for the last few hours. All day, they'd
barely eaten. They'd barely stopped.

They'd hunted.

And the man they'd needed—Wesley Kaiser—had
been right there. Under their noses at the cabin. He'd
just slipped away from them. Vanished.

The guy knew the mountains. He knew the area
too well. They'd searched but hadn't been able to find
him. The Smokies were just full of too many hiding
spaces. The guy's rented car had still been parked in
the lot at the trailhead, and they'd left a guard there
to see if he came out.

But so far, there'd been no news on him.

Bowen had showered, trying to wash the hell of
the day off his skin and now, clad in a pair of loose
sweats, he found himself walking toward the door
that connected his room to Macey's.

His hand lifted to curl around the doorknob. He
unlocked the door.

She said I was her choice.

But he hesitated. He—

The door opened. Macey stood there, her hair wet around her shoulders, wearing a T-shirt with *FBI* written across the chest. The blue shirt ended at the middle of her thighs.

"I kept waiting for you to come to me." She looked at the hand he still had raised. "Guess I should have waited a few more minutes."

No, he never wanted her to wait—

"I want to sleep with you." A faint smile curved her lips, but the smile never reached her eyes. "This time, I'm not here asking you to fuck me. I just want to fall asleep in your arms and know that, for a few moments, I'm safe. Because that's what you are to me, Bowen." Her smile had faded. "You're my safety in a storm."

He reached for her hand and his fingers feathered over her wrist. Without a word, he pulled her into his room and, with his hand still gentle on her, he guided her to his bed. She slipped beneath the covers, and he followed her, stopping only long enough to turn out the light.

When he was in bed, she immediately rolled toward him. She put her head on his chest.

"I like to hear your heartbeat," Macey murmured. "So steady and strong. Just like you." Then she gave a faint sigh. "No matter what you might say to the contrary, I know the truth about you. I've always known it."

His arm curled around her.

"Tomorrow will be better, won't it?" Macey asked him.

"It will be better." He would have given her any promise. Did she still not realize it? He'd make tomorrow better. For her. *Anything*, for her.

He held her as her breathing slowed. As she slipped into slumber. And only then did he close his own eyes.

It will be better.

JONAH RUSHED THROUGH the woods, tilting his head back as he stared up at the stars. He needed those fucking constellations right then. Because he had no clue where the hell he was. He'd escaped, and now he had to plan.

Plan, plan.

Because that little prick was going to come after him again.

I've got to stop him.

But first, first he had to stay alive.

His gaze frantically scanned the stars overhead. When he'd been a kid, his dad had told him all about the constellations.

Look at Orion's Belt, son. See it up there? One of the brightest patterns in the sky. Alnilam, Mintaka and Alnitak. Those are the ones that gleam up there in his belt. Orion, see, he was a great hunter. So powerful. It's important to be powerful, son. Because the weak...the weak will always be prey to everyone else.

Jonah's body shook as he tried to banish his father's voice from his head. He didn't need those memories. Didn't need the shit his father had tried to teach him.

He didn't need *any* of it.

He looked down at his hands, and…for just a moment, he noticed…*there's blood on my hands.*

He staggered back, then realized, the blood… right, *right.* It was just coming from his wrists. He'd struggled against that rope for so long that his wrists had started bleeding. That was why he had blood there.

No other reason.

The weak will always be prey to everyone else.

He surged forward. He wasn't weak. He'd proved that, over and over again. He'd get out of those woods. He'd find Macey. He'd stop the freak with the nails.

I'm. Not. Weak.

THE LIGHT WAS in her eyes, blinding her. Macey couldn't see past that too bright light. She was strapped onto the operating room table, but it wasn't the straps that held her immobile.

He'd drugged her.

"I could stare into your eyes forever." His rumbling voice came from behind the light. "So unusual, but then, you realize just how special you are, right, Dr. Night?"

She couldn't talk. He'd gagged her. They were in the basement of the hospital, in a wing that hadn't been used for years. Or at least, she'd thought it hadn't been used. She'd been wrong. About so many things.

"Red hair is always rare, but to find a redhead with heterochromia...it's like I hit the jackpot."

A tear leaked from her eye.

"Don't worry. I've made sure that you will feel everything that happens to you. I just—well, the drugs were to make sure that you wouldn't fight back. That's all. Not to impair the experience for you. Fighting back just ruins everything. I know what I'm talking about, believe me." He sighed. "I had a few patients early on—they were special like you. Well, not quite like you, but I think you get the idea. They fought and things got messy."

A whimper sounded behind her gag because he'd just taken his scalpel and cut her on the left arm, a long, slow slice from her inner wrist all the way up to her elbow.

"How was that?" he asked her.

It hurt. She was in hell. And she was staring at the devil.

"I'll start slowly, just so you know what's going to happen." He'd moved around the table, going to her right side now. "I keep my slices light at first. I like to see how the patient reacts to the pain stimulus."

She wasn't a patient. Nothing was wrong with her. She just wanted him to stop!

But he'd sliced her again. A mirror image of the wound he'd given to her before, a slice on her right arm that began at her inner wrist and slid all the way up to her elbow.

"Later, the slices will get deeper. I have a gift with the scalpel, haven't you heard?" He laughed. He was laughing at her pain. Laughing at her horror. Laughing at her.

"Every time I work on a patient, I wonder...what is it like without the anesthesia?"

Sick freak.

"But not just any patient works for me. I need the special ones." He moved toward her face and she knew he was going to slice her again. He lifted the scalpel and pressed it to her cheek.

The fingers on her right hand jerked.

"You and I are going to have so much fun, and those beautiful eyes of yours will show me everything that you feel." He paused a moment. *"I'll be taking those eyes before I'm done."*

It was a dream. No, a memory. Macey knew that, but she couldn't make herself wake up.

When he leaned forward once more, Macey realized that something was wrong with Daniel's eyes.

There were nails in them.

"You never see the monster coming... You can't see him, not until it's too late."

She shot up in bed, sucking in a deep breath.

"Macey?" Bowen's arms wrapped around her. His touch was warm. "You okay?"

No, she was so incredibly far from okay. A glance at the clock on the bedside showed she'd been sleeping for three hours.

"Bad dream?" Bowen rasped.

"I was on his table again. But this time, I remembered something he'd said to me." God. "He said he was going to take my eyes."

"Macey…"

"I didn't tell the cops that part." There'd been so much else to tell them. "My eyes… God, when I was a kid, I hated that they were different. That I was so different. I wore contacts when I was a teenager, just like Gale Collins did, because I wanted to fit in with everyone else."

"I think your eyes are beautiful."

Her gaze jerked toward him, but she couldn't see him clearly, not in the dark.

"To be honest, though, I've always thought everything about you was beautiful."

Her heart warmed. "You never said *anything*. You made me come to you—"

"Because I knew you weren't ready, and I would have rather been your friend, your partner, than fucking nothing at all."

She could feel tears stinging her eyes. "Why? Why, Bowen? Why me?"

"Because you're strong and you're smart and when you got dealt one of the worst hands life can give you…Macey, you went out and tried to help other people. You didn't run. You didn't hide. You didn't let the need for vengeance destroy you. You just—you got even stronger. Fuck, but I admired that."

She hadn't felt strong. She'd felt like a ghost, just trying to be alive again.

But Bowen had reminded her of all the things that were waiting in life. There wasn't just pain out there.

Pleasure.

Hope.

Second chances.

Love?

She found her hands rising, curling around his jaw and she put her lips against his. She'd gone to his room not for sex, just for…for his touch. For his comfort. But right then, things were different.

And still…

It's not about sex. We're not just having sex.

She'd told him once that it was just fucking, and now Macey realized what a liar she'd been. It had never been that, had it?

Not for her…

Not for him?

Her tongue slid into his mouth. She kissed him slowly, and she savored him. His hands settled along her hips and he pulled her against him. He was still sitting up, and she straddled his legs. She could feel his cock growing against her as they kissed. The kiss became harder, stronger, and his hands rose up to stroke her breasts.

"Make love to me." She'd whispered those words and she wouldn't take them back. Love, not fucking. Love, not sex.

"Always, Mace," he promised her, the nickname sounded like an endearment rolling from his tongue, and she had to blink away the tears that wanted to fill her eyes. The eyes he'd called beautiful.

His hands caressed her breasts, and her nipples were tight and aching for his touch. He kissed his way down her throat, stopping in those spots that he knew she liked. Down, down…and her breath panted out. Her nails dug into his shoulders as she held on tight.

Her panties were getting wet. His cock—it was rock hard. She arched her hips and slid her sex over him, loving the friction but wanting so much more. Wanting him in her.

Wanting everything.

Wanting *him*.

His right hand trailed down her body. He slid his fingers beneath the hem of her panties and then he was thrusting them inside of her. Macey lifted up onto her knees, sucking in a sharp breath, as his fingers slid in and out of her. Her eyes squeezed shut. "I want *you*. All of you."

His fingers slid out. She bit her bottom lip. Her body was bow tight, already on the edge and they'd just begun. But then…

She heard a rip in the darkness. He'd torn her panties and Macey almost wanted to laugh. But she couldn't. The desire she felt was too intense. The need too raw.

She pushed his sweats out of the way and his cock surged toward her. Her fist closed around him, and Macey stroked his erect length. Once, twice, again and again, she pumped him.

"You're driving me…out of my…mind…"

Good. That was how she wanted him. How she wanted to be.

"Need to get...protection," Bowen growled.

"I'm clean. And there's...no risk of pregnancy." She couldn't believe she was even saying those words. Couldn't believe she was suggesting that they—

"Macey."

"This one time, I want you." She needed this connection. Needed him.

"I'm clean," he told her, his voice nearly guttural. "There is no risk with me."

No, there wasn't.

She eased higher onto her knees. His cock pushed against her, and then Macey arched down, taking him in deep. He filled her completely, and she moaned because he felt so good.

She wanted to savor him. To drive him wild.

Then she wanted the pleasure to rip through them both, destroying what had been. Leaving something new.

His hands were tight and hard on her waist as he lifted her up, then surged deep into her core. Again and again, he plunged into her, and the angle of his thrusts had his cock sliding right over her clit. Macey wanted to go slow. She wanted that savoring—

But the pleasure wasn't stopping. She couldn't hold back the maelstrom of release. She came around him, her whole body shaking as her sex spasmed. She cried out his name and her body shuddered.

Then she felt him come inside of her, a hot splash

that just made her own pleasure so much more intense.

She kissed him, and this time, the kiss was different. Something…softer.

Something sweeter.

A connection was there, she could feel it between them.

A link that had bonded them.

Her heartbeat stopped thundering in her ears. She eased back down, moving to lay beside him. His arms curled around her.

And she knew, with utter certainty…

This is where I belong. With him.

HIS PHONE WAS RINGING. Bowen slowly turned his head and saw the phone vibrating as it slid across the top of the nightstand. His hand flew out and he grabbed the phone.

Four a.m. No way this call is good.

"Murphy," he said, voice gruff. Beside him, Macey stirred in the bed.

"I need…help…"

Bowen sat up, fast.

"I'm…" A rough rasp of breath. "At the ranger station…only one here with me is Zack…D-Douglas…"

"Jonah?" Bowen snapped. "Is that you?"

"N-need help," he rasped again. "Bastard…held me…tied up…no food…"

Macey jumped out of bed and flashed on the lights.

"Jonah, I'll call the rest of the team." He didn't

mention anything about the team's growing suspicions or what they'd found at Jonah's home. "You're at the ranger station with Zack Douglas, right? That's what you said?"

"Y-yes…"

"Stay there. We're coming to get you."

Macey was at the foot of the bed.

Jonah had hung up.

"What's happening?" she demanded.

"Jonah's at Ranger Douglas's station. He wants help." He dialed Samantha and, despite the insane hour, she answered on the second ring. "Samantha, Jonah just called." And he rattled off the details as fast as he could.

His gut was clenched, his hand too tight around the phone, and he still wondered…

What the fuck is really going on here?

"Tucker and I will get a team from the PD and get en route," Samantha said, her voice sharp. "You and Macey get there, too. I want all hands on deck for this one." Her words were grim. Tight. "I don't like this… Be on guard…*every moment*, got me?"

He understood exactly what she meant.

He and Macey had mistaken Curtis Zale for a victim. But he hadn't been. As for Jonah…

"Understood," Bowen replied quietly. Then he was jumping from the bed and grabbing his clothes as quickly as he could. Macey had already dressed and gotten her gun from the other room. They hauled ass out of that lodge and jumped into the SUV. It was dark outside, but a thousand stars seemed to glitter overhead.

They rushed down the winding roads, heading for the mountains, easing toward the ranger station, and Bowen's hands were fisted around the wheel as he tried to navigate those tight, twisting roads in the dark.

"Victim or killer?" The words burst from him.

Macey had gone dead silent.

"He called for help," Bowen said, "but everything we've learned since Jonah's disappearance... Damn it! Damn it!" *Everything makes him look like a suspect and not one of our own.*

"We go in and we treat him as both." Macey's voice was soft. "Victim and killer, that's what we have to do, until we learn more."

The road branched up ahead. It was so dark that he almost missed the right turn. He slammed on the brake and jerked the wheel, and then they started heading up, up the mountain. Reflectors were on the side of the road, warning of a steep drop-off as they glinted on an old guardrail. It was barely a two-lane road. More like just one, and he was damn glad no other cars were headed his way. His headlights cut through the darkness.

Higher, higher they went. He could feel his ears popping.

The earth seemed to have fallen away on the right...on Macey's side of the car.

It was the only path to take in order to reach the ranger's station. It was—

He heard the growl of an engine, and then bright lights were suddenly right in front of him. He could see the frame of an oversize truck, one with tires that were too big and headlights mounted on the roof of the vehicle. That truck came right for him, swerving to hit him.

"Bowen!" Macey screamed.

But there wasn't any time to stop. There was nowhere to turn, the road was too narrow, and that truck…it was as if it had been waiting for them.

The truck slammed into him, as hard as it could, and Bowen's SUV flew toward the reflectors—the reflectors that had warned of danger, the weak guardrail that wouldn't keep them safe.

The SUV crashed right through that flimsy old railing.

His head turned, not toward that fucking truck, but toward Macey. She'd screamed his name. She'd sounded so afraid. He tried to reach for her.

But the SUV was rolling, tumbling down that mountain, over and over and the screams he heard then…they were the screams of metal as the SUV crashed.

CHAPTER EIGHTEEN

THE LIGHT WAS in her eyes, blinding her. Macey couldn't see past that too bright light. She squinted, trying to see the man behind the light, because she knew he was there.

The monster was always there.

She was trapped, strapped onto the operating room table—

No, no, I'm not fucking on that table.

Macey blinked, but the bright light didn't vanish. She was trapped, all right, but not on Daniel Haddox's table of torture. She was pinned in the SUV, still held in place by her seat belt. Her door had twisted inward and metal seemed to surround her. Broken glass was on her clothes, in her hair, and she could feel blood sliding down her cheek.

The light was still in her eyes. She squinted, trying to see past it.

"Macey, you're going to be all right!"

She knew that voice.

"Oh, God, Douglas, hurry the hell up!" that familiar voice shouted. "She's still alive but, God, he isn't."

That was Jonah's voice. High and desperate. Shouting out for help from—Ranger Douglas?

But then his words registered.

She's still alive but, God, he isn't.

Her head turned to the left. The light pouring into the car let her see Bowen. Bowen—with blood all over him. Bowen, with a deployed air bag slowly sagging beneath him. A giant chunk of metal hung from his chest.

"Bowen?" Macey whispered.

He didn't move. She wasn't even sure he was breathing.

"Bowen!" Frantic, she began clawing at her seat belt. It wouldn't give. She was trapped, strapped down. Her arms were bleeding from a dozen cuts, the metal from her bent door dug into her side and she couldn't get free to help Bowen. He was right there, inches away, and all she could do was put her hands on his face. "Look at me!"

But he didn't. His eyes didn't open. And he felt... cold.

"Macey!" Jonah's voice snapped like a whip. "I've got to get you out of that vehicle. It's not stable. The fucking thing could keep rolling any moment."

What? Weren't they already at the bottom of the mountain? She wasn't sure. Her temple ached, and she knew she'd hit her head. A deployed air bag was near her, too, but it had slit open in several spots.

"A tree stopped your free fall, but the trunk is already cracking. You have to get out!" Then a knife was reaching through her broken window.

Macey screamed.

But the knife just cut through her seat belt.

Had he used the knife to cut into the air bag, too? Was that why it was flat now? Or had the chunks of sharp metal done that?

"I'm pulling her out!" Jonah suddenly yelled. "Douglas, get your ass over here! We'll haul her to safety, then we'll get Bowen."

Yes, yes, they had to get Bowen. She was still touching Bowen. Now that her seat belt was gone, she could move more and her fumbling fingers slid down his throat. She felt his pulse—

Beating. Slowly, but still beating.

Bowen was alive!

"Got you," Jonah said. His arms curled around her and he hauled her from the wreckage. The metal scraped over her hip and she felt the rise of more blood soak her clothes. His hold was tight as he got her out, and then he still held her in his arms, hurrying for safety as he called out to Douglas for help.

Only... Douglas wasn't there.

It took a few moments for that unsettling truth to set in.

"I saved you," Jonah said. He lowered Macey to her feet. The bright light was gone. He must have dropped it or shoved it into his pocket when he'd pulled her out. "You're going to be okay."

She didn't speak for a moment, straining to hear— to hear some small sound that would tell her that Zack Douglas was *actually* there.

"You left your weapon in the car, Macey."

Her hand flew to her side.

"Or rather, I cut the holster off you. Didn't even see that coming, did you?" He backed up a step and the light was shining on her again. Bright. Right in her eyes.

She lifted her hand and turned her face away. "Douglas isn't here."

"No..." He laughed. "Zack Douglas isn't here. No one is here but me and you."

And Bowen. He's still here.

"I'm glad you survived the crash, Mace."

Mace. He was using Bowen's nickname for her, and her skin crawled.

"Wasn't sure you would, but that was a chance I had to take. I mean, how else was I going to get close enough to take out Bowen? There he was, rushing so fast to find me, and I knew it was perfect."

She tried to see into the darkness around her. He'd been telling the truth when he said that the SUV hadn't fallen all the way down the mountain. It was perched halfway against a tree, and if that tree snapped, Bowen would keep falling.

I have to get him out.

"The feds know, don't they, Mace?"

"Know what?" Her voice was trembling. She wanted him to think that she was afraid. That she was weak. Then he'd never see her attack coming.

But he sighed. "They know about me. That dick Tucker gave the game away back at the museum. I mean, shit, I'd just proven myself. I'd shot the bad guy—and believe me, Peter Carter *was* bad. Did you see that shit he did to his girlfriend? He *kept* her skull at his museum. Obviously, he was psychotic." He paused. "And that's why I don't get it. You had the chance to put him out of his misery, but you choked. Again. Tucker didn't want me on the team but you—the woman who couldn't carry out a kill when it was deserved? He and Samantha both waved you in with open arms."

She took a step toward the SUV. The light followed her.

"Tucker tipped his hand. The guy had always ridden my ass, but that day he just came out and said he thought I was a killer. He *said* that shit."

She stared at him and took another slow step toward the SUV. *You are a fucking killer.*

"Knew trouble was coming," Jonah muttered, "when he said I couldn't empathize with the victims. Fuck, fuck, fuck. That was the one word. Shrinks always use that word. *Empathize.* No, I can't empathize. I don't feel shit for them. But I still do the job, don't I? I still get the work done."

Macey's breath slid out. "That's why you hacked the files at the FBI. You…you mimic, don't you?" *Oh, hell.* That was a coping mechanism that psychopaths often used. They didn't feel the way normal individuals did, so they just mimicked the behavior. They acted as if they got angry, as if they were hurt, as if they loved. But it was all just acting.

He hadn't known how to act like the other agents

in the team, so he'd cracked into their files so that his responses would become like theirs. She could see now. Finally.

"Asshole said I wasn't acting right because my hands weren't shaking. I mean, hello! I was doing what good agents do, you know? Standing calm in the face of danger. That's how Bowen always acts!"

Another step brought her even closer to the SUV.

"But Tucker fucking Frost was standing there judging me. Saying I was *off* with my response. Like he can talk! The whole world knows what a screwup his brother was. But the guy…he started asking about my family. Saying I'd just stood there, waiting to watch Peter Carter kill himself, the same way I stood there and watched my family die."

"He was wrong," Macey said, forcing those words past lips that felt numb. It was cold out there, and she was still bleeding from so many cuts. Her body ached. Her temple throbbed. Nausea rolled in her stomach and she knew that she was staring at another monster.

"Yes." Jonah seemed pleased. "He was wrong. He didn't get me at all, did he? I *loved* my father. Was I supposed to hurt him?"

As he killed everyone else?

Maybe that was when Jonah had stopped being able to feel. Maybe he hadn't been born without emotions. Maybe they'd just died when his family had.

"He loved me, too. Said he loved me the most.

That was why he smiled right before he shot himself. Because he'd saved me."

No, he hadn't saved you. He just hadn't killed you.

"Tucker was asking about my program, saying that seemed like the perfect way for our perp to find the serials." He laughed. "On that, he was right."

"You told me the program didn't work," she rasped out even as she inched closer to the SUV. As long as she kept him talking, he didn't seem to even notice her movements.

"I lied."

The light was still on her.

"It worked. I found Daniel. Gale Collins wasn't the first to die in that little North Carolina town. She was just the bait I sent in for him. *I* found him, a doctor practicing off the grid, giving pain pills out like candy, using a new name and still slicing and dicing. I sent Gale to him. I told her it was an undercover FBI operation, but it wasn't. She was just some hick girl who thought she was doing something big—when she was the one who was the pawn to get our game in motion."

Another tremble rolled through her body. This one was only half faked. "She had my eyes."

"Yes! Yes—and I knew that he would have to grab her. So I waited in town, I watched, and the instant he had her…I had *him*. I let him have his fun, seemed only fair, and when he was getting ready to finish her up, I snuck up behind him with my hammer. One hit. Bang. And he was down."

She licked her busted lips. "And Gale?" Because he'd said *getting ready to finish her up*.

"I slit her throat. I mean, I couldn't very well have her admitting to anyone that she knew me, could I? That would just screw everything up."

She was close enough to the SUV. Macey spun and ran for the driver's-side door. She yanked on it as hard as she could and it popped open.

"Macey, fuck, get away from him! The SUV will roll! Stop it!"

She fumbled inside, shoving against what was left of the air bag, grabbing for Bowen as she hung half in the vehicle.

But Jonah's arms closed around her waist and with a loud growl, he yanked her back against him. "I'm trying to save you! It's all been for fucking you!"

She kicked out at him, slamming back with her heels to hit his legs and throwing her head back to ram the bastard in the nose. He howled in pain, but didn't let her go.

If anything, his hold tightened.

"I killed Haddox...*for you*! I knew you'd never do it on your own, and I wasn't going to let him stay out there after what he'd done to you!"

She stilled.

"My program worked! I could find those bastards! I found Remus!"

She didn't struggle at all. When she struggled, he just tightened his hold. When she stilled...

His hold is loosening.

"He killed his girlfriend's stepmother," he whispered, his breath blowing over her ear. He seemed to be hugging her now, not restraining her. "I knew it was him. And the dumbass just trotted right up here to me like a lamb to a slaughter."

"How did you know about Curtis Zale? Your program?"

He laughed, the rumble shaking her. "I knew there was a killer here. Had to be, but I didn't know where he was hiding his victims. Not until I got a little help."

Had she just seen movement in the SUV? The door was open. Yes, yes, she thought Bowen was moving on the inside.

"Help," Macey repeated. "You mean help...from Wesley Kaiser?" Because she knew he had to be part of this mess.

"No, actually, I don't mean him at all. My help came from someone else entirely." He laughed. "But I'll never tell."

Fuck him. He'd made the mistake of easing his hold and the dumbass hadn't even realized...

Macey spun toward him and the chunk of sharp metal that she'd palmed right before he'd yanked her out of the SUV? She swiped that makeshift weapon at him, and it sliced across his hands.

"Blood on my fucking hands!" Jonah yelled.

"Yeah, there's plenty of that." Then she hit him again. Only this time, she drove that metal at his stomach. She twisted it, jerked it up and—

His fist slammed into her face.

Macey didn't let that stop her. She stabbed him again, and he was screaming and yelling and—

"You'll want—" Bowen's voice growled "—to get the fuck away from her now."

Jonah stilled.

Macey didn't. She kept a grip on her makeshift weapon and rushed back toward Bowen's voice, thinking she needed to protect him—

But there was enough starlight for her to see the gun he gripped in his hand. Metal was still in his chest, and that terrified her, but Bowen was on his feet. And his weapon was aimed at the wolf who'd been among them all along.

Only Jonah started to laugh. Again. "You used the Haddox trick!" He sounded...impressed? "The Doctor stayed alive because he didn't take Macey's knife out of him. He would have bled to death if he had. Haddox waited and got a friend to stitch him up. Did you know that, Mace? Another doc at the hospital stitched him up that night and never said a word to anyone. But don't worry, that fellow is on my list, too."

"Stop," she ordered.

He didn't. "You used the Haddox trick," Jonah said again. "Keep the metal in...and you can live longer. Take it out...you're dead. You bleed, bleed, bleed. And that metal—it's in you far deeper than that knife was in Haddox. I can tell. It's so deep I bet...I bet you're a dead man walking. You don't even know..."

"Where is Zack Douglas?" Macey demanded.

"At the ranger station. Just like I said. He really did find me."

Goose bumps were all over her arms. "What did you do to him?"

"He should have noticed all those hikers were making a pattern. If he'd noticed sooner, lives would have been saved." Jonah's bloody hands were at his sides. "I figured he deserved what he got."

"You staged your abduction from the museum," Bowen snarled.

"No!" A roar from Jonah. "That fucking twit Wesley did that! He came to *me* for help! No one else at the FBI would give him the time of day. He came to me—we worked on that fucking program together! And then...then he didn't like the results. He was trying to stop *me*. Hit me with the hammer...tied me up... *His mistake. I got away.* And he'll be next."

"No," Bowen rasped. "You will be."

Jonah laughed at those words. "Are you gonna do it? Right in front of her? Kill me in cold blood? I gave you the chance, over and over, to prove you were the better agent. You failed every single time. Now you won't even be the better man. You'll shoot in cold blood, hitting an unarmed man. The same way you hit an unarmed man when you killed Arnold Shaw, right? I mean, hey, I read the file, I could see the bullshit. You planted that knife on him, didn't you? And that poor desperate victim on the scene, she was so grateful she lied for you."

"Get on your knees…and put your hands *up*," Bowen barked but his voice was sounding weak.

Macey moved closer to him, her shoulder brushing against his arm. "Let me take the gun," she whispered to Bowen.

"See!" Jonah yelled. "She wants the gun because she knows you'll shoot to kill! Macey won't! Macey isn't like you!"

Bowen's body trembled harder. He staggered and she thought he was going to fall. Her left arm flew around his waist as she tried to steady him.

"It's true, Mace!" Jonah called out. "That night in the dark alley, Bowen shot an unarmed man. He covered up the crime, and he's been doing it for years."

"Give me the gun, Bowen," Macey said, voice stronger.

His head turned. His eyes gleamed in the darkness. "Want to…protect you…"

She could feel his blood soaking the side of her body. He was hurt so badly. Too badly. Macey swallowed. "You've always protected me." *It's my turn to protect you.* "Give me the gun."

"It's because she knows what you are now. You're done, Bowen! Done! *Dead man walking…*"

Bowen still gripped the gun.

Jonah had bent to his knees, but his hands…his hands were inching toward the coat he wore. Was that a park ranger's coat?

And what's under his damn coat?

"Mace..." Bowen gasped her name. *"Love...you."*

Her lips shook. "Give me the gun."

Bowen's hand slid toward hers.

From the corner of her eye, she saw Jonah lunge to his feet.

Bowen began to fall. His hand was still on the gun. Hers was around his. Her head turned, snapping toward Jonah. He was pulling out a weapon from beneath his coat.

Macey's hands jerked around Bowen's, but he was already firing. They shot together. He pulled the trigger. She aimed the gun.

The bullet blasted right into Jonah's head. He fell back, his body twitching.

And then Bowen fell, sinking to his knees.

"Bowen!"

"Make sure..." Each word seemed like a struggle. "He's...done..."

She rushed toward Jonah. His body was still jerking and a gun was just inches from his outstretched hand. Macey grabbed the gun and tucked it into her waistband. She could tell by the wound...

He's done.

She ran back to Bowen. His hands were wrapped around the chunk of metal in his chest and he was trying to pull it out. *"No!"* Once more, her hands closed around his. "Don't! He was right. Don't pull it out now."

"I'm...cold, Mace."

And she was terrified. She wanted the metal to stay where it was because she feared it had hit his heart. But, oh, God, he was covered in so much blood. So many wounds.

"Meant it…" Bowen mumbled. "Love you…"

"And I love you and you're going to be all right, do you hear me? You just—you have to stay calm. You lie still and I'm going to get help." She ran to the battered SUV, looking for a phone. *Please be there, please be…*

The SUV groaned around her. Metal screeched and she snatched up the phone as fast as she could. The screen was broken, a rough crack like a spider's web across the surface, but it still worked. It was glowing, giving her light, and she stumbled back, swiping her finger across that broken screen, and then—

No service. No fucking service. Because she was halfway down a mountain in the woods. *In the middle of nowhere.*

Macey rushed back to Bowen and she sank to her knees beside him. "It's going to be okay," she told him again as her hand curled around his.

"You…lie…like hell…"

Tears were sliding down her cheeks. "No, everything is fine. I'm a doctor, remember?" She leaned forward and pressed a kiss to his lips. "I'll take care of you."

"Love…you…"

"And I love you." Her hand squeezed his. "So if

you think, even for a second, that I am not going to make sure that you stay alive, you're wrong."

He didn't speak.

"Do you hear me, Bowen? You're going to stay alive. You are going to stay—"

His hand was limp in her grasp.

Alive.

She pulled her hand away from his and began using the phone she'd retrieved as a flashlight so she could evaluate all of his wounds. *Oh, my God.*

They were bad. So bad...

Then her chin lifted.

And she got to work.

CHAPTER NINETEEN

SAMANTHA AND TUCKER rushed into the dark ranger's station. The place was pitch-black. Samantha knew that was a sign of trouble, so they went in fast and hard and silently. If Jonah was there, getting help from Ranger Douglas, she knew the lights would be shining in that place. Since it was pitch-black...

Trouble.

And why hadn't the ranger called for help himself? That piece of the puzzle had been nagging at her. She'd tried to get the ranger station again and again during her ride up there. Sure, phone service could be damn spotty, but she'd had the PD radio in.

No response.

No one was in the dark waiting area. Empty. She had a flashlight in her hand as she swept the scene. The flashlight was right above her gun.

Tucker kicked open the door that led to the office behind the check-in desk.

"Help..." A weak, pain-filled cry.

Tucker rushed in, and Samantha was right behind him. But their flashlights didn't fall on Jonah's haggard face. Instead, they illuminated the blood-soaked form of Ranger Zack Douglas.

"Help..." he begged again.

"Bowen?" Macey had his blood all over her hands. "I need to get help for you." She bit her lip and looked up at the top of the mountain. *But I hate to leave you.* She was putting pressure on some of his worst wounds. She'd ripped her clothes apart and bound up the terrible gash in his thigh, the one that made her worry he'd nipped an artery. No wonder his legs had given way on him before.

She hadn't touched the metal in his chest. But her hands were shoving against the deep slice across his ribs. The slice that had cut his skin wide-open.

She needed help, needed to climb up that mountain. "You can't move," she whispered. "Understand? If I leave you, you can't move at all."

Her left hand swept over him once more, moving down to make sure that wound in his leg—

It was bleeding again. Too much.

Apply pressure, elevation, pressure points... She knew all the immediate ways to help and she was doing everything she could. But that was the problem—she had to keep working on him, almost constantly. If she left him, even for the few moments it would take to climb to the top and potentially get cell service or hail down a car—

He could die.

And if she just stayed there, doing the best she could with him—no medical gear, no tools...

Maybe I'll buy him time this way. He'll stay alive until others come.

Only...what if the others didn't come?

SAMANTHA RAN BACK outside of the ranger station. "We need a medic in there!"

And the team who'd followed her and Tucker up the mountain sprang into action. They'd gone in silently, but there were cops there, EMTs, plenty of backup waiting in the wings.

But Jonah isn't here.

They'd swept the rest of the station. It was clear.

"Where in the hell is he?" Tucker demanded as he stalked to Samantha's side.

The assembled team had lights on in the small lot now—lights from the cruisers, from the ambulance. Her gaze swept the area. "Douglas would have kept his personal vehicle up here." She marched around the building and there…her flashlight hit the fresh tire tracks. It had rained lightly and the ground was still soft. Soft enough for her to see the tire tracks left behind. Big ones, probably the off-roading type that a large truck would use.

She stared at those tracks and the fear in her grew worse. "Macey and Bowen should have been here by now."

"I still can't get either one of them on their phones. My call just goes to voice mail." Tucker's voice was grim. "I don't get it—they would have needed to drive up the same mountain road we did. There's only one way up to this station."

Yes, one way. And Jonah had made sure that they were all coming that way. Had he known that Macey and Bowen would be coming first?

Of course. He called Bowen directly.

The perp they were after had been calling Bowen from the very beginning. Taunting him. Challenging him. Watching him.

Because Bowen was always a target?

"Bowen was in the way," she said as she turned sharply and rushed back for her vehicle. She could just see the faintest tendrils of light beginning to streak across the sky. The night was finally ending. "He was calling Bowen at first, challenging him, because he needed to prove he was better." She was almost running as she ran for her rental. "Now he's going to eliminate Bowen because he stands between Jonah and the one he really wanted all along."

Who was closest to Bowen? Who did Bowen protect?

"Macey." Tucker jumped into the vehicle with her. "Fuck, that's why the Doctor was the first victim. It was about her. All along—her."

She cranked the SUV, revved the engine and got the hell out of there even as the local cops shouted for her.

I have to find my team.

"We thought it was Bowen. That the focus was him, but Jonah was just taunting him. Macey... *Macey* was his end game."

And Samantha was very, very afraid the end had come.

They rushed down that mountain, with Tucker still trying to get Macey or Bowen on the line. Faint rays of light cut through the treetops, and as she rounded a curve—

Her headlights—it was still dark enough to need them—hit the broken guardrail. Samantha slammed on her brakes. "Did you see that on the way up?"

"I could barely see any-fucking-thing on the way up."

She reversed the SUV and parked it near that broken railing. When she jumped out, her flashlight automatically swept the scene…

And she saw the big truck that had been parked off road, partially hidden behind a patch of trees. "Tucker," she snapped, warning him with a motion of her hand.

His gaze immediately zeroed in on the truck. He rushed toward it with his weapon drawn.

"Empty," he barked.

It was empty. There was a freaking car-sized hole in the guardrail, and her two agents—her friends—weren't answering their phones. They hadn't arrived at the ranger station because they *couldn't*.

She and Tucker immediately began scaling down that mountain. Their lights swept out, and she could smell gasoline.

Hold on, Macey. Hold on, Bowen. We're coming.

Down, down they went, slipping and falling because it was so steep. Rocks tripped her and branches cut into Samantha and then—

Her light hit the wreckage. She staggered to a stop. Oh, Jesus. Sweet Jesus. Tucker was right beside her. His flashlight swept to the left and there—covered in blood—they saw Macey.

She blinked against their light, for a moment looking lost. Blood soaked her—her shirt, her hands and—

"He can feel everything." A sob shook her body. "But I didn't have a choice! He was dying! I had to work on him!"

Bowen lay on the ground before Macey. A chunk of metal was in his chest. A tourniquet was wrapped around his legs and the blood…

"Get back up the mountain," Samantha ordered Tucker as she ran to Macey. "Get help!"

"YOU CAN LET him go, ma'am," the medic said as he secured Bowen. "We've got him!"

They were airlifting him to safety. She should take her hands off Bowen. Macey knew that. The scene was chaotic around her and the *whoop-whoop-whoop* of the helicopter blades filled her ears.

Bowen was still alive. His eyes hadn't opened. He hadn't looked at her. But he was alive.

She'd made sure of it.

Her body ached because her muscles had been clenched with tension for so long. She'd had to do things to him…hold his veins, fight so hard…

No anesthesia.

She'd hurt him. She knew it. Daniel had once promised her…

I've made sure that you will feel everything that happens to you… I'll start slowly, just so you know what's going to happen. I keep my slices light at first. I like to see how the patient reacts to the pain stimulus…

"Ma'am, you have to let him go."

Her hands slowly lifted. "I'll see you soon, Bowen," she promised him.

But he didn't look at her.

Because he couldn't.

"MACEY."

She blinked. She was sitting in the back of an ambulance. A female EMT was cleaning the wound on her face, and the scene around her seemed completely surreal.

The night was gone. The sun had poured into the mountains. She was back on the road, away from the wreckage. She could see a team hauling up a body bag.

Jonah. They'd found their missing agent.

"Macey, tell me what happened." Samantha's voice was strained.

"Bowen is going to be all right."

"Macey—"

Her head turned as she stared at her boss—and her friend. "Bowen is going to be all right?"

Samantha hesitated, and Macey felt as if her heart had just been clawed out.

"You took care of him," Samantha assured her softly. "No one else could have done what you did. You kept him alive, Macey. Now he's going to the hospital. They'll work on him. They'll do their best."

"Removing that metal is going to be tricky. They have to be sure—"

Samantha's hand closed around hers. "You kept him alive."

A tear leaked down her cheek. "Even wounded so badly, he got out of the vehicle because he wanted to save *me*. I don't know how he did it. Shouldn't have happened. But he got out of that wrecked SUV. He pulled a gun on Jonah. He *stopped* Jonah."

"So Bowen is the one who shot him?"

Give me the gun. She'd asked him that, again and again. Because Macey had known exactly what she needed to do. "I did it." She'd been the one to aim. Bowen had been too weak then, he'd been falling. "I shot Jonah in the head because he was going for his weapon." That weapon had been taken from her. "You have it now…it's proof…"

"About Jonah's gun…" There was a hesitant note in Samantha's voice.

Macey stared at her.

"It wasn't loaded."

Her breath choked out. "He…he forced us off the road, nearly killed us both…" *And his gun wasn't loaded?* Her eyes squeezed shut. "Just like his father." Oh, God. He'd been so much like his father. Killing everyone and then…

Killing himself. "Jonah wanted to die." Because the end had been there for him. Only, he'd wanted to take out Bowen, too. He'd wanted her to see Bowen for what he was.

And I do. Bowen is the man I love. The man I'll always love.

"Did he confess, Macey?" Samantha pushed.

The EMT cleared her throat. "She really needs to get to the hospital."

The hospital. Yes. Macey nodded, still feeling dazed. *Adrenaline. Fear. Pain.* She had to get to the hospital because Bowen was going to be at the hospital. She needed to see him. "Bowen is going to be all right…"

"Did Jonah confess, Macey?" Samantha asked once more.

Macey realized that she'd closed her eyes. Macey opened them, blinked. "He admitted to killing Daniel Haddox. He even… Jonah was the one who slit the throat of Gale Collins."

She heard a dark curse from her right and realized Tucker was there, too.

"She was bait," Macey explained. Her hand rose and pointed to her eyes. "Because she was like me. Jonah used her, made her think…" Nausea was rising in her, but she swallowed it down. She was an FBI agent. She could do this. She'd give her statement, even covered in Bowen's blood. *Bowen!* She'd tell them what happened. She'd wrap this scene…

"She needs a hospital." The EMT sounded angry now.

"Jonah used Gale. Convinced her that…convinced her that she was working with the FBI. Then he killed her…" Her breath rushed out. "His program worked. Said he'd…he'd found Patrick. Took him out, too."

"Did his fucking program predict Curtis Zale, too?" Tucker had moved closer.

She strained to remember on this part. "Yes, but

he…needed help finding the victims." It was hard for her to think clearly. She'd asked him if Wesley had helped but…

I'll never tell.

"Where is Wesley Kaiser?" Samantha wanted to know. "We noticed there were bind marks around Jonah's wrists and ankles. Was that staged?"

"No…he said…said Wesley had taken him, but that he'd gotten away."

Tucker and Samantha shared a long, hard look. "So they *were* working together."

A shudder worked along her body. Was everyone as cold as she was? No, no, of course not. *Shock.* "He said… Jonah said he was the only one at the FBI who listened to Wesley's story."

"Where is that kid now?" Tucker fumed. "If Wesley's still out there, the public is in danger."

She shook her head. "He…he took Jonah. Jonah said the guy…that Wesley was trying to…to stop him."

Tucker gave a low whistle. "Wesley went to Jonah seeking justice for his sister. Looks like he got a whole lot more than he bargained for."

"I—I need to see Bowen," Macey whispered. "I need him."

Samantha nodded curtly. "We've got this scene." She motioned to the glaring EMT. "Take her to the hospital."

"About time," the woman muttered.

They loaded Macey into the ambulance and right before those doors closed—

"Wait!" Macey called.

She saw Samantha and Tucker turn back to her. "There's someone else involved," she managed. "Not just Wesley…something else…some*one* else…"

Samantha and Tucker shared a dark look.

The doors closed.

CHAPTER TWENTY

Bowen felt like hell. Absolute freaking hell. He was lying in the hospital bed, bandages were all over him, and the light coming through the blinds fell right into his eyes.

And Macey isn't here. Where is Macey?

He'd woken in that room, and his last memory had been of Macey's fingers closing around his as she jerked the gun toward Jonah.

Had they shot the other agent? Had the bullet found its target?

Where. Is. Macey?

He grabbed for the side of the bed and began to haul himself up. Pain lanced through him, but he didn't care. There was an IV line pumping into his vein, but he grabbed for it—

"Are you trying to undo all the hard work that the doctors here did? That *I* did on that godforsaken mountain?"

Macey.

His head whipped to the right. She was standing there, bruises on her beautiful skin, a bandage on her cheek and a faint smile on her face.

He could only stare at her.

"Bowen?" Her smile slipped away as she hurried to him.

He grabbed her; the IV burned, and he didn't give a fuck. He pulled Macey closer, wobbling there on the edge of the bed.

"No, Bowen, you don't even *want* to know how many stitches you have!" The beep of machines was wild around him. "Stop!" Gently, she pushed him back. "You have to take it easy."

He didn't want easy. He didn't want anything but her. "Couldn't...remember what happened."

Her eyes widened. Such perfect eyes. Eyes he could stare into forever. "We shot Jonah."

Okay, so they *had* shot him.

"Then you almost died." Her lips pressed together and pain flashed on her face. "And I have never, ever been so scared in my life." She eased him back onto the bed. "Not even when I thought Daniel Haddox was *taking* my life." She started to back away.

But his hand flew out and curled around her wrist. "Thought...Jonah was going to...kill you."

"I don't believe that was ever his intention." Her lashes swept down. "He was very twisted up. He managed to get past us all, for so long. Managed to work *at the FBI.* I'd sworn I wouldn't be fooled again—"

Bowen brought her hand to his mouth and kissed her fingers.

"I wasn't going to let him get away with what he'd done." She stared into his eyes. "I wasn't letting you die on that mountain."

His Macey was safe. They'd both made it.

"You were in surgery for over six hours." Her left hand rose and pressed to his chest. "That chunk of metal missed your heart."

"Because you already had it."

Her head tilted. "Bowen…"

"I know we won't be together in the field anymore." His words rushed out. His throat was sore, his voice a bit raspy—he figured they'd had some tube shoved down his throat during surgery—but he had to keep talking. "If we can't be partners there…"

She was shaking her head.

"Then I want us to be partners…I want us to be partners in *life*." He was screwing this up. Still sick from surgery, weak, but the words needed to be said. He'd come too close to losing the one thing that mattered most to him.

Macey.

She wasn't shaking her head any longer.

"Will you marry me, Macey?" He could barely breathe.

"This isn't some delirious proposal that you won't remember later, after your pain meds wear off?"

"Will you marry me?"

"Yes."

Fuck, yeah! He yanked her closer and his mouth pressed to hers. He didn't care about the pain he felt because he had Macey in his arms. Macey in his life, and she'd just promised him forever.

No pain could ever compete with that.

"I love you, Bowen," Macey whispered against his lips.

He knew they'd come through the darkness. Knew that they'd survived. And now...now he had Macey.

He would fight like hell to always keep her at his side.

As his friend, as his partner, as the woman he loved more than any-fucking-thing.

His Macey.

And he held her even tighter.

DR. AMELIA LANG hurried back to her motel room. She'd just heard on the radio that FBI Agent Jonah Loxley had been killed—and that the man was the suspected perpetrator in several homicides.

Wesley Kaiser was wanted by authorities.

Wesley... Carlisle.

Oh, God.

She'd worked side by side with him. She'd thought she knew him, but apparently, the guy had abducted Jonah Loxley.

The cops didn't know where Wesley was. They'd put out an APB for him. She'd had a guard on her last night, but she'd sent him away that morning, thinking she was safe.

I don't feel so safe any longer. Her hand tightened on her purse. She had a license to carry a concealed weapon. She'd told the cops about her license and the guy who'd taken her to the motel the night before—that cop—had told her it was a good idea to keep the weapon close.

She fumbled with the lock on her room and hurried inside. She shut the door, flipped on the lights and—

"Hello, Dr. Lang."

Carlisle. No, Wesley. He was there. Screaming, she yanked the gun from her purse and whirled around. He was standing near the window. Sadness covered his face.

"It didn't work. Susannah is dead, so many people are dead…and I don't feel better. I just feel *worse*." His hands fisted at his sides and he took a lurching step toward her. "Why won't the pain stop?"

The gun shook in her hands.

"Why won't it fucking stop?" He stared at her with wild eyes—and then he ran at her.

Amelia fired. He kept coming at her. So she kept firing. Over and over. Until he stopped running.

Until her gun was empty.

The next day…

"You should be in the hospital, Macey," Tucker muttered, shooting her a hard glare as she stood in the Gatlinburg police station.

"I'm okay." But Bowen? He wasn't *as* okay. He'd have to stay in the hospital for quite a while longer, but he *would* recover. He'd survive.

Then she'd marry that man.

"I can do this interrogation," Tucker continued, motioning toward the one-way mirror. They were in the observation room, and Dr. Amelia Lang—a very pale Dr. Lang—sat in the interrogation room. Her shoulders were hunched and her hands were on the cup of coffee that rested on the table before her. "You don't have to go in there."

Yes, she did. "The case is almost closed." A case that had drawn national attention. An FBI agent as a killer? Of course that story was on every TV channel.

But the story wasn't over, not yet.

"I just need to ask her a few questions." Macey gave him a quick nod. "I *need* to do this."

The faint lines near his mouth tightened, but Tucker nodded. Macey turned away from him and walked slowly into the hallway. Samantha was waiting for her. When Samantha saw her, one dark brow arched. "I hear congratulations are in order."

I said yes. I have a life to look forward to. So many good things...not just darkness. "Yes."

Samantha pulled her close in a hug. "Congratulations," she said, and her voice was warm. But when she eased back, a shadow had fallen over her face. "I will always remember seeing you on the side of that mountain, your body covered in blood as you fought to save him." Her chin lifted. "I hope that man understands just how much you love him."

"He does," Macey told her, believing this with all of her being. "Because he feels the same way about me."

Samantha considered that. "Yes, I believe he does." Her gaze slid to the closed interrogation room door. "I'm assuming you want the honors?"

"I think I deserve them."

Again, Samantha seemed to consider her words. "Yes, you do." She opened the door for Macey. "I'll be watching. If you need me, I'm there."

Because Samantha had her back. Just as Bowen did. As Tucker did. They were more than just a team. They were a family.

And woe be unto anyone who messed with her family.

Macey walked into the interrogation room. Her heels tapped lightly on the floor. She didn't have a manila file in her hand. Didn't have an evidence bag. She didn't need one.

Dr. Lang glanced up as she entered. Relief swept over her face. "I'm so glad you're okay, Agent Night!" She rose, almost spilling her coffee cup because her hands were shaking so badly. "I heard about what happened to you and Agent Bowen. It's a miracle you both survived!"

Macey stopped near the table. "I believe in miracles, Dr. Lang."

Dr. Lang smiled, a quick flash, but then it was gone. "Please…just make it Amelia. We're long past the formal point, aren't we?"

Yes, they were. "I believe," Macey continued, her voice calm and easy, "that there are good people in the world. People who want to help others. People who want to be happy and help their families and their friends to be happy. People who want to make the world a legitimately better place."

Amelia still stood, uncertain.

"And I also believe that there are monsters in this world. People who seek out darkness. People who thrive on pain and chaos."

"You think, Carlisle—I mean, Wesley—was one of those people?"

Macey pulled out her chair and sat at the table. Amelia slowly lowered into her own seat. She pushed her coffee cup away.

"I think Wesley Kaiser was a man driven to the brink of his sanity by grief. He'd lost his sister. He knew that she was dead, that she'd been murdered, but no one would believe him."

Amelia's hands fisted before her. "I shot him." Her voice was weak. "He was in my room, and I—I shot him."

"I know." Six of her bullets had hit him. He'd died on the scene.

Amelia's shoulders sagged. "He never talked to me about his sister. I wish…oh, God, I wish things had ended differently. If he'd told me the truth, I could have helped him! It didn't have to end this way."

"No," Macey agreed with her completely. "It didn't."

A tear leaked from Amelia's right eye. "What happens now? Will I go to jail?" Before Macey could continue, Amelia said, "It was self-defense, I swear! He was running at me—coming for me. He didn't have a gun, not that I could see, but I was so scared." A sob burst from her. "I knew what he'd done. And I didn't want him to k-kill me."

Macey reached across the table. A tissue box had been placed there. She offered Amelia a tissue. Amelia swiped it over her streaming eyes. Macey waited for the other woman to compose herself.

After a few moments, Amelia seemed to get her control back. "I'm sorry. It's been a really rough twenty-four hours, you know?"

I know. Macey offered her a smile. "I *know* you would have helped Wesley."

Some of the tension left Amelia's face.

"Actually," Macey remarked, "I think you did help him."

"I—I don't understand—"

"Jonah Loxley told me that someone else helped him. He knew that hikers were disappearing here in Gatlinburg, but he had no idea where their bodies were being hidden. He didn't know that part of the puzzle, you see. The program that he'd created to find potential serials just showed him a victim pattern in the area. It didn't show him where those victims were buried. It didn't show him who his killer was."

A faint line appeared between Amelia's brows. "I don't understand."

"I didn't, either, not at first, but then I remembered... You are really, really good at finding bodies."

Amelia's lips parted, but she didn't speak.

Macey gave her another smile. "Let me tell you what I think happened..."

"I—I didn't—"

"I think Wesley came to you. He came to you *not* as Carlisle, but as himself. He'd figured out that his sister was dead. He'd figured out that Peter Carter had murdered her, but he had no proof. So he went to someone who knew how to find bodies. He went to you."

Amelia shook her head. "I—I— *No. That never happened.*"

Macey squared her shoulders and rolled up her sleeves. She caught a glimpse of her scars and, for the first time, they made her feel stronger. "Peter Carter—in his very warped and twisted way— loved Susannah. So maybe you used that as a starting point. Maybe you went to him and appealed to the emotions he'd had for her. But while you were at the museum, you happen to notice the new exhibit, didn't you? The hate nails...and the skull."

Amelia was staring at her with wide, shocked eyes.

"Did a little digging on you," Macey said, inclining her head. "You're a forensic geophysicist now, but when you were an undergrad, you were focused on forensic anthropology."

"Y-yes…"

"That means you know your way around bones. I'm betting with just one glance, you knew you weren't looking at some two-hundred-year-old skull. You were staring at a recent victim. You were staring at Susannah."

Amelia's breath came faster. She was almost panting.

"But then the problem became...where was her

body? You realized that Peter was still obsessed with her, and maybe…maybe during that visit he mentioned the spot that Susannah liked to visit. Her favorite place. Her *safe* place. You headed out there with Wesley, because, of course, he remembered that his sister had loved that spot when they were kids, and you took your equipment with you. You found the cabin and you started searching."

"This is crazy," Amelia whispered. She stared at Macey in horror. "You're crazy."

Macey glanced down at her scars, and she smiled. "You found a lot that day. Not just Susannah…but so many more bodies. I bet you nearly went wild when you found all of those readings."

Amelia was shaking her head—

"Did you wonder if Peter was the one who'd killed them all? Bet you did, so you went to Wesley's contact at the FBI. You met Jonah. You shared what you knew, he shared what he knew…and you realized that you'd found the burial grounds for a serial killer." She shrugged. "At that point, well, I'm betting Jonah just staked out the cabin, huh? Probably put up some recording devices because he sure seemed to love those." She knew now that Jonah had been the one to put the devices in her cabin. They'd found the receivers for those devices—in the cabin he shared with Tucker. *He was right under our noses the whole time.* "Jonah liked to watch. He liked to find sins. So he waited and he watched and he found Curtis Zale."

Amelia shot to her feet. "This is ridiculous! You were *at* that cabin! None of those bodies had been dug up! There was no way for me to know that Susannah was there—no way for me to know about—"

"You detected the bodies with your equipment. Most of them were in a nice, neat little line behind the cabin. Those were the work of Curtis Zale. Susannah was all alone, underneath her favorite tree. Her brother would have known that tree was her favorite, right?"

Amelia didn't speak.

"You saw them, and, no, you didn't dig them up. Because you had a…well, a team of sorts, I guess. And you all had a plan. That plan involved killing Curtis Zale."

Amelia was still standing and her body was completely stiff. "Agent Murphy is the one who killed that man! I wasn't even there! I didn't arrive until after—"

"After you had Agent Murphy do your dirty work. After you and your *team* had staged the scene. You liked the nails, huh? Took that from Peter, didn't you? A nice little 'fuck you' every time you used it."

"I'm— I don't want to talk to you any longer. You're lying! Making up *lies*!"

Macey just stared at her.

"You have no proof about *any* of this!" Amelia nearly yelled. "Nothing! You're just making up stories!"

Macey tilted back her head. "Wesley didn't like what you were doing. He'd started all this—only because he wanted justice for his sister. But somewhere along the line, that got lost. He didn't realize until too late that the FBI agent he'd turned to for help? That guy was the *last* person he should have trusted. Jonah Loxley was a monster—"

Amelia's nostrils flared.

"And Wesley, he was looking for a white knight. Unfortunately for him, he wound up with *two* monsters." She rose to her feet and flattened her hands on the table. "He was in your motel room today, without any weapon at all, and you shot him six times. You did that to stop him from talking about what *you* did."

"You," Amelia argued back, her voice strangled. "You shot Jonah, and I heard he didn't even have bullets in his gun." Then, before Macey could speak, she made a rough, chopping motion with her hand. "Doesn't matter. We were both *scared*. Don't you see that, Agent Night? You and I are the same. We had to fight back to save our lives."

They were nothing alike. "Wesley left a full, written confession beneath his sister's birch tree. He told us everything, including how you helped to give him a false identity. He implicated you completely."

"No." Amelia backed up a step and absolute horror flashed on her face. "No!" Then she cried, "That fucking *bastard*!" Fury blasted in her words. "I did everything for him! No one else was helping that little prick! Me, I did it! Jonah and I were the ones who found the killers. We were the ones who were going to make sure that Peter paid—we were making sure they all paid! We were finally giving those killers the payback they deserved!" She shoved her hair back. "Do you know how many bodies I've found? Kids, men, women? Thrown away like garbage? It was time someone stood up for them! Time someone fought back!"

"With torture…and by using innocent people as bait?" An image of Gale Collins flashed before her eyes. "How does what you did make you any better than the monsters you paid back?"

Amelia's frantic gaze flew around the interrogation room. "I want a deal! I want—"

"There is no deal for you. You murdered Wesley Kaiser in cold blood. You saw him, and you feared he'd tell us about your involvement. So you killed him."

Amelia's lips trembled. "My whole life was on the l-line. What was I supposed to do?"

Macey didn't move.

"I didn't know he'd written a confession." Amelia's eyes squeezed shut. "Oh, God, I didn't know!"

Macey watched her for a moment. Amelia's body was swaying, tears sparking on her lashes. "He didn't." Her voice was so quiet.

But Amelia heard those soft words. Her eyes immediately flew open.

"He didn't leave a confession, but you just made one."

Amelia's mouth dropped. "You…you lied?"

"And you killed." Macey turned her back on the other woman. "But you won't be doing that anymore. You won't be doing anything but spending the rest of your life behind bars."

"No!" Amelia screamed.

Macey didn't look back. She'd gotten what she needed. She opened the door. A uniformed cop waited on the threshold. "Take her back to holding," Macey told him. "And be sure you read Dr. Lang her rights."

MACEY PULLED IN a deep, bracing breath as she stood in the hospital corridor. She'd already checked on Dr. McKinley—he was healing nicely. And Zack Douglas was going to pull through, too, thank goodness. Samantha and Tucker had found him just in time.

There were no more killers for her to hunt right then. No more victims to discover. The case was over.

Three killers—Jonah, Amelia and Wesley. A twisted team that had hunted dark predators but had themselves become lost in the darkness.

Sometimes Macey had worried that she was letting her own darkness consume her. The pain from her past, the need for vengeance...

She opened the hospital room door.

Bowen was sitting up in bed. He smiled when he saw her.

She didn't worry about getting lost in the darkness anymore. She'd come out of that cage, and she'd gone into the light.

Bowen had shown her the way.

"We got her," she told him.

Bowen lifted his hand toward her. She hurried to him and her hand extended. Her sleeves were still up. She could see her scars. She didn't want to hide anymore. Not the good or the bad. Not her fears. Not her hopes. She wanted to take life, to hold it tight. To savor every single moment.

Her fingers curled with his.

And Macey knew her nightmares didn't matter anymore. The future—that mattered. Her life with Bowen mattered.

What would come next...

That mattered.

* * * * *

Alexei's whispered words sent a chill racing up Britt's spine, and she gripped the edge of the table. Oh, God, she was sitting across from a maniac.

"I... You... Who are you?" She half rose out of her chair and then thumped back down.

He covered one of her hands with his, and if she'd given in to her first instinct, she would've snatched it away. But Alexei's hand felt warm, secure. He'd protected her, kept her safe...and lied to her.

"I'm Alexei Ivanov, US Navy SEAL sniper. That's all still true, but I'm also the son of Aleksandr Ivanov, who was murdered by Olav Belkin, and I'm here to avenge that murder."

She licked her dry lips and sucked down some iced tea through her straw. "So, there's no connection between the Belkins and terrorists? You're just trying to get close enough to Belkin to... kill him?"

"There is a connection. The Belkins have worked with terrorists before, in Russia. It's not new territory for them. If I can take down Olav Belkin, his terrorist connections will run scared." He spread his hands. "It's a win-win."

"Except what you're doing is illegal. If you're caught, it will end your career, regardless of the favor you're doing the world." She grabbed his hand, digging her nails into his skin. "Is your vengeance worth that? Everything you worked so hard to achieve?"

His gaze dropped to his hand in her possession. "You know, I never even met my father. My mother was pregnant when my father was murdered, and I was born in New York after relatives got her out of Russia."

"How did it happen?" Maybe if she could get him to talk about it matter-of-factly, putting his Russian passion aside… "How did your father know Belkin, or was it random?"

His head jerked when the waitress showed up to take their plates. "Anything else?"

"Coffee for both of us." Britt wagged her finger between herself and Alexei.

He shoved his dark hair back from his face with one hand. "It wasn't random. My father was a shopkeeper in St. Petersburg. Belkin was a member of the Vory v Zakone."

Britt raised her eyebrows. "The what?"

"Vory v Zakone. The Russian mob in the old Soviet Union. It literally means thieves in law. They were involved in all criminal activities—drugs, girls, extortion. And my father—" he lifted one shoulder in that very Russian manner of his "—objected to those activities. The Vory answered his objections by slitting his throat one night in his shop."

Britt covered her mouth with both hands. No wonder Alexei wanted revenge. She'd been ready to do violence against Sergei for lying about her sister, and she didn't even know if he was involved in Leanna's disappearance yet.

"That's awful. I mean, I have no words, really." She pressed her lips together when the waitress returned with their coffee.

Alexei dumped some sugar into his coffee with a shaky hand, his jaw tight.

So much for tamping down that temper.

Don't miss
SECURED BY THE SEAL by Carol Ericson,
available February 2018 wherever
Harlequin Intrigue® books and ebooks are sold.

www.Harlequin.com

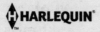

INTRIGUE

EDGE-OF-YOUR-SEAT INTRIGUE, FEARLESS ROMANCE.

Save $1.00

on the purchase of ANY Harlequin® Intrigue book.

Available wherever books are sold, including most bookstores, supermarkets, drugstores and discount stores.

Save $1.00

on the purchase of any Harlequin® Intrigue book.

Coupon valid until May 31, 2018.
Redeemable at participating outlets in the U.S. and Canada only.
Not redeemable at Barnes & Noble stores. Limit one coupon per customer.

52615489

5 65373 00076 2 **(8100)0 12341**

® and ™ are trademarks owned and used by the trademark owner and/or its licensee.

© 2018 Harlequin Enterprises Limited

HICECOUPBPA0118

Get 2 Free Books,
Plus 2 Free Gifts -
just for trying the _Reader Service!_

Get 2 Free Books,
Plus 2 Free Gifts—
just for trying the Reader Service!

HARLEQUIN
INTRIGUE

Get 2 Free Books,